Tim Pears is an award-winning British author. Born in 1956, he grew up in Devon, left school at sixteen, and had a wide variety of jobs before studying at the National Film and Television School. His novel *In a Land of Plenty* was made into a ten-part BBC TV series in 2001. He has been Writer in Residence at the Cheltenham Festival of Literature, and Royal Literary Fund Fellow at Oxford Brookes University, and has taught creative writing at Ruskin College and elsewhere. Tim lives in Oxford with his wife and children.

You can discover more about the author at www.timpears.com

THE HORSEMAN

1911: In a forgotten valley on the Devon-Somerset border, the seasons unfold, marked only by the rituals of the farming calendar. Twelve-year-old Leopold Sercombe skips school to help his father, a carter. Skinny and pale, with eyes the colour of blackberries, Leo dreams of a job on the master's stud farm. As ploughs furrow the hard January fields, the master's daughter, young Miss Charlotte, shocks the estate's tenants by wielding a gun at the annual shoot. One day Leo is breaking a colt for his father when a boy in breeches and riding boots appears — and peering under the stranger's hat, Leo discovers Charlotte. So a friendship begins, bound by a deep love of horses, but divided by rigid social boundaries — boundaries that become increasingly difficult to navigate as the couple approach adolescence.

TIM PEARS

———————— ◆ ————————

THE
HORSEMAN

Complete and Unabridged

CHARNWOOD
Leicester

First published in Great Britain in 2017 by
Bloomsbury
An imprint of Bloomsbury Publishing Plc
London

First Charnwood Edition
published 2017
by arrangement with
Bloomsbury Publishing Plc
London

A catalogue record for this book is available
from the British Library.

ISBN 978–1–4448–3358–4

Published by
F. A. Thorpe (Publishing)
Anstey, Leicestershire

Set by Words & Graphics Ltd.
Anstey, Leicestershire
Printed and bound in Great Britain by
T. J. International Ltd., Padstow, Cornwall

This book is printed on acid-free paper

For Craig and Ineke

I saw in the night, and behold, a man riding upon a red horse! He was standing among the myrtle trees in the glen; and behind him were red, sorrel, and white horses. Then I said, 'What are these, my lord?' The angel who talked with me said to me, 'I will show you what they are.' So the man who was standing among the myrtle trees answered, 'These are they whom the Lord has sent to patrol the earth.'

Zechariah, 1:8–10

Prologue

The boy, Leopold Jonas Sercombe, stood by his father at the open doorway to the smithy. Jacob Crocker's younger son, the gangly one, fed a circle of metal into the furnace. Outside, behind the boy, the earth was frozen. His feet were numb and his arse throbbed with the cold but he could feel the heat on his face. His father's gaze was rapt and hawkish, he'd come to scrutinise, for these wheels were for the great waggon and he'd let naught shoddy by. Merely by his presence he gave Jacob Crocker to know that if Albert Sercombe found fault, nothing would please him more than to reject the lot for the master.

The stocks had been shaped from oak logs and rested in the seasoning chamber five years. The wheels and their parts were carved from oak and stored another three. The dates were nicked into the wood by the wheelwright next door. Jacob Crocker laid a wooden wheel down on the tyring platform.

The boy had been here many times with the horses. In the corner sat the old fellow as he always sat, astride a childish stool, sharpening the horseshoe nails a Crocker son had cut from an iron rod; hunched over an ancient anvil this gaffer sat beneath a window festooned with cobwebs, and put a point on the nails with a small hammer. Did the old man ever move from

1

that spot, night or day, or was he welded to it? Perhaps he had been there for ever, tapping at the nails since the first horses were shod a thousand years ago, crouching with his little hammer like a hobgoblin smith at the oldest forge in the known world.

Jacob Crocker was wet with sweat. His younger son now worked the bellows. Standing in the doorway the boy could feel the temperature rise. When the smith moved, the boy could see the ground damp where sweat had run out of the soles of his boots. A white fowl pranced slowly amongst the litter of rusty iron on the coal-dusty ground, inspecting the clinker as if for tasty morsels. Horseshoes hung on nails spaced along the roof joists according to their size. The boy's backside tingled. His nostrils itched.

The smith's elder son, the one with the livid scar across his cheek that drew your eyes to it, reached in his pliers and drew the iron tyre out of the furnace, white hot. Crocker pincered it on the other side. The blacksmiths had made it three inches too small but in the heat of the fire it expanded. They eased it down onto the rim of the wooden wheel. As it seared the wood the great wheel burst into flame.

The wheel was on fire but the smiths ignored the blaze, calmly knocked the iron tyre into place, tapping it with their hammers here, and here. Each became satisfied that the fit was snug at the same unspoken moment and took a step back off the platform. Crocker signalled with a minute inclination of his head to his second son, who pressed a lever. The platform dropped, the

2

wheel was plunged into a trough of water.

Fierce plumes of steam rose hissing and bubbling from the tempering trough. And now there came a loud knocking and cracking from under the water, as the metal tyre contracted and squeezed the component parts of the wheel impossibly tight together, driving the spokes into position. The men stood. The boy listened slack-mouthed to the sounds like those of a ghost rapping out a message for him.

The banging muted and gradually ceased, as the blacksmiths stood by, and the boy's father peered, till the water was still and the forge was silent, the first of four wooden wheels stifled into submission.

January 1911

The boy walked through the cold darkness behind his father and older brother Fred. None spoke but at the farm Fred went to the other stable. Albert lit hurricane lanterns. The boy heard his cousin Herbert's footsteps as he came running towards them. Herbert appeared out of the dark and went directly to the feed room. Into the barrow he shovelled chaff and oat flour. The boy assisted him, pitching mangolds into the pulping machine whose handle Herbert turned. When it was done he added the pulp to the chaff. The boy mixed it up as best he could with a fork then Herbert wheeled the barrow to the stable and went from one stall to the next, shovelling the horses' breakfast into their feeding troughs.

The boy's father Albert came into the stable with a dense wodge of hay balanced on his head. He climbed the ladder into the tallet loft. From there the carter pitched summer-scented hay into the mangers, whistling through his teeth to his horses below. With their lips they pulled wisps and strands of the fodder through the wooden racks.

'Seein as you is here, boy, you can give em some corn. Give Noble double.'

The boy opened the metal bin. The clanking of the lid caused each of the horses to turn towards the sound. The biggest carthorse, Red, was nearest. In the cold stall he exhaled and his breath poured in two plumes from his nostrils. The boy scooped the corn.

★ ★ ★

They walked back to the cottage. The boy's mother Ruth gave them bread and boiled bacon. They ate in silence, the numb parts of their bodies tingling back to painful feeling. Ruth adjusted the wick of the paraffin lamp upon the table as light seeped into the room. This table upon which the doctor had removed Fred's tonsils some years back. The boy searched for the bloodstain. Perhaps it was no longer there.

Albert drained his mug of tea. 'They ploughs won't lead theirselves,' he said, and stood up. Fred stood too. They took up their croust bags that Ruth had placed upon the table, and left. The boy Leo followed. His mother did not try to stop him but said that his sister Kizzie would bring his lunch to school and that he'd best not be late again or he'd feel the switch from Miss Pugsley, and his mother would not object.

★ ★ ★

In the tack room the boy watched his father gather implements. A heavy plough spanner. Whip cord. Thongs of leather to repair harness. Shut links to mend the plough traces. He placed these in a canvas basket. Horse nail stubs to fix spreaders, cart nails for cleats to hold the plough wheels for a time.

Herbert geared up two of the horses, Red and one of the two-year-old black geldings, Coal, as requested by his carter.

Albert applied grease to the mould board of the plough, and they set off as light seeped into the world around them.

'Give you a leg up,' Albert told his son. The boy sat side-wise atop Red, the nearside horse. Albert walked next to him. He carried a plough paddle, using it as a walking stick though none was needed. His corduroy trousers were tied with string below the knee. Herbert chose not to follow this fashion. The carter's and his lad's croust bags hung from Red's hames.

'Not a bleedin cloud above us,' Herbert called from behind. 'Clean and raw today.'

They reached Higher Redlands, a pasture to be ploughed for corn. The boy rolled onto his stomach and slid off the carthorse. Herbert hung their bags from the branch of an elm tree by the gate. Albert set the plough. When Herbert was ready Albert handed him the paddle. 'Aim for that ash tree in yon hedge,' he said. 'Red's steady but if Coal lags, crack the whip.'

'Yes, gaffer, I knows that.'

'Don't touch him, mind, just crack it by his ears.'

Albert turned and walked back through the gateway. Herbert shook his head, then he clicked his tongue and called to the horses to move. The coulter bit into the turf and as the plough moved forward so the turf rose and turned over. The boy walked to the gate and on to school.

★ ★ ★

In the afternoon he walked home the same way. The sun lowered in the sky and some parts of the hillocky land were in shadow, others in harsh light. Four plough teams now worked in four small sloping, ill-shaped fields. His uncle Enoch and brother Fred drove two horses each. Herbert still ploughed Higher Redlands behind Red and Coal. His father Albert had put the other gelding next to Pleasant the old mare. He worked Lower Redlands, the steepest of the fields in that part of Manor Farm. He used a one-way plough, stopping at the end of each furrow to tilt the plough and so engage the alternate mould board. Ploughing one way across the slope of the hill the furrow was turned to the left, the other way to the right, both ways downhill as gravity demanded. The uppermost horse took most of the strain but the gelding did not shirk. The boy's father told him that the old mare was their best exemplar. She had some quality that inclined young horses to copy her. He did not know what it was. The boy watched. He could not see it either but he believed his father, that it existed.

The turf rose up and curled over like a long thin wave breaking on the beach of Bridgwater Bay. This pasture had not been a fruitful one, it was full of stroil grass. The horses' feet thudded, the whippletrees swung, the coulter ripped through speedwell, bindweed, dandelion. In one direction, walking west across the field, the sun was glaring and his father bent his head. He

8

walked with a rolling, sideways carriage, shoulders swaying. A gait he could no longer rid himself of even when walking unencumbered in the yard or lane.

None noticed the boy watching them for each man and lad aspired to the straightest lines, on which depended his reputation. They would plough one acre in the day, each walking fifteen miles.

The new soil came up dark brown, reddish, for the frost and ice to break it up. Behind his father, as behind each of the other three ploughmen, swirling blizzards of gulls fell swooping to the ground for wire-worms and chafer-grubs. They had not been there this morning.

In the field where Herbert ploughed, other birds scavenged and the boy walked through the gate to study them. Wagtails. A chaffinch. Two or three lapwings strutted quickly forwards to peck up insects. He spotted curlews, starlings, golden plovers, stalking the upturned earth, but they were outnumbered by the gulls who bullied them for the worms in their beaks and chased them, screeching with a noise like metal scraped across metal.

Herbert reached the hedge and called to the horses to turn and set back once more in parallel to his previous course. The coulter jumped out of the furrow. The boy could not see if it had hit a stone. Perhaps it had. Herbert called the horses to a halt. He looked down at the ground. He kicked the soil over with his foot. As if surprised by this erratic unexpected behaviour the gulls ceased squawking for a moment. Without the sound of horses' footsteps, jangling harness, the coulter ringing as it cut the ground, there was a sudden quiet. No such sounds from the next field either where Albert ploughed.

'That won't show,' Herbert said out loud to himself as he toed the furrow straight.

Something, a sound or movement, caused the boy to turn towards the hedge. He saw his father's face through branches, some leafless and others the bright dark green of holly, like some wintry Green Man akin to that carved into the end of one of the choir stalls in the village church; only seen by boys seeking it. A bodiless head in the foliage. His father's expression was blank. What he did there in the hedgerow was a mystery. Then his head shifted and the boy understood his father was buttoning his flies.

Albert walked along the hedge and came through the open gateway into the field. He did not see the boy or if he did he paid no heed. He walked up the furrow behind Herbert, who had resumed his course, and yelled for him to stop. The lad called the horses to whoa and turned. Albert asked him for the whip, and Herbert handed it over. He looked neither anxious nor surprised but merely at a loss. Albert told him to remove his coat.

Herbert frowned. There was in this grimace of fear some kind of sarcasm, almost a smile, as well.

'Take off your jacket, lad,' Albert said.

Slowly, button by button, Herbert undid his jacket and shrugged it off. He hung it over one of the handles of the plough.

'And your waistcoat,' Albert said.

The lad hesitated, then he unbuttoned his waistcoat. His expression became surly, petulant.

'And your shirt.'

Herbert seemed to shake his head though it might have been a shiver. 'Tis fuckin cold, uncle,' he said.

'Take it off.'

Herbert scooped his braces off his shoulders and let them fall to hang by his sides. He pulled the bottom of his shirt out of his trousers. He undid the top buttons of his white sweat- and mud-streaked cotton shirt and, leaning forward, pulled it over his head. Then he hung it with the waistcoat on the other handle of the plough.

He stood looking at his carter, waiting. His scrawny torso was white and bare save for a scribble of hair midway between his brown nipples.

Albert gazed at his lad. Then he took two steps forward, at a diagonal away from Herbert, as if to march off across the field. But then as he came level with the lad he raised the whip and turned and cracked it hard upon his back. Herbert squealed and turned away but Albert pursued him, following round after him and striking him once more across the back.

Herbert cursed and cried out in pain. Albert laid the whip carefully across the handles of the plough.

'That won't show neither,' he said. 'Now put your garments on and plough the furrow.'

The boy watched his father walk back into his own field. He watched Herbert pulling on his clothes in a desultory manner, sniffing to himself. A glimpse of red weal already on the white skin. Herbert buttoned up the waistcoat with trembling fingers. He looked up and saw Leo watching him. It seemed he would say something but he did not. He put on his coat and turned to the plough. He picked up the whip and cracked it close to Coal's rump and told the horses to go on.

The boy heard a sudden tumultuous cacophony of birds bickering and squawking, and understood that they had made this noise all the while, but he had not heard nor seen them even though now they filled the air. He turned and walked homeward.

January

There were six farms on the estate. No two fields among them were of like size or configuration. No tracks ran straight but dipped and wove around the tumps and hummocks of land. Some hedges were laid, others left tall and wild. Conifers grew in neat yet oddly shaped plantations. Oak and ash and beech trees seeded themselves in hidden combes. Streams meandered in no discernible direction, cutting deep narrow gullies here, trickling over gravel beds there. Erratic walkways crisscrossed the estate. The boy's father Albert told him that when God created this corner of the world He'd just helped himself to a well-earned tipple. His mother Ruth derided that blasphemy and said that much of their peninsula was so contoured, her husband had seen little of it. To the west the land rose to the Brendon Hills and the moor beyond. To the east the Quantocks loomed.

★ ★ ★

Today, all was quiet. Horses remained in their stables. No machinery ran on the estate. No work was allowed on the land, for fear of disturbing the game. The master had few rules. This was one, on the second Friday in January.

13

After they'd fed and groomed the horses, Albert Sercombe and his carters oiled harness in the tack room. In the cottage, Ruth baked bread, Kizzie kneading the dough, and she cooked pork pies. The boy left them and walked across the estate to the keeper's cottage in Pigeon Wood, in sight of the big house. The keeper's wife told him she thought they would be back home for breakfast soon and he could wait. He thanked her and sat outside, warming himself by hugging the keeper's Springers chained in the back yard. The spaniels welcomed his attention.

Presently the man and lad appeared. When he saw the boy the big man said, 'We only feeds one Sercombe here if that's what your weest brother's thinkin.' As he passed, he ruffled the boy's hair, chuckling, and said, 'Looks like he needs feedin up, mind, you can give im alf a yourn.'

Leo sat while they ate their breakfast, thick slices of hot bread and butter, and boiled bacon with much fat upon it. Mrs Budgell insisted that he ate a slice of bread and when he shook his head she put the plate in front of him anyhow and he consumed it, to the last crumb. It was the same colour as his mother's bread but more chewy in its texture and with a flavour of something. Honey? She poured four mugs of tea and placed one before him. Then she sat. She asked her husband whether all went well. He said it did and that he would go to the house shortly and walk the drives with the master. He asked Sid if his brother had come to help him.

'If he ain't, he's made a mistake, Mister

Budgell, since he's goin to.'

They ate and drank. Aaron Budgell said to Leo, 'Do you wish to feel it? You been glancin at it like a little tit.' Leo looked at him blankly for a moment. Then he nodded. Aaron Budgell put a hand upon the table and leaned towards the boy. Leo ran his fingers over the knobbly ridge in the middle of the keeper's bald skull.

'The last poacher what laid a hand on me,' Budgell said. 'Docker Furze. The autumn of nineteen o seven. Whacked me with his cudgel, and it was made of oak. When people see this, you know what it makes em think of, boy?' Leo shook his head. 'It reminds em of the state Docker was in when I was done with the old boy, that's what. He's still only able to eat liquids to this day, I'm told.'

★   ★   ★

After breakfast Sid took Leo to the keeper's barn. On the table was a bolt of red cloth from which he cut a square some two feet by two with a pair of scissors. 'Use that for size to cut another one, and carry on for me,' he told Leo. The scissors were sharp and cut the red cloth with ease. Sid punched holes in two adjacent corners of each square and tied them with string to ash sticks cut to size and with two nicks cut ready for the string to bite into. 'We've twenty beaters, and I'll make up five spare,' Sid said.

The boy's brother Sid was sixteen and sole under keeper for the head gamekeeper Aaron Budgell. Sid was fascinated by all animals, not

15

horses in particular; it was the other way round for Leo.

'There's six Guns tomorrow,' he said. 'One a they's a woman, if you can believe that. Lord Grenvil's daughter. Mister Budgell reckons t'will give us bad luck. Her's here like as a chaperone, so the master's daughter can shoot this year and not look out a place, for she did insist upon it and as we all know the master cannot refuse Miss Charlotte nothin.'

Leo asked whether he would be carrying the cartridge bag for Lord Grenvil's daughter.

'I don't reckon so,' Sid said. 'Us should give her a woman for loadin, and a cartridge girl, and some other traper for pickin up an all, see how she gets on. Mister Budgell reckons her's too pretty to be able to shoot straight. Maybe Lady Grenvil's tryin to marry her off. Thinks her'll meet a good man on the shootin field.'

Leo cut the red cloth. As his father's tack room was filled with the accoutrements of the carter's profession so this keeper's barn possessed an assortment of strange tools and devices. Traps of different kinds, some surely antiquated, half gone to rust. Spades with hooks at the end of their long handles. Nets. Bird scarers.

'The master and Miss Charlotte. Lord Grenvil. The Miss Grenvil. Colonel Giffard from over the Quantocks. And a Mister Carew — he's some London toff not been here before. Arrived last night. I don't know nothin about him. Tis his bag you'll carry.'

Leo finished cutting the flags. He offered to help tie them to the ash sticks but Sid said that he should do them himself. It was not that he did not trust his younger brother but rather that if one came loose he had no one to blame but himself, that was it. Leo studied the keeper's implements while Sid talked. A shelf of canisters. Renardine, creosote, paraffin. Strychnine, arsenic. A knuckle-duster with two spikes.

'I do believe the master has shoot days out a social obligation. He could do without em, I reckon. What he loves is goin out with me or Mister Budgell, walkin up the hedgerows and havin a pot-shot at a pheasant or two. A hare. They old Labs a his potterin alongside.'

Leo asked his brother if he knew how much he stank. Sid said he believed it for he'd been skinning stoats. They had some new steel gins that worked a treat. 'I'll make a few bob,' he said. 'Stoats, weasels, to go with the rabbits. We've had a few cats come into our coverts and all. Mister Budgell sends the skins off up to London. He gets a shillin or two for a stoat, four shillin for a good cat, and he shares it all with me.'

When the flags were finished Sid rolled each one around its thin pole and stacked them in a corner. Then he had Leo carry another pile of wooden posts to the cart outside. Each post had a number painted in yellow upon it, one to six. While he waited Leo counted the posts. There were eighteen numbered in all, plus two blanks. Sid returned leading the keeper's donkey, which he attached to the cart. Then he pulled the donkey's halter, and cursed her until she had made plain her reluctance to work, and then she plodded forward. 'Once she knows we're comin

17

back home, she'll move quick then all right.'

Sid led the donkey through the wood, Leo beside him. Leo asked if they had caught moles. 'Moles?' Sid said. 'Moles don't hurt no one, you idiot. So long's they keep off the master's lawns. And then the mole catcher comes in, and he gets their skins. We had good sport with rats, though, you should a been here last week. All round the stables. We found their holes and put barley meal down. Next day, Wednesday, come back and did the same. They loved us, the little bastards. Thursday we give em nothin. Then Friday Mister Budgell mixed barley flour with caster sugar and arsenic. Had me put it down their holes with a spoon tied to a long stick.'

Sid spoke as they walked. The donkey plodded along. Sid Sercombe was loquacious as Leo was shy and taciturn. Their mother Ruth used to tell Sid he was taking the words out of his younger brother's mouth and leaving none for him, to kindly shut his trap for just one minute, but he would not.

'I had a dead jackdaw, Leo. Tied it to a line. We waited till these blasted crows was comin in to roost and I dragged it across the field. The crows come down to mob the bloody thing, dead as it was, and Mister Budgell scattershot em by the score. Magpies, you can't take em so easy. You have to find their roost for one thing. They like a patch a brambles to hide in, in a big wood. I waited for a good wind and then I went and shot a few. I got eight of em one afternoon.'

Sid unloaded a number of the posts, then carried on across the estate. He pointed out a

18

gibbet of vermin of which he was mighty proud. There sparrowhawks hung with their wings outspread. There was a dog fox, a vixen, cubs. Ravens. Sid admitted he did not know whether the main purpose of the gibbet was to deter other vermin or to let the master know that his keepers were doing their job. He told Leo how owls would take the head off a young bird. They'd trapped tawny owls in a ginn, but used pole traps for brown owls. Mister Budgell would never kill a white owl, he said. No, he never would, Sid could swear on the Bible to that, and neither would Sid himself. He said that sparrowhawks were easy to shoot for they always came back to where they'd last killed, but kestrels were unpredictable. You just had to keep an eye out, and if you saw one when you had your gun, you nabbed it if you could.

Most vermin control took place in the summer and autumn, of course, but Mister Budgell kept it up all year round. During his two years on the job, Sid said, they'd put harriers, merlins and the hobby on the gibbet, and once a peregrine falcon he reckoned he'd mentioned before to Leo, and there weren't many keepers who could say as much.

They laid a bunch of posts at the second drive, and continued. As long as his brother spoke, the boy was happy to listen. Like Leo, Sid had meeched off school and would cross the estate to help out Mister Budgell. As soon as Sid was old enough the head keeper had requested that his under keeper be let go and Sid Sercombe taken on. The master had obliged.

★ ★ ★

On the day following, the second Saturday in January, the boy walked back to the keeper's cottage before first light. There was a frost on the ground, the world was silent and new, he perceived it being born out of the darkness around him. The air was cold and clear. There were skeins of mist in the low fields that were like the breath of the land made visible, like his own. The last stars of the night sky disappeared above him into the pale blue. He might have been the first human upon the earth, striding through the garden. He doubted whether there were any places so beautiful in all the planets known or unknown to man, or to God.

Outside the gamekeeper's cottage, boys and men gathered. Some girls, ever hopeful. Most off the estate, Fred and Herbert among them, a few from the village. Aaron Budgell allotted them their roles. Sid gave a red flag to each beater. Boys and old men would be stops. Six cartridge boys, six pickers-up. The Guns would have their own loaders. One man had brought his dog along. Mister Budgell sent him home.

Most shoot owners and keepers believed that partridge shooting should finish by Christmas, for the birds began to pair in early January. The master instead shot none before. He believed that partridges drove better off land that lay quiet, and anyhow, partridges were incidental in this crooked landscape. Pheasant was the main quarry.

* ★ ★

They walked en masse to the first beat. The boy's brother Sid wore corduroy breeches, pigskin leggings, ankle-length tea-drinker boots of horsehide, a thorn-proof tweed jacket. Aaron Budgell was accoutred likewise and he rode a cob at the head of the crowd. They reached the covert from which the first battue would proceed. Aaron Budgell explained that they would beat the birds out of this wood that was their home, and in the afternoon would drive them back. He told the stops that if they wished they could light small fires to keep warm, not because he gave a tinker's cuss for their comfort but because in moving about in search of twigs and branches they would do more to keep the pheasants from sneaking out of the sides of the wood than in standing about doing nothing but shiver. The smoke too would help.

Mister Budgell left Sid to place the stops and the beaters. But first he said that some had been doing this job three Saturdays in January for many years, and might not take kindly to orders given them by such a youth. Mister Budgell said that if anyone had a problem with his under keeper then they had one with him, and should step forward now. None did. The remainder followed him on his pony down into the combe from which the Guns would shoot.

The boy's brother Fred was to be a picker-up, and walked beside him. He spoke quietly. 'See some a they beatin lads have big pockets in their coats?' Leo nodded. 'And I wouldn't be

21

surprised if Herb put a bird or two by to collect later on.'

They waited at the pegs, the numbered stakes, which must have been hammered into place after the master and the gamekeeper had held their conference. Aaron Budgell told the cartridge boys and the pickers-up who their Guns were. He told them how the master deplored the drawing of pegs, a hit-and-miss method. The master and he had set the pegs with care, and Lord Prideaux had allotted the Guns to them as he best judged it. Leo would carry the cartridges for the stranger, Mister Carew. His brother would pick up for Lord Grenvil's daughter. One of the others said Fred Sercombe would have a restful day, it was money for old rope for some. As the laughter died down Aaron Budgell said, 'Now, now,' but he himself was still grinning. He rode the cob away and tied it to a tree some way distant and returned.

They heard a waggon trundling along and then they saw it, conveying the Guns towards them, the boy's uncle Enoch driving. One horse between the poles, Enoch's oldest Shire. The loaders walked behind. Enoch brought the waggon to a halt. The Guns were seated upon benches put in place for the purpose. They rose and alighted from the waggon. Loaders stepped gallantly forward to assist their ladies. Miss Charlotte reached the ground before hers could do so. The master introduced his guests to the head gamekeeper, Budgell, who for those who did not know him had been with the family for many years. He had taught the master to shoot,

22

and was teaching Lottie with the same gun, a small, single-barrelled muzzle loader she would use today.

Lord Grenvil told Budgell that he hoped he was doing a better job with the daughter than he'd managed with the father. If it were so, he should like to offer him the post on his own estate with a view to a similar improvement. He nodded to his daughter Alice, who smiled and shook her head. Colonel Giffard pronounced it nonsense, though what precisely no one knew.

Aaron Budgell explained to the Guns where the birds would come from. He asked the gentlemen to leave the low-flying pheasants for the ladies. He said they would have four drives this morning and two this afternoon. After lunch they would shoot only cock pheasants, but this morning they may shoot hens as well.

The master invited his guests to warm their blood with a sloe gin before they began. The cartridge boys and pickers-up joined the loaders at the back of the cart. Fred knew something of guns and admired them. The master used a pair of Charles Lancaster 28-inch 12-bores, their stocks rubbed to a smooth and shining patina. Lord Grenvil used a pair of Purdeys, his daughter very light Churchill 12s with 2-inch chambers. Colonel Giffard had a pair of Holland & Holland guns. Fred asked the man handling the remaining guns, which he lifted carefully from two wooden cases, whose and what they were. The man said they were Mister Carew's and had been made for him on his eighteenth birthday, in nineteen o seven, by Cogswell &

Harrison. He said they were hammerless, of course, and had 30-inch barrels. Leo stared at them. They were inlaid with gold, and had intricate scroll engraving on the barrel. The monogram on the stock was also embossed on the leather bag he was to carry, containing two hundred cartridges.

The Guns took their places at the pegs. Behind each stood their loader, holding the second gun, then the cartridge boy, and finally the picker-up, who would have nothing to do but watch until the shooting was over. The master's black Labradors were the only dogs present, to Mister Carew's left. Leo looked at the master's daughter at the next peg to the right. She only had the one gun, and it only had one barrel. She would have to wait to have it reloaded after every shot. She was not much taller than he was. He did not know her age. Her gun, though small, looked too big for her, yet she held it confidently, her left hand gripping the forestock, the fingers of her right hand around the trigger guard. She stood with her left leg forward, her long dark skirt brushing the grass.

Aaron Budgell stepped forward from the Guns and blew a battered old hunting horn up the slope in front of them, then he stepped back and walked to the rear of the pegs.

They stood in the cold quiet morning, in the shadowed combe, waiting for the beaters to drive the birds from their covert. After some while they heard a whistle, which Leo knew must be blown by his brother Sid. The shots raised their guns in readiness and stared at the empty sky.

24

There was silence, broken only by the panting of one of the master's dogs who stood a few feet away. Suddenly the dog went quiet and held its breath, and then the first birds came over the bank above them.

★ ★ ★

The Guns had their lunch in the head keeper's cottage. The loaders and beaters and stops crowded into the barn. The stops were given a big lump of cheese and a pork pie each. Boys had small loaves or buns of bread with a chunk cut out of the middle and a lump of butter stuffed inside. The loaders and beaters ate salt beef sandwiches and pickled onions. There was a barrel of pale ale and another of mild, and bottles of pop. They spoke of the morning. Mister Carew had said not a word to anyone, whether those assisting him or his host or fellow guests. His loader was his valet and had accompanied him from London. The man assured the company that the reason was shyness rather than arrogance. Be that as it may, all the pickers-up agreed he was the best shot they had ever seen. One of the old stops said the previous Lord Prideaux, the master's father, was a finer shot, but all laughed at him for as a stop in the wood he could not have witnessed a single shot of young Carew's. All that the beaters and stops saw of the entertainment was the occasional bird falling in front of them, and the loaders and cartridge boys were too involved in their work to watch.

Mister Carew's picker-up, who'd stood behind Leo all morning, asked if anyone else had seen the two birds he'd brought down on the second drive, one barrel after the other up in front of the sun. He said that Mister Budgell had asked the Guns to leave low-flying birds but it seemed this young marksman left everything below thirty yards. He said some were so high, seventy yards he reckoned, that he could hear the pellets rattling the pheasants' wings as they flew on, unscathed. Someone asked Mister Budgell whether there might be a bonus paid if more than a hundred pheasants were shot today. Mister Budgell said no, the stops would receive a shilling and the cartridge boys the same, and the beaters one and six, as he had already made clear.

It was agreed that the master's young daughter had bagged more pheasants with that child's gun than was feasible. Three, if not four. Fred said that the only birds shot on his, Miss Grenvil's, peg were those swiped by Colonel Giffard next door, and many laughed and nodded in agreement, for it was a well-known, ill-mannered habit of the old Quantocks codger. Sid went outside and when he came back he said he fancied a breeze was coming up, which could make for a brisk afternoon. Mister Budgell said that speaking of the afternoon it was upon them, and time to go.

★　★　★

The final beat took place back in the combe where they'd started, as the light began to fail.

The pheasants were beaten homeward, out of the hanging woods. They were driven gradually, steadily, to avoid flushes and give the Guns as many single birds as possible. When Leo heard Aaron Budgell, standing between Mister Carew's peg and the master's, say, 'He's doin it right,' he understood that the keeper was referring to Sid. Some birds flew straight across the little valley, no more than twenty or twenty-five yards above them, but the wind was indeed blowing, many birds were lifted and flew higher and faster. Mister Carew's loader worked so fast that the boy could hardly manage to keep him supplied with cartridges. He was too busy to witness Mister Carew's skill but he had certainly not seen such quick loading as from this valet.

He did not know how long they shot for but it was constant. When at last Mister Carew lowered his gun the boy saw flames pouring out of the ends of the barrels. Both guns were so hot that Mister Carew and his loader laid them down upon the ground, where they scorched the grass. The pickers-up did their work and the Labradors too padded around collecting the downed birds. Leo asked the loader how many Mister Carew had shot. The loader grinned and pointed to his ears. He shrugged and shook his head. Then the boy smiled too for he realised that he was deaf as well and had not heard a word of what he himself had said.

February

The bell sounded like a warning to the population that children had escaped. They came out of the school-house to a world still fogged and frozen. They took one direction or the other in two keen unruly crowds. Some attempted to skate on the frozen ruts. Others broke off icicles and sucked them, winter sweets, or used them as weapons. Many ran to keep warm or simply for the sake of it. The boy did not. He walked, sucked in the sharp cold air, and breathed it out in plumes of steam.

Children dispersed homeward, the rabble thinned. They left the village. Around him children yelled and yelped. He did not hear them. He listened to the quietness. The birds that had left for more clement territory, the horses at rest, animals in hibernation, dogs asleep, men pottering. He listened to the emptiness.

His sister caught them up. A monitor, she stayed behind to help the teacher tidy, received in return a piece of cake or biscuit. A number turned off the road for the farms and cottages of the estate. One of the Sparke girls asked Kizzie whether she had any cake left. 'Was you given summat taffety?'

'That's for me to know and you to wonder,' Kizzie said. 'And if one day you be monitor then you may know yourself.'

In Higher Redlands where he believed they intended to sow turnips the boy saw smoking piles dotted across the bare ploughed earth. Red stood between the poles of one of the two-wheeled carts. Cousin Herbert forked manure off the cart into a heap. Beyond, the boy's brother Fred did likewise. Pleasant the old mare stood patiently waiting for him to finish. The muck-carts were the smallest the horses ever had to pull. They made the Shires look huge, giants towing toys. An easy job for the horses, less so for these lads. They had been doing it when the boy left for school and would doubtless do so until the day grew dark, spreading at the rate of twenty tons an acre. One or two of the girls waved, and the carting lads waved back, briefly.

⋆　⋆　⋆

Kizzie headed for their cottage but the boy walked on to Manor Farm. In the frozen world smell, like sound, was muted, but from where they'd shovelled muck came rich aromas. From Isaac Wooland's cowhouse the smell was sweet, like hay and meadow grass. By the stables the air was harsh with ammonia. Noble was in her stall and the boy went to her. Her foal was due within a month. Her belly hung swollen beneath her and the boy imagined her foal within, its spindly limbs folded, eyes closed, slung between the Shire mare's great haunches, her sturdy legs. The boy spoke to her. He told her she was the finest horse on his carter father's farm. The name she had been given at her own birth befitted her.

He took the stool that hung from a hook on the wall and stood on it beside her. He scratched a point low on her neck he had discovered by chance she liked as no other horse he knew of seemed to. The mare was still and listened to him speaking to her. He said he looked forward to seeing her give birth and he told her of his secret wish, that his father would involve him in the handling of her foal, for it was something he wished for above all things now. He believed he was ready, whatever others might say of his age or stature or other immaturity.

The boy heard voices. He did not know whether they had only just entered the range of his hearing or whether they had been there for some while and he had only just become aware of them. He listened now. The voices of men. They came from the tack room, on the far side of the stall next door.

His father and one other.

Two others.

The boy climbed up into the manger and around the partition to Red's empty stall. He picked his way over Red's manger and crouched there beside the wall to the tack room. There was a foot of space between the wood partition walls and the back brick wall, left so that the carter could hear his horses.

'They over Home Farm builds middens in the yard and they takes them as serious as their corn or hay stacks, and so they should.'

It was his uncle Enoch speaking. The boy pressed one hand against the partition wall, the other on the wooden screen upon which he crouched. He leaned forward and peered into the tack room. None of the three men were seated, all stood. The stove had been lit but only Amos Tucker stood beside it. The others were in separate corners.

'This is how they build em, gaffer,' Enoch said. 'They lays a square about the size a this room.' He described the shape with his hands. 'Build as high as a man can reach, then they starts another square aside of it. Bin doin so for two year now. No takin it out a bit at a time, half rotted.' Enoch opened wide his arms. 'One great midden.'

'Is he done?' Albert said.

'Tis all mixed up so tis all the same. Not patchy like ours.'

'Is he finished?' Albert asked Amos Tucker.

'No, I isn't,' Enoch said. 'It gets so hot in there all the damn seeds perish, every last one.'

Albert laughed. Amos Tucker said, 'Combustion.'

'I want no fires in my yard, gaffer,' Albert said.

'Will you look at the midden on Home Farm?' Enoch said.

'I will not,' said the boy's father. The men stood in silence, as if taking in what had been said and thinking deeply on it.

'Yon brother a mine knows about horses, gaffer,' Enoch said. 'Don't mean he knows bugger all else about farmin.'

The coal stove made no noise. The carters

31

waited for the farmer to say something. To resolve the dispute one way or the other. He said nothing. Perhaps he was waiting for the words but they would not come to him. Instead he stepped slowly to the door and opened it and walked away.

The carters watched him leave. Enoch Sercombe shook his head. 'You's lucky the gaffer's a coward,' he said quietly. 'He's scared to give you a single fuckin order or get you to change one single thing in case you walks away.'

Albert pondered what his brother meant. 'He's right,' he said. 'I would.'

March

The boy stood in the field. He did not move. A statue of himself. What would someone think should they see him? A boy who, like the wife of Lot, had been walking across the field but looked back and been petrified to salt? Or had he been carried there for a scarecrow? Boys were paid to keep crows off seeds but they generally made a noise. Waved their arms about, or ran at the crows as if believing, like puppies, they could catch them. If they had catapults so much the better.

The boy stood still. He watched hares at play. The buck hares chasing the does. Hither and thither. An endless game of tag. He never saw the bucks catch up and receive their prize. They must couple later somewhere hidden.

He watched a fox chase a hare. Only for the sport, for hare meat did not agree with the vulpine palate. The fox would gain on its prey, then the hare turned sharply. The fox could not do this but rather jumped up, turning in the air. It landed and chased the hare again, who had opened up the gap between them once more. The effect was comical. Eventually the fox tired of its sport, headed for a hedge and vanished.

The boy did not move. A hare came across the field. It headed straight for him. It did not veer to left or right. It had happened once before a hare had run almost into him. He did not know whether it had been blind, or sick. He stood in the field. The hare came on towards him. He held his breath. A few yards away it got his scent and turned its head a little, and saw him, and ran off. So, each species of animal had its own peculiarities of vision. This world we surveyed was not as it was but as it was seen, in many different guises.

Back at the cottage he found all their mattresses taken downstairs and stood up outside, leaning against walls or hedges, like tablets brought down from the mountain. Perhaps there were Commandments writ in the stains. A voice sounded from above.

'Come and give us a hand then, Leo,' his mother said, leaning out of a window.

'Yes,' said Kizzie, from another. 'Don't stand there gawpin.'

Leo climbed the stairs. There were three bedrooms. Kizzie was sweeping the bare boards of their parents' room. Chairs, bedside tables, washstand were piled upon the slats of the bed. Ruth was in the room he shared with his brother Fred. She called him in. This room had been swept already. Ruth shifted one of the beds, wedging it against a wall at right angles to the other.

'What do you think?' she asked. 'Like this?'

The boy frowned. 'T'was all right how it was.'

'Don't be zart, Leo,' his mother said. 'How's about next to each other but facin opposite ways? Then you and Fred can sit up and have a gab together.'

Ruth called it spring-cleaning but all knew this to be an excuse for rearranging furniture, creating a new configuration of their wooden beds and tables in the small rooms. Their mother did this every year. Perhaps such activity placated some restless spirit within her.

When the men came home from the farm, Kizzie whispered to her father what he might not otherwise have noticed. Albert looked around the cottage and returned to the kitchen and told their mother what an improvement she had made, and the children all agreed.

March

Albert Sercombe slept on a cot in the stable. So too the boy, on a bed of straw beneath a blanket in the tack room. He would not leave.

'Ye'll be like Dunstone, can't see the point a home.' But the boy was at home. He gazed upon the sets of waggon harness with their back-bands and belly bands, the breechings and the riding saddle. The halters and blinkers. Many pairs of reins. There was a smell of leather and saddle soap. Plough strings, cart saddles, cobble trees and swingletrees, each hung on wooden pegs in its allotted place. These were icons of beauty to the boy like the painted crockery his mother had brought in her dowry and kept in their parlour.

He would not leave until Noble's foal was born. He attempted the habit of his father of rising at hourly intervals, more or less, during the night to check upon the mare. Was able to regain slumber upon his return to the straw. Then he was woken suddenly by voices, and understood even as he looked around him in the bright light pouring into the tack room that he had missed it. His father had not woken him.

Leopold walked to the loose box. The master stood beside his father, looking in over the open upper door.

'A fine mare, carter. How many's she given us?'

36

'This'll be her sixth foal, master,' his father replied. 'The last one was yon filly in the next box.'

The boy quietly approached, and stood beside his father. A girl stood beside the master. His daughter. 'I can't believe he'll grow to be a carthorse,' she said. 'He looks so delicate.'

'All babies do,' her father said.

Miss Charlotte was at church every Sunday, sat in the front pew beside her father. The dowager countess, the master's grandmother, no longer accompanied them. Otherwise Leo rarely saw the girl, though she lived on the estate as they all did. The shoot was a rare occurrence. Miss Charlotte did not go to the village school but had her own governess, a teacher all to herself who lived in the big house with her. He did not believe she had ever been on the farm before.

'I've water warmin for the mare,' Albert said.

The boy, hearing this, went to the stable room. He felt the water in the urn with his finger. It was lukewarm. He poured a quantity into a bucket and heaved it along the yard. He could not help it swinging. Water sloshed out at either side. The master turned and said, 'One of your sons, carter?'

His father took the bucket from him in one strong hand. 'Not so big's he thinks he is, master.'

'No, no, carter, he's willing. We like that, we applaud it.'

The boy did not look up yet he knew the girl watched him. His father opened the door and entered the loose box. Noble bared her teeth.

37

She made a sound that was a kind of low growling.

'Easy, girl, easy now.' He put the bucket on the ground and backed out of the box, and the mare drank.

'The most gentle mare I've ever had, master, but when she's with a young foal . . . '

'Will she have to work again?' the girl asked.

'We'll let her rest for ten days, miss,' Albert said. 'I'll give her plenty a warm bran mash, and one or two other things besides.'

They watched the foal become accustomed by degrees to standing on his spindly legs. He probed beneath his mother's belly and sucked her milk. The mare bent down on occasion and briefly nuzzled or licked him. He leaned his head against her side and stroked it against her skin. As the foal explored the circumscribed territory of the loose box he sometimes staggered and looked as if he might fall but he never did.

The master chuckled. 'I can tell my daughter would like to pet your foal. But I believe the carter here,' he said to her, 'will no more let you touch the creature than its mother will. Isn't that true, carter?'

Albert Sercombe nodded. 'Aye, master. We don't handle them afore they're broken.'

The boy glanced across at the girl. She was looking at her father and then away, her eyes narrow slits of anger, suggesting that what he had presumed of her was false, or else that his assumption was correct but she did not wish him to share it with their servants, the boy did not know which.

38

April

Though the windows were high and he could see but sky through them the boy gazed upward rather than before him.

'Are you listening?' Miss Pugsley said. She called his name and he turned and she asked him to name the capital of a certain country in such a tone as to suggest she had asked him already once or more. She wore her black-and-white hair in a tight bun upon her head. For his distraction or his ignorance, which he was not sure, she told him to hold out his hand and stung his palm with the switch she kept for that purpose.

★   ★   ★

The school day had begun with the children rung into the room by the bell in the roof. Jane Sparke played a harmonium and they sang the morning hymn. *Awake, my soul, and with the sun, Thy daily stage of duty run.* Miss Pugsley said a prayer then mounted her platform desk and filled in the register while a monitor read a lesson from the first book of the Old Testament about some of the many clans of the sons of Noah. She read them out. The Jebusites, Amorites, Girgashites, Hivites, Arkites. The

Sinites, Arvadites, Zemarites and Hamathites. Would all be slaughtered to make room for the Israelites, the chosen people of God? At intervals the monitor stopped and asked questions of those she deemed inattentive, and those who answered wrongly were called from their seats to stand in line at the front. Following the reading Miss Pugsley caned these miscreants.

They practised their writing every day. Studied arithmetic, reading and grammar.

Miss Pine tended to the younger children, herded to the back of the room. Today Miss Pugsley had taken the older ones through history then mathematics. During the first lesson she rebuked Leo for confusing Christopher Columbus with Ferdinand Magellan, and in the second she chastised him for making no attempt to calculate the simple equations chalked upon the board. The boy was right-handed. He held out his left palm; with each blow the pain intensified. In the lunch break some went home, some ate their bread and cheese or pie in the playground. Leo walked out of the village and watched farmhands at their labours, with their animals, as was his habit.

When Leo returned, Alfred Haswell approached him flanked by others and said, 'Here he comes, the yay-nay what talks more to beasts than he do to us.' The others laughed and Alfred said, 'Why's that then, Sercombe, is you a fuckin beast? With the brain of a beast and the mind a one too?'

Then his sister was beside Leo, saying, 'He'll get more sense from any a them creatures than he will from ye.'

More had gathered, and some chuckled at Kizzie's wit, but one of those flanking Alfred, Gilbert Prowse, son of the baker, said, 'And is big sister as to speak for e.' He turned to seek the approval of his coterie. Kizzie struck him on his jaw presented side-on to her, and he staggered sideways into the crowd pushed up close around them. The bell rang. They looked over and saw Miss Pine by the door, shaking the bell so vigorously it belied her consumptive frame. They trundled across the playground and shuffled back into the classroom.

In the afternoon the swallows continued to build their nests in the eaves of the school. They flew away from the building and returned with plant fibre between their beaks or with nothing visible and Leo presumed their mouths were full of mud, though he did not know for sure. The subjects studied were geometry and Latin. He was not the only one to be chastised but he received the switch more than anyone and he was the last, shortly before the end of the final lesson. He walked back to his place and studied his hand, the way the blood seemed to seep to the surface, drawn upwards by the impact of the switch upon his skin. Perhaps by the heat of it.

As the class made their way out Miss Pugsley requested that he remain behind. He sat in his place. The desks and tables were scoured with initials. Kizzie told him she had found the letters ES and was convinced they were those of their uncle Enoch, carved there when he was a child like them. Miss Pugsley dismissed Miss Pine, and when she had gone the schoolmistress called

41

Leo once more to the front. Her voice echoed in the high roof in a way it had not when the room was full.

'Leopold Sercombe,' she said, more quietly than she habitually spoke. 'What am I to do with you? You do understand, I hope, that punishing you gives me no pleasure? You will soon be one of the eldest and so you must set an example, or I must set one of you. I would much rather not.'

The boy stood with his head lowered.

'Do you understand?'

'Yes, miss.'

'Please speak clearly.'

'Yes, miss.'

'I can't hear you. Do not mumble, boy.'

'Yes, miss.'

'And look at me when I'm talking to you. Oh, Leopold, you are not simple, I'm convinced of it. Can you not see that the world reveals itself to children who study? We walk in the footsteps of those who've studied before us and thus civilisation is created. The Empire thrives. Its peoples prosper.' Miss Pugsley sighed.

The boy watched her feet as she turned and walked some paces to the side, then came back to where she'd stood before. Her shoes were of brown leather and they had a pattern punched and stitched in their sides. They had been polished in recent days if not this very one.

'Your truancy is foolish and you must know how it saddens your mother. But at the very least, when you do come here, can you not concentrate? I wonder if you even try, Leopold. Instead you gaze at the sky and daydream.'

42

'I'm sorry, miss,' he said. 'The swallows don't be long in their labours this time a year.'

Miss Pugsley frowned. 'Swallows?'

Leo told her of their nests in the eaves of the school house, and how they built them or renovated old ones from the year before.

'You were studying birds?'

'Most of the time I be listenin.'

'To what, may I ask, if not to me?'

'I believe, miss, there be an owl in yon chimney.' He glanced across to the chimney breast above the iron stove. He saw Miss Pugsley turn that way too. 'This time a year, one day you lights it, another day you don't. Owls like the shelter of a chimney. They don't know if they likes the heat. It gets too hot, they fly off. Then they comes back and it's cooled down and they don't know where they is.'

'I see.'

Leo looked down at Miss Pugsley's orna-mented shoes. The cotton thread of her black stockings was finer than that of his sister's or his mother's. He knew she was no longer gazing at the chimney breast but was studying him.

'I believe that is the most I've heard you utter in all these years,' she said. 'And you were listening to the owl come and go?'

'No,' he said. 'She never went today. She bin there the whole time, I reckon. I could hear her frettin.'

'Oh, Leopold,' Miss Pugsley said. She stepped towards him. He felt her hands at the back of his head and her arms sliding around and drawing him towards her chest. He felt her neck against his mouth. He could smell a sweetness of powder and of the perspiration of her skin. She kissed the top of his head as she squeezed him to her. 'Oh, Leopold,' she said. 'What am I to do with you?' She clasped him to her. He stood with his arms at his sides. As long as he kept his head down he could breathe unobstructed. He feared that she would lift his head, what would happen if she did. But she only held him tight and kissed the top of his skull through his hair and then she let him go, and stepped back. He looked up at her.

'What will become of you, Leopold?' she said.

'I shall work on one a the master's farms,' he said.

'For your father, I suppose?' she asked. 'He does not mind your truancy as your mother does.'

'No,' he said. 'Sons do not work for their fathers. The master won't allow it. He said it be a sure recipe for discord. I could not be Father's lad, nor his under carter. I should like to work on the master's stud farm.'

'Yes,' she said. 'Then you surely will. You may go. Go home, Leopold.'

He turned and walked to the door, and opened it, and closed it behind him, and trotted out of the playground and along the lane.

April

'He gets up and goes with you to help with your early chores, it's no wonder he forgets to go to school.'

'Would you stop him?'

The boy listened as they spoke of him though he was there beside them. Ruth put a log in the stove and closed the lid. 'I'd rather he slept longer, yes, and woke later, like Kizzie,' she said, wiping her hands on her apron. 'And went to school with her.'

His father considered this long before answering. By the time he did so, Ruth was seated at the table too. 'If you can keep him sleepin, good luck, mother.'

When either of them spoke their breath disturbed the candle flame, and the light fluttered in the room. His father sipped his tea.

'Do you hear your mother?' he said at length. 'T'would be a help to the gaffer if I could write out orders and that. You needs to read and write, for certain, to be a carter these days.'

'Or something better,' said his mother.

The boy looked up and saw the colour in his father's face darken as the blood rose. One of his hands clenched into a fist upon the table.

Leo looked down. In time his father's voice

45

came, steady and low. 'Stay here this mornin. We'll be turnin out tonight. Come then. Is that a bargain, boy? Go to school today.'

After Albert and Fred had left, Leo rose to go back upstairs. His mother took his hand and he turned. She gazed at him. 'Your eyes are dark as sloes,' she said. Her own were pale blue. 'How strange that you all have your father's eyes.' She raised his hand to her lips and kissed it. 'Go,' she said. 'Sleep a little longer if you can.'

Leo tried but he could not. In time he heard Kizzie stir and came directly downstairs once more. Ruth still sat at the kitchen table, sipping at her tea though it had long gone cold. She gazed at the wall. The boy asked his mother what she was thinking. She told him she remembered the days of her childhood. The sea, the restless churning waves, breaking on the esplanade. He asked her where it was she grew up, though he knew the answer, for he liked to hear her say the word, 'Penzance.'

She had come east for work and met the young carter and married him in haste. Leo had not met any of her family. 'My mother and my father,' she told him, 'your grandparents, are long gone in the ground. But I have a brother, if he be there still.'

★ ★ ★

Leo waited in the yard. He heard horses' hooves in the lane and saw Herbert leading Noble, Red and Captain. He took them to the stable, and gave them each corn in their stalls.

46

'You want to groom one a the big pair?' Herbert said.

There was a box of grooming implements the boy had the use of, since in his grandfather's time there'd been a second lad in each team. He brushed down Red as the great carthorse ate. Leo lifted the horse's front left foot and removed mud and grit from it with the hoof pick. He worked down towards the toe, so that the point of the pick might not penetrate the soft parts of the frog. He cleared the cleft of the frog and studied it for signs of thrush but found none. He tapped the shoe to see that it was secure and ran the tips of his fingers round the clenches to see that none had risen. The Shire horse helped him, holding his leg up so that the boy did not carry the whole of the weight.

'Yon horse been workin on the offside today,' Herbert called over from the next stall. 'Every time I turned em on the headland the bugger tried to grab young buds in the hedge with his teeth.'

The boy took up the dandy brush and climbed onto the stool he'd brought into the stall for this purpose. He began at the poll behind the crest of Red's head on the nearside. He brushed to and fro with all the vigour at his disposal, shifting caked dirt and sweat marks from the horse's coat. He brushed Red's belly, then moved to the legs and brushed the dirt from the points of the hocks, from the matted fetlocks and pasterns. As he worked on the hind limbs the boy held the horse's tail out of the way with his free hand.

'I don't know who's more keen to get em out a

the stable, them or I.' Herbert's voice came from further away. He'd finished Noble and was now in the stall of Captain the black gelding.

Leo took up the body brush, with its short and close-set hairs. He threw Red's mane across to the other side of his neck and brushed the crest. He brought back the mane and commenced work upon it at the lower end by the withers. Using a finger of his free hand to separate some locks of hair, he brushed first the ends of the hairs to remove tangles and then the roots in the same way. He worked slowly up the neck, dealing with a few locks at a time. He inhaled the smell of the horse as he did so. The incomparable concoction of hay, dust, flesh and sweat. The scent was best just behind Red's ears. Each horse had its own smell. Red's was sweeter than most, but all that Leo had encountered were good. His father reckoned that the smell of a horse sometimes offered the first sign of illness.

When the mane was clear the boy passed to the body, now taking up the curry comb in his right hand. He began once more at the poll region on the nearside, brushing in short circular strokes in the direction of the lay of the coat, leaning the weight of his body behind the brush. After every fourth stroke he drew the brush across the teeth of the curry comb to dislodge the dirt. He tapped the comb on the floor to clean it out in its turn. When he had completed the nearside he walked around behind the horse and began on the offside, switching hands.

When he had finished the body the boy unstrapped the halter and tied the rope around

Red's neck. He returned the curry comb to the box and with his free hand steadied the horse's head. He worked more gently now and spoke quietly to the carthorse as he did so. When he had brushed its head he replaced the halter.

The tail the boy dealt with as he had the mane, a few strands of hair at a time, teasing and shaking the locks out.

'Your old man's harrowin. Be in soon, let's hope. He says we's turnin em out tonight. Captain's frisky summat awful. I reckon they know, somehow.'

The boy took up a wisp, a fresh one that he reckoned had not been used before. He filled a bucket of water, wet his fingers and shook them over the wisp, in a way the Bishop had sprinkled holy water at Confirmation. He told the horse what he was about to do and showed Red the wisp and then he brought it down with a bang upon the side of the horse's neck and ran it across his skin in the direction of the lay of his coat. He banged the horse in the same way ten times, counting them off, then he moved on to the horse's quarters, and thighs, the hard flat muscular regions of his body. Then round to the other side.

Albert Sercombe came in from harrowing with Coal and Pleasant. 'Finished already?' the boy heard him say. 'You've got Leopold groomin Red?'

'Your boy's only a little tacker, uncle. A course it takes him longer.'

'Thought you'd give him the big horse, did you?'

'Yes, and he has to keep gettin on and off that stool, poor little sod.'

Leo dipped the sponge in the bucket of water and wrung it out. He pushed the stool with his foot against the wall by Red's head and stepped up onto it. He sponged away from the corners of the horse's eyes and around the eyelids. He stepped down and wrung out the sponge and stepped back up and sponged the muzzle region, cleaning the carthorse's lips and the inside and the outside of his nostrils. Again he watered the sponge and wrung it out then moved to the other end of the horse. He lifted the tail and gently cleaned the dock region.

The horse breathed contentedly. The boy found the jar of his father's hoof oil. He dipped the small brush in it and lifted the horse's foot and gave a thin coat of oil to the whole of the hoof and the bulbs of the heel as far up as the coronet, each hoof in turn. Then he returned the jar and all the equipment to their cupboard in the stable room.

Leo returned to Red's stall and spoke to him and then climbed the partition between that stall and the next. He climbed along the cribs past Noble and Captain and squatted on the next partition to watch his father complete the grooming of Pleasant. Beyond, Herbert worked on Coal, the second black gelding. Albert sponged the old mare's face. Then he stopped and peered into her eyes. The mare gazed straight ahead, munching her corn, and to the boy it appeared that man and horse looked long into each other's eyes. His father shifted position slightly, studying the mare's eyeballs from different angles. Then he stepped away and leaned down, filled his sponge with water and wrung it out, and began to clean the horse's muzzle.

Albert glanced up. He did not openly acknowledge his son's looming presence but said, 'I been to the Glenthorne Estate when I were a lad. Had to deliver a horse there for the master. A big hunter, he was. I got lost, I reckon, and I come to it along a track through a gateway in the middle a nowhere. The hunter spotted somethin above us and reared up beneath me.' Albert raised his arms above his head and spread his hands apart. Water dripped down his sleeve. 'A great archway over our heads. On top of each a the pillars was a crouchin gargoyle.' He resumed cleaning the old mare's mouth. 'Never seen nothin like it. That's what you's like up there, boy. A crouchin damn' gargoyle.' Albert chuckled to himself. 'Why I was lookin in her eyes was to see if her lens is cloudy. I'm thinkin there's the start a cataracts.' He picked up the bucket and moved to the back of the horse. 'Nothin to be done about it if there is.'

When Albert had finished he said, 'Let's get em out, then,' and they took the horses, the carters with a pair each, Noble's foal following her, the filly too, the boy leading Red, towering above him, out of the stable and through the yard and into Back Meadow where they let them loose.

'You and me better sweep the stables out,' Albert said to Herbert. They returned to the yard

51

but the boy stayed and watched the horses. The young black geldings galloped around the field. Noble rolled on her back. Old Pleasant, cataracts or not, could smell the new grass and pulled it from the ground and munched it. Leopold saw that for her it was like the new potatoes of early summer eaten with no more than a knob of butter and a leaf or two of mint, or like the first green peas his mother shelled from their pods and boiled and which he savoured in his mouth. So was this first meal of pasture grass of the spring for the old mare.

Red came up to Noble and nibbled at her withers. Noble turned her head to her fellow Shire horse but she did not move. The foal stuck close to his mother. Captain trotted over towards the fence and then twenty yards away passed directly across in front of Leo, kicking his legs behind him as if in some balletic display for the boy, to show him of what acrobatics a big horse is capable.

'Their antics is amusin.'

The boy had not seen or heard Amos Tucker approach. The farmer leaned against the fence pole upon which Leo sat.

'Just turned out?' Amos said.

Leo nodded.

The farmer and the boy watched the horses. Enoch and Fred brought their own groomed animals, the four Shires and the two young bay geldings, to the pasture and let them loose, then returned to sweep their stable. The two teams of horses, who saw little of each other at close quarters through the winter, began to reacquaint themselves in their liberty. They cantered to and fro across or around the pasture on a particular course, from this point to that point, with great purpose that no human being could quite fathom. The boy doubted whether any horse other than the one in motion could either.

'Your father will let em out each evenin, then let em out all night come Friday, I reckon. That's what he does. What his old man did an all.'

Amos Tucker lit his pipe. The horses grazed each a while then took off again. Dusk began to fall. The carters came and collected their horses. It took them longer than they wished for whatever awaited in the cribs, however deep the straw in the stalls, nothing could compare to fresh grass and open space. But the evening cooled, and darkness fell, and the horses allowed themselves to be haltered, and led back to the yard.

April

In the morning, rain fell light but steady upon the land. Leopold and Kizzie walked to school as did other pupils off the estate and round about. Kizzie spoke with girls from the other farms. The boy looked around him. Cattle gathered on the least windswept side of their grazing pasture. Sheep sought shelter in bushes or in the lea of walls. Horses stood in the rain with their heads down as if suffering punishment. Or perhaps showing defiance. Leo took a detour through the wood. Birds did not fly but huddled on branches. Each shrank within a carapace of its wings and feathers. Rain dripped through the leaves.

The children ran through the schoolyard. They were glad to be in the warm dry schoolhouse, but the boy was not. At lunchtime he walked back to the farm.

★   ★   ★

In the afternoon the rain fell harder.

'There's harness to be oiled, gaffer,' Herbert said.

'Aye,' Albert replied.

'I'll light the fire if you want, gaffer.'

'Don't push it, lad, don't push it. Never too wet to cart muck.'

Albert sought out his brother Enoch, the under carter, and told him he would take the black geldings to the blacksmith for it was near as dammit time for their shoes to be refitted. Enoch said he believed it was. Albert told him that Herbert would follow with Noble and Red, and that Leopold was here and would bring Pleasant who was due new ones as hers were a quarter-year old. Enoch said he and Fred would oil tack in the saddle room. Albert nodded his approval.

They took empty canvas sacks, cut gaps along the seams for head and arms and wore them as capes against the weather. Herbert and the boy, leading their horses, passed Albert in the lane, leading Coal and Captain in their refitted shoes, though the falling rain splashing on the stone of the road muffled the noise of them.

'Wait,' Albert Sercombe called to his son. Herbert did not hear and carried on. The boy halted the mare and stood. The carter tied his horses to branches in the hedge. He came back and took the mare's halter from the boy. 'I'll walk her up the lane and walk her back. Watch and tell me what you see.'

He walked his great old mare up the lane. The rain fell upon them all. After the length of a cricket wicket, which was as far as Leo could see before the rain blotted out all things visible, Albert turned and walked back. 'What did you see?' he asked. 'Did you notice owt?'

The boy nodded.

'When?' his father asked. His eyes were narrowed against the rain that beat against his face and ran in the wrinkled fissures of his weathered skin.

'When she put her hind leg to the ground,' the boy said. 'Nearside.'

'Good. Tell the smith to study it.'

★   ★   ★

Others too had come. Herbert tied the horses to iron rings on the outside wall of the smithy and left them standing patiently in the rain.

The boy stood between the bay mare and Red, the nearest of the Shires, sheltered from the cold rain by their great bodies and warmed by them likewise, if only a little. He peered inside the forge. He could see Herbert with other lads and men. They stood, morose, steam rising from them as their wet clothes dried out in the heat of the smithy, speaking doubtless to complain of their lot and to share bad news of their fellows. Then Herbert spoke and the lad nearest to him swung his arm around behind Herbert and slapped the back of his head. His head bowed forward and his damp cap flew off, and the men laughed. Herbert bent forward to retrieve his cap and as he rose with it in his hand he was laughing too.

When his turn came Herbert took first one then the other of the carthorses. The boy remained outside. When it was done Herbert said he would not wait but would see Leo back at the farm, and the boy led the old mare into the forge. The smith Jacob Crocker greeted the boy and he greeted the horse. He told his tall younger son to fetch shoes for Pleasant and if he didn't yet know what size shoes, front and hind, Manor Farm carter's old mare required by now he should seek an alternative profession. The son reached up and made his selection from shoes that hung on nails on the roof joists. In the heat of the forge on this busy day he was naked from the waist up. Crocker saw the boy watching his son and said, 'Tis the one job here he's good for, innit, reachin up high. His back's no good for this work. Tis causin him grief already. He'll never lift an anvil.'

Jacob Crocker's own strength was a legend. His chest was said to measure fifty inches. He could hold two carthorses while they struggled to break away. His neck was so thick, he would let two men wind rope around it and do their best to strangle him. He would challenge any man to lift with their two hands what he could hold above his head with one. Leo himself had seen him bend a poker over his own bare arm, and straighten a horseshoe with his hands.

'My father says to look at her hind foot nearside,' the boy said. 'Her's noddin when her puts it down.'

Crocker shared this request with his elder son, the farrier. They were alike, two barrel-chested men who could lift a horse, a hunter at least if not a Shire. The son was scarred from some infant accident in the forge, the second son was made crooked and their father was as wide as he was tall, too squat, almost dwarf. Yet their flaws or oddities only made it seem to the boy more likely they had been forged by the Lord, who

57

according to Isaiah created the smith, who blew the fire of coals and produced shoes for the horses of chariots, and the wheels, and the weapons of those who rode them to inflict the wrath of God.

The tall second son who had chosen the new shoes put them in the blazing furnace. He shovelled coal and worked the bellows. His spine when he stood was not entirely straight.

The elder son leaned back against the mare's front left flank, bent forward, ran his hand down her leg, squeezed the tendon above the fetlock and lifted the hoof. The mare shifted her weight, distributing it across her other three feet. She allowed the farrier to hold her front left leg between his knees. He chiselled straight the tips of the nails then levered and pulled the old shoe off with pliers, throwing it onto a pile of such discards. He took up his hoof pick and cleaned out the hoof. He laid down the pick and took up his knife and cut the top layer of horn. He laid down the knife and took up his nippers and trimmed the hoof wall. When this was done he used a rasp to flatten and smooth the bottom of the hoof.

The boy looked away from the scar on the side of the young farrier's face. He found himself gazing at the misshapen spine of the second son, and looked away. His gaze returned unbidden to the first son's countenance. The farrier gestured to his brother, who brought the hot shoe to him. The farrier took the pliers and applied the shoe to the mare's hoof. The wall of the hoof hissed and smoked, the stench of the burning matter

58

filling the boy's nostrils.

The farrier took nails from the pocket of his apron and drove them through the shoe and the wall of the hoof. The boy saw the tips protrude through the wall. The farrier used nippers to bend and clip the tips of the nails. Then with the hammer he clinched each nail with a single blow. He then reshod the second and the third hoof likewise. When he came to the near hind foot he removed the shoe and cleaned the hoof then dug into it, until pus came out.

His father, watching, said, 'He's found it. I knew it'd be there. Your old man's not often wrong.'

The boy believed that his father was never wrong when it came to horses but he did not say so.

Jacob Crocker wrapped the old mare's foot in a poultice of bran, in a leather bag secured with string tightened around her pastern.

'Walk her home slow, boy. Apply a new poultice three times a day for the next couple a days, then bring her back here. Tell your old man to put a drop a washin soda in it and all.' Crocker patted the mare's flank. 'A good un, this old girl. Must be comin up near to twenty.'

The boy nodded. 'Eighteen.'

'Er's got a little sidebone down at the coronet there, you might have noticed. I'm keepin an eye on it. We'll adapt her shoe if we has to. She must be gettin stiff in her joints but she's never pulled her foot away from us yet.'

May

James Sparke of Wood Farm kept a breeding
sow. She farrowed in the early spring. The boy's
mother Ruth announced one evening that a
dozen sucklings had been born during the
previous night. How their mother received such
information was a mystery for she seemed rarely
to leave home or garden. Word on such matters
travelled around the tied cottages on the estate
by some mystical means.

Over the days and weeks following, the boy
and his sister Kizzie took a detour via Wood
Farm on their way home from school. They
leaned over the pig-sty fence and gazed at the
great black sow, who lay like some proud obese
monarch on the cleanish straw. Her sleek black
piglets slept or crawled sleepily over her and each
other or suckled at her teats.

After nine weeks Ruth accompanied them to
Wood Farm. Leo carried the sack. Two of the
litter had already gone. James Sparke and Ruth
Sercombe enquired after each other's families.
They spoke about the weather, animals, crops,
church. The names of many people known and
unknown to the children were mentioned and
discussed. Leo watched his sister fall asleep
standing up, as ponies do. Perhaps the gabbering
pair would go on to talk of the people of other

countries, other races, those upon the earth and those below, why not? But then the children's mother asked how much Mister Sparke wanted for this runt over here and he asked Mrs Sercombe whether she truly expected him to be as generous as he was last year, surely she did not wish to take such advantage of a man's good nature again, and so they got to haggling.

James Sparke named a price of two shillings for the fattening pig. Ruth Sercombe burst into laughter as if Mister Sparke had cracked a rattling joke too subtle for the children to comprehend, and said she was glad that despite all the trials and tribulations of this past year he had not lost his sense of humour. She offered one shilling. Mister Sparke said Mrs Sercombe must have little to occupy herself, no? — perhaps her daughter here had taken over the household chores — if she enjoyed wasting a busy farmer's time for her own amusement. He would not go below one shilling and elevenpence. Ruth said, yes, she was quite happy to walk to and fro, she would leave now and would come back when he was serious. She offered one shilling and one penny. So they continued to barter until all of a sudden James Sparke spat on his palm and Ruth spat on hers, and they shook on a deal.

James Sparke leaned over the fence of the sty and caught a black piglet by one of its hind legs. It squealed, shrill and plaintive. Its mother protested with deep-throated grunts. Leo opened the sack. Mister Sparke lifted the piglet and fed it into the sack. The Sercombes walked home three abreast, Leo with the sack over his shoulder, Kizzie beside him speaking to the piglet with words of consolation and promises of how much he would relish his new home. The boy struggled with his load as the piglet wriggled in the sack until he found the breathing hole, and then he lay still with his snout sticking out and listened to the girl's words of reassurance.

May

Pigeons roosted on the beams under the roof of the open shed in the stable yard. The boy fancied their cooing soothed the horses through the long hours of winter darkness. Their number would increase periodically. Albert Sercombe decreed that their tribe be kept to a dozen, twelve apostles, their cooing the incantation of some bird-like gospel of their own.

'Do we fancy pigeon pie, mother?' he asked Ruth. The day following he shot the surplus and presented her with their carcases.

The pigeons gathered small twigs in their beaks and constructed their nests on the rafters. The nests grew by immeasurable, laborious increments. By the following spring they would be dilapidated and the birds would start again. When the chicks were hatched the boy climbed up and studied them. They grew wings. Before they could fly he collected them one Tuesday in a small crate, which he covered with a piece of cloth. This he put in the cart to which he harnessed the pony and so carried it to the crossroads near Home Farm on the eastern side of the estate. There he waited and in time a light horse and cart appeared from the direction of the village. It slowed as it approached him.

'Got something for me, boy?' the huckster asked. 'Let's see.'

The boy showed him the pigeon chicks, seventeen in total.

The huckster wore a chequered yellow waistcoat beneath his grey jacket. He looked around, tipped the front of his hat back. 'You're the carter's younger boy,' he said. 'I want no argument with your father.'

The huckster bought surplus poultry, butter, eggs from the farms on the estate and doubtless others. He also sold all manner of items without order or reason. A year ago he'd sold a pair of laces to the boy's brother Fred. They broke within days for they were made of cotton not of leather such as were required for hobnailed boots, and the following Tuesday Albert Sercombe waited for him. Leo went with him. The carter demanded back the ballast Fred had paid for the cotton laces. The huckster said it was an honest sale and warned Albert not to lay a hand upon him. Not withstanding this request, with a single punch Albert broke his nose and the huckster handed over the coin, all bloody as was the yellow waistcoat.

'I'll give ye half a crown,' he told the boy now. 'Don't make a face, boy, that's two pennies for every chick near's dammit. If ye wish to walk to Taunton or bloody Bridgwater to find yourself a fairer price, you're welcome.'

Leopold nodded and the huckster gave him the coin. He shook his head. 'Don't think you can spend it on my cart. I'll buy but I'll sell to neither you nor your kin.'

64

He made sure the crate was secure on his cart and then rode away along the lane. The boy watched. The odd items stacked upon the cart knocked and jostled against each other, making an almost musical sound as of a band of tambourines fading into the distance.

June

Gideon Sparke, son of James, announced to the cohort of his contemporaries stood around the schoolyard at breaktime that his father had acquired a new pony. He said it was better than any other such animal upon the estate and his father had bought it chiefly for his, Gideon's, use. Leo found this believable. James Sparke also gave his son pig bladders, which Gideon brought to school for football. If he found himself on the losing side he was inclined to grab the bladder and take it home.

Alfred Haswell said he supposed this pony had no vices. Gideon agreed. She was willing, well schooled, comfortable, and had the softest mouth you could dream of. Farm machinery did not rattle her.

Kizzie asked if the pony was pretty too and Gideon assured her that she was. 'A lovely bay mare, I should say, with a good bit a Welsh in her — lovelier than any a your lot over Manor Farm.' He said that she was seven years old, the perfect age. A touch under fourteen hands, an ideal height. That she came to call and boxed easy.

'Sounds just right for you.'

'No, she ain't a novice's pony, that's true.'

Gideon was a tall and portly boy, cumbersome, for not only did his father give him whatever he desired, his mother likewise refused him nothing, which in her case amounted to food. The other boys preferred to tease than to cross him, for though he was no natural fighter, in a brawl his sheer size could prove awkward.

'I'll bet she's fast, though, Giddy, ain't she?' Gilbert Prowse offered.

'Fast?' said Gideon. 'Faster than any a yourn.'

'You should breed from her.'

'She's already bred, when she were three. A lovely black foal, filly t'was.'

'You saw it, did you?'

'I heard about it. A wonderful mother, she were.'

'Don't let the master see such a prize,' said Alfred. 'Why, he'll confiscate a fitty mare like that for hisself.'

'You don't believe me?' Gideon said. 'I'll prove it. Get Sercombe there to bring his nag Saturday and I'll race him. Father'll give us one a his pasture fields. Bring your brass and I'll bet the bloody lot a you.'

With that the bell rang and Gideon marched ahead into the schoolroom.

★　★　★

They congregated at Wood Farm on the morning of the appointed day, the children of the estate and of the village and one or two adults with naught better to do. Dunstone was one, Isaiah Vagges another. Kizzie had volunteered her services as bookmaker for the event.

Leo had not asked for the contest, but it did

67

not occur to him to refuse. The boy walked their pony along the track. He was a skewbald gelding, less than thirteen hands high, a strong little cob who liked to work. He could be harnessed to the small cart in a moment for Ruth to take to the village or if Amos Tucker needed something fetching. Unlike the cart-horses he had no name. Leo did not know why. It was as if a horse had to be of sufficient height to warrant one. He was happy for Leo to ride him. But he was not fast.

Gideon or perhaps his father had marked out a race track in a field of grass. The field was crooked like most hereabouts but there were half a dozen places where the hedge turned sharply, and at each of these corners they had planted a stake some five yards out. Leo led the cob around the temporary course. He watched Gideon seated upon his bay mare in the middle of the field, allowing other children to come and pat the horse and otherwise pay homage. Unless there was something faulty with the bay she would surely be swifter than Leo's cob, but she had to carry far more weight and perhaps this would equalise the contest.

Kizzie took note of the bets. People bet against her pot and they bet against Gideon too, according to his challenge in the schoolyard. In order to be allowed to bet on a horse with Kizzie they had to bet a farthing against him. That was the deal.

The boys and girls put down their farthings or half-pennies. Gilbert Prowse, son of the baker, put down threepence. According to what proportion of stakes were put on which horse, Kizzie determined the odds. They began even but shifted with each wager. She noted the amount a person laid and their odds at that moment. Most, seeing the new pony, forgot how good a rider Leo Sercombe was and put their money on Gideon. Since they had also to stand Gideon's wager it was a way to spread their bet.

Kizzie did not know how bookmakers operated on professional race tracks but here on the estate the children had devised this system and it had become accepted as their custom. It required an older child such as herself, competent in mathematics, to administer it. After the race she would take her cut of five per cent then divide the rest according to a subtle combination of the odds and the amount in the pot. She would also either hand over farthings to Gideon or give him a list of those to each of whom he owed this sum.

★ ★ ★

When the master's daughter walked into the field all stopped what they were doing and watched her come towards them. She did not falter. She asked the first person she reached, Gilbert Prowse, if those two ponies were the only ones taking part. How she knew about the race was a mystery, yet it was hardly profound, for one or two of the maids in the big house were elder sisters of those here present.

Miss Prideaux wore a blue skirt and white blouse. The skirt had neither pleat nor trim and the blouse was plain yet as she walked amongst them it was as if her presence were a gift conferred upon the assembled company. Leo was not sure how. She wore a straw boater tilted back upon her head and from beneath it her light brown hair fell loose upon her shoulders. When she saw Kizzie with the money she stepped forward and said, 'Put this on the bigger horse.'

Kizzie stared at the coin now on her palm. She had seen a sovereign before, but not held one herself. It was oddly insubstantial, lighter than a florin. 'Beg pardon, Miss Charlotte,' she said. 'We cannot cover it.'

The master's daughter frowned. She took back the coin and returned it to her purse, producing a sixpence instead, which Kizzie accepted. She licked her pencil and wrote down the name.

★ ★ ★

Alfred Haswell asked Gideon how many times they intended to circumnavigate the field. Gideon said they would ride twice around. Leo nodded in agreement. He figured the field was between one and two acres. There were two stakes to mark the start line, which would also be the finish. Gideon rode his bay mare towards it. Leo watched him and knew at once that he and his cob would win the race, for the chubby older boy's bareback mount upon the horse was loose and unbalanced. If Gideon let his mare go, he would be unable to stay upon her. That was all there was to it.

Leo looked around. The morning was overcast

70

but warm, the grey sky would surely clear soon. He jumped onto his pony's back and grasping the mane pivoted his body and swung his right leg over, and followed after Gideon.

There was no official starter. The riders made ready and Gideon yelled and took off. The boy let him go. The mare set off at a cracking pace. Gideon held on as best he could. Soon he was holding his arms as far around the bay mare's neck as he could, while also pulling on the reins to slow her down. Leo let his cob canter behind some yards distant, for if the corpulent boy fell he did not wish to trample him. He wondered whether the others in the middle of the field realised Gideon's predicament. Perhaps they found the sight impressive and thought he was riding his bay mare like a jockey. Leo looked across and saw that they were yelling and waving encouragement, though to whom he could not tell.

They circled the field once. Gideon pressed his legs against his horse's belly for balance. He still hung on her neck, and was jouncing or wobbling upon her spine. Halfway round the second time Leo himself leaned forward. He brought his knees up and crouched forward on the cob's withers. It was not a style he had copied, or been taught. He cantered past the bay mare and glanced towards the spectators, for he hoped the master's daughter was watching. But, riding hard, he could not pick her out in the crowd.

June

The boy's father strode up the track to Little Rats Hill. The boy fell behind, trotted a few steps to catch up. Walked beside his father. Grey sky. Lagged again. Trotted forward. They ascended the track in this manner.

On the hill the boy's father took a plug of tobacco from his pouch, filled and lit his clay pipe. They waited.

Amos Tucker rode his cob across Haw Park towards them. They watched him kick the horse periodically though it made no difference to the beast's laggardly pace. The farmer's legs looked puny beneath the barrel of his body.

'Albert,' Amos said.

'Gaffer,' said the boy's father. The boy took the reins of the cob as Tucker leaned forward on to the horse's neck grasping its mane, and rolled his weight over the saddle and down to the ground.

'What's our reckonin, Albert? Be we ready?'

The two men stood in close proximity to each other. Each studied the earth around him and as far as he could see, turning at intervals to cast his eye in a fresh direction. The sky was overcast, streaked with grey, a little hazy. The boy held the reins and watched the two men. The cob wanted to munch the lush grass but the boy gripped the bridle beside the bit and kept her head up.

'I reckon tis makin its way,' said his father quietly.

Tucker looked around about, as if with these words seeing the scene afresh. He nodded, and spoke in little more than a whisper. 'I reckon so too. It's risin, innit?'

The boy's father frowned. 'Seems so to me, gaffer.'

Tucker took a step closer. The boy strained to hear him. 'Let us make a beginnin,' he said.

They spoke in whispers, as if some malevolent spirit in the upper sphere might overhear and punish their presumption. Or as if words uttered carelessly might dart like arrows upward and puncture the wispy clouds, provoking rain.

'Go forth, Albert,' Tucker said. 'Make ready.' He clambered aboard his mare, took the reins from the boy and steered back towards the farmhouse in the bed of the valley, kicking the cob's flanks on occasion, to no discernible effect.

Albert Sercombe set off down the track. The boy could see the village in the distance and the families returning from church to the farms on the estate. Pilgrims walking home. He heard a sound, turned and scanned the air searching for its origin. The song of a skylark. He could not see the bird but its chirping liquid song teased him. He stared. His cousin, son of Enoch, elder brother of Herbert, was a soldier. He had been home on leave one month before, shunned by his elders, dandy in red tunic and round cap. The lads and boys gathered round him. While he hid they closed their eyes then tried to find him but they never could. He also stripped naked then wagered he could reclothe himself entire, fit for parade, in the time it took a lad to hold a lit match. Thus he took their pennies.

The boy looked about him patiently, the skylark's running stream of song impossible to pinpoint, until he saw the bird dropping, plummeting towards the ground, and then before it seemed to reach the grass it vanished. The boy turned and trotted after his father.

★   ★   ★

The men rose and moved like shades in the dark cottage. His father Albert, his brother Fred. The boy followed them. They stumbled along the lane from the cottage to the farm, dew materialising on their caps and shoulders.

Fred hived off to the stables. At the gate to the pasture the boy's father called the horses. They came up out of the darkness.

Fred had climbed into the loft, poured corn and chaff into the manger. He threw the last of the clover from the year before into their racks as the horses came into the stable, five of them, one after another in the order they observed amongst themselves. Red, the big ten-year-old Shire, then eight-year-old Noble with her foal and the filly, then the old mare Pleasant, then the two black three year olds, first Captain, then Coal. They entered their customary stalls one by one.

While Albert prepared the harness and tackle, the boy followed Noble into her stall. He spoke to her to tell her of his approach, that she be not

74

startled as she fed. He speculated as to whether she missed her foal in the daytime while she worked. He told her he thought she would be in harness with her brother, Red, today, driven by the lad Herbert, his cousin, but that when the cereal harvest came she'd be put abreast with the young ones, and he wondered whether when she pulled beside Captain she would know that he was her son. He thought not.

He heard the clatter of hobnailed boots. Then his father's voice addressing the new arrivals. 'Good a you to join us fore the evenin.'

'I see no fuckin light ayet in that sky,' the boy's uncle, Enoch, replied. 'I'm here. Your lad's here.'

'He'll find Fred's filled the manger.'

Herbert ran in. He geared up Red with chain harness, groping in the gloom, then came into Noble's stall. 'Will you lead her out for me?' he asked.

They led the heavy horses to the stone drinking trough. The boy's father stood in the rickyard by the two-horse mower, cleaned, oiled, knife-sharp. In the half-light the mower gave the first colour of the day, red and canary yellow.

'Hup! Back!' Herbert spoke loudly to each horse in turn until they stood either side of the mowing machine's pole. He lifted this and Albert strapped it to the underside of the horses' collars, the weight of the machine on their necks. He fastened the traces to the swinging whippletrees, and put a wooden coupling stick between the horses' bridles, fastening it with spring clips.

Albert tied the rope reins with a slip knot to

75

the left ring of Noble's bridle and the right ring of Red's. Herbert fetched an armful of old clover and placed it on the iron seat.

'Think I'm gettin old and soft, lad?' Albert asked him.

'I've no wish for a sore arse, uncle,' Herbert said. 'See no need for thee to have one neither.'

'We'll start over Watercress Meadow. Bring a rake, another knife and the file.' Albert mounted the machine, made a clicking sound by blowing air through his teeth sharply against his cheek, and flicked the reins. The horses moved slowly forward and he drove them out of the yard, past the farmhouse still in darkness, into the lane by Long Close, the boy Leo following.

At the gate to Watercress Meadow, Albert Sercombe waited. He did not look behind. The boy trotted past and unlatched the gate, and swung it open. Albert dropped the bedding of the mower. He pushed the lever at his side forward to pitch the fingers and knocked the gear knob to the on position. He ordered the horses to walk on. The meadow was heavy with dew. Light seeped into the morning, the sky was clear, the boy watched the mowing machine clatter around the outside of the meadow tight to the hedge in a clockwise direction, the long knife cutting the grass on the right-hand side of the machine. Rabbits scuttered to their burrows.

The boy walked back to the yard. He passed Herbert on the way, weighed down with implements. He saw his uncle Enoch riding the second mower, he guessed to the Berry Fields. The boy's brother Fred followed in a cart.

From the tool shed Leo took a sickle and sharpening stone and returned to the field. He watched the rattling mower. Grass, cornflower, clover, meadow-sweet, fell before the agitating knife. Herbert raked the outermost swathe in away from the hedge. The boy walked through the field. He found a wasps' nest and cut around it with the sickle. His father had not asked him to do this but he took it upon himself.

Albert Sercombe drove the horses, the horses pulled the mower, the mower cut the grass. At times he stopped and climbed down and freed the knife that was clogged with wet grass or with soil from molehills. Herbert Sercombe raked the swathe away from the hedge. Starlings gathered and scoured the newly mown grass for worms and insects. Leo Sercombe investigated the long grass. His father brought the horses to a stop and called out to Herbert to bring the new knife. He disengaged the gear and raised the bedding.

Herbert came with the long knife. Albert felt the blade. 'You've not sharpened it,' he said.

'You didn't say.'

'Did you not think, you lazy sod?'

'You said to rake the hedge swathe.'

The boy thought his father might strike the lad, but he did not. 'Where's the file?'

Herbert said nothing.

Albert nodded in the direction of the oak tree at the base of which Herbert had stowed the implements. 'You left the file over there?'

'You said to fetch the knife.' Herbert turned and walked towards the oak, muttering to himself. Albert watched him, shaking his head, as if someone were speaking in his ear pointing out the lad's merits yet he disagreed.

The boy noticed that the first bluebottles and horseflies of the morning had appeared, worrying the horses. He went to the hedge, reached up and pulled off lanterns of elderflower. He walked back and laced them into the horses' bridles. His father filed the blade of the new knife. Herbert removed the used knife from the machine, and replaced it with the freshly sharpened one. He squirted oil from the long-spouted can along the blade and between the metal fingers, then he oiled the driving bar, and lastly he filled the reservoir for the cogs that drove the mower from the wheels of the vehicle.

'You know well what to do,' Albert told him. 'So do it.'

They hung their jackets on the hedge and resumed their labours. The boy watched his father circle the field in diminishing irregular loops. Periodically the carter slapped the skin of his neck or arm. From a distance he appeared to be castigating himself.

The boy's sister Kizzie stood beneath the oak tree. She held up a basket. No one knew how long she had been standing there.

'You should a called us,' Herbert yelled.

Kizzie did not answer. She had recently taken a vow of silence. The school monitors had been nominated to go to the Coronation fête, given to a horde of the nation's children at the Crystal Palace. Kizzie could not be spared at this, the busiest time of year. Miss Pugsley and Mabel Prowse had gone without her.

Herbert unhooked the pair of horses from the mower. Leo carried handfuls of freshly cut grass into the shade and the horses munched it, their tails swinging.

They ate the cottage loaf and cheese and onion the girl had brought, drank water, and tea, still lukewarm from the pot.

'Feels like it should be lunchtime,' said Herbert. 'And tis only the mornin break.'

'These are the long days,' Albert agreed. They ate in silence.

Farmer Tucker came walking into the field. 'Mornin, Albert,' he said. 'You've made a good start. Here, I brought you a drop a cider.'

'Welcome, gaffer.' Albert took the flagon and drank deeply, then passed it to Herbert who did likewise.

'Heard the clatter of the mower as I ate my breakfast,' Amos Tucker said. 'What a racket. And it makes no difference how low you set it, you'll never shave as fine as a good man with a scythe.'

Albert Sercombe nodded slowly. 'Aye, gaffer, and it took as I recall eight men to cut this meadow.'

The boy and his sister and the lad their cousin Herbert said nothing.

'Aye, Albert,' Tucker said. 'And if I listen now . . . ' He ceased speaking and raised his head aslant, ears cocked, alert in the manner of a plump cock pheasant. ' . . . I can hear the music of those scythes being sharpened.'

Kizzie passed around jam tarts.

'Remember, Albert, when the master brought

79

the first mowing machine on to the estate? He'd only just took over, after the old Lord Prideaux died on us.'

'Was it here on Manor Farm, gaffer?' Herbert said.

'No. Home Farm. Albert's father, Jonas, told me, 'The men won't endure it.' Right enough, they stuck iron harrow tines upright in the grass. Ruined the machine.' Amos Tucker shook his head. 'Who was the master to punish? The men or the farmer?'

Albert swallowed a draught of cider.

'What did the master do, gaffer?' Herbert asked.

Farmer Tucker cast about him. As if there were a greater, invisible audience for his recollections beyond this small band. 'One old boy was a bachelor. He was put under arrest, and taken to court in Taunton. Sent down a while in Exeter gaol. Never heard from again, was he, Albert?'

The boy's father shook his head.

'Died in the workhouse, like as not,' said Amos. 'And the farmer, one Gresley by name, the master moved on after harvest.'

'Some of they others was lucky, I'd say,' Herbert opined.

'Our master is a wise man,' Albert assured his lad. He rose unsteady to his feet. They stepped out of the shade of the oak branches.

'Hot for the horses, ain't it, carter?' Herbert said.

Albert looked up at the sun, squinting.

Herbert nodded towards Noble and Red. 'The

80

blood-suckers is botherin em bad.'

'We'll finish this meadow.'

The girl took the basket away. Tucker carried off his empty flagon. Herbert filed the blade. When the time came to replace it he did so. The mower rattled around the field. The boy watched his father ride the mower. A wispy cloud of steam rose from his sweating body. He was like one of those Canaanites who lived in the valley land and had chariots of iron; they were not driven out by the Israelites but lived in the midst of them, and they became forced labourers. They lived thus, still, here in the West Country.

Periodically rabbits ran across the stubble, birds rose from the grass. When the residual clump in the middle of the meadow was cut Albert Sercombe drove his pair out around the outside of the field in an anti-clockwise direction: the grass over which the horses had ridden initially had recovered a little and now itself was mown.

When he reached the gate Albert brought the horses to a halt, raised the knife and fingers of the mower, put them out of gear. The boy saw bloodstains on the blade. His father drove the horses back into the lane. Herbert gathered the implements. The boy turned back into the field and followed the hedge where the machine had most recently mowed. He found the dismembered carcase of a partridge, and a little further on its nest, built by chance in a slight depression of the earth. He counted nine olive-brown eggs, smooth and glossy. Only three were broken. He removed his jacket and tied the ends of the two sleeves together. He looped the sleeves as a collar round his neck, and lifted the nest carefully, entire, and carried it in his jacket like a sling slowly home.

★ ★ ★

The boy's mother was responsible for their poultry. She had two hen huts, each housing thirty hens and one cockerel. Annually in March the cockerels were replaced by others of different breeds. Thus she did invigorate her flock of birds. The yard and the orchard were populated by many different strains, Albion, Brahmin, Dorking, Leghorn, Spanish and Wyandottes clucking and squawking in a confusion of tongues like the doomed builders of Babel.

Ruth fed young chicks with rice. Each spring she sold the two-year-old hens and replaced them with pullets hatched the previous year. The boy searched among them now for the black Minorca hen. She had never been sold; his mother deemed her as co-operative a sitter as she had ever known. The bird believed every egg placed beneath her was her own. He found her in the orchard and bribed her with grain to her nesting place behind the wood shed. He laid the partridge eggs down, still in their nest, and the hen took a turn or two around them then stood and looked about her as if to an imaginary audience of her own kind, to show them this impressive production. Then she sat upon the eggs.

* * *

On the day following, Herbert took one of the three year olds, Captain, leading the swathe turner to Watercress Meadow. The hot sun had bleached the outermost of the green herbage and was turning it to hay already. The clover in red bloom was now a fawn colour, the yellow trefoil had wilted, and Herbert followed the same route as his carter had the day before, turning the grass, which smelled so sweet a man could imagine becoming a ruminant munching upon it, contented.

Leo had agreed to go to school but he tracked back. At the farm he collected the same implements Herbert had used the day before and carried them past the Meadow to Ferny Piece from where he could hear his father mowing. The boy raked the swathe out away from the hedge. When Albert stopped for his morning break he did not speak of his son's presence, neither to thank nor to berate him, but he broke his bread and cut the cheese and the onion and shared them with Leo, and he shared the water.

The hay in the field gave off heat as it dried. The boy watched birds as they flew through the air above and were unexpectedly disturbed, how their flight was upset and how they responded. Some struggled ill-naturedly then resumed their intended direction. One yellow wagtail, however, returned to this unexpected thermal and let itself fall and glide. The boy watched it playing with the air.

★ ★ ★

When they ate again, Leo produced his packed school lunch. The boy pulled his boiled bacon sandwich apart and offered his father the larger part. His father passed him his knife and the boy cut his jam pie in half. His father reached across and ruffled the boy's head and hair; his hand was huge, flattened by labour, the skin callused and tough like hide.

★ ★ ★

On the morning of the third day Albert paced out a rectangle in the rick yard, thirty feet long by fifteen feet wide, and marked it with old straw.

They began to gather the hay. Albert hitched Noble in the shafts of one waggon and drove it to the Meadow. Herbert hitched Red to the second and towed it likewise.

The boy and his mother and his sister raked the swathes of hay into cocks. The heads of the rakes were as wide as those who wielded them were tall. Their wooden teeth were each eight inches long. Albert stood in the bed of the first waggon. His son Fred on one side and Herbert on the other pitched hay up to him with their long forks. Dunstone led Noble between the cocks of hay. His mother saw the boy watching the horses.

'I know you'd rather have yon job, Leo,' she said. 'Poor Dunstone would take it to heart.'

Dunstone was a vagabond upon the estate. He

84

had no place to sleep but each night chose a new spot. At a glance he could pass for a boy but then one saw his face. Or one might see him stiff and limping in the morning and take him for an old man, and be likewise duped. He was neither young nor old, and he was both. They said of him there was not much up in the attic. His ragged clothes were the cast-offs of other men. Given him by women ashamed for their husbands to wear them any longer. They were ill-fitting upon poor Dunstone. The sleeves of his jacket reached almost to his fingers. The hems of the trousers had been cut off and were frayed above his ankles. He lifted wisps of hay and fed them to the horse.

The job was short-handed but Albert Sercombe could not abide his brother working in the same field and Tucker put up with the restriction. Enoch Sercombe mowed the Back Meadow. They could hear the machine clattering on the other side of the hedge on the eastern side of Watercress Meadow.

The boy as he raked glanced often at his father. Albert rose by degrees upon the hay he stacked beneath himself, levitating like the Prophet Ezekiel or some ecstatic saint contemplating the mystery of the Lord's harvest. When he nodded, the boy trotted to the farm and entered the stables. Captain had already had his halter put upon him. The boy led him back out to the Meadow. Amos Tucker was at the gate and said to him, ''The wolf also shall dwell with the lamb, and a child will lead them.'' He grinned and called to the boy's mother, 'See him lead the beast, Ruth. I swear he's no need for the halter. Is it not a wonder?'

Leo did not look to either side and did not acknowledge those who now considered him but led the great black Shire gelding to the waggon, where Herbert hitched Captain to the front of Noble as the trace horse. Dunstone watched, moving from one foot to the other.

'He talks to the creatures, Dunstone,' Herbert said. 'Don't you, Leo? Speak to the dumb creatures more than thou speakest to man?'

Dunstone could not keep still. 'What shall I do?' he asked of Herbert. There were no more than half a dozen teeth left in his mouth. He turned to the boy and said, 'What shall I do?'

Fred tied ropes to the sides of the waggon and threw them to his father atop the load. Amos Tucker wound them around the pins on the other side and threw them back to Albert, and so did they criss-cross the mound of hay and secure the load. Albert stood and looked about him for a moment, enjoying this unusual perspective on the land he knew. Then he came over the side: grasping a rope, he lowered himself hand over hand to the ground. Ruth raked down the sides of the load and Amos Tucker applauded her neatness.

Leo climbed up and rode Noble side-saddle, his father beside the horse's bridle, holding Captain's long leading rein. He ordered the horses forward. The boy looked back and saw that Amos Tucker was now in the second waggon, loading with a sheaf pike the hay thrown up by Herbert and Fred. Dunstone led the horse, Red, forward when told to. The boy's mother and his sister raked another line of hay into cocks.

The waggon joggled and swayed across the field, through the gateway, along the lane. Hay caught in the hedge and was pulled off the load, decorating the branches like the scattering of some midsummer festivity. As they approached the long slope towards the farm the horses sped up, though Albert Sercombe had said nothing and pulled the full waggon up the incline and into the yard.

Ernest Cudmore the shepherd and Isaac Wooland the stockman were waiting for them. When the waggon was in position Isaac leaned a ladder against it and they climbed on top of the load of hay. Albert unhitched the ropes from the pins and the other two men began to pitch forkfuls down to him, into the foundation Albert had laid at the break of day.

The boy fetched the second gelding, Coal, from the stable and walked him to the Meadow. Herbert walked towards him and they passed each other through the gateway.

The field was quiet. Amos Tucker's daughters had joined the boy's mother and sister in raking the swathes into cocks across the great meadow. Their white smocks and bonnets were smirched with dirt. His uncle Enoch had taken over from Herbert, pitching forkfuls up to Amos Tucker. The boy led the horse to the front of the waggon. Enoch hitched it to the traces. When they had tied the load down, Dunstone led Red and Coal close to the gateway and stood them

87

there. The men slaked their thirst with cold tea. Herbert returned with the empty waggon, standing aboard it, driving Noble and Captain with their separate reins. He brought them to where his father Enoch indicated. The boy held the horses. Herbert walked to the gateway and took the reins from Dunstone and led the second, full waggon out and along the lane. Dunstone came trotting over and took Red's bridle from the boy.

So they worked through the afternoon and the warm evening. As the light ebbed, the women left the field. The men completed a load in the fading light. They followed the last waggon into the yard, sweat-soaked flannel shirts cooling on their backs.

A second rick had begun. The boy watched his father put the roof on the first rick in the dying light. He came down the ladder. 'Let it settle,' he told Herbert. 'Then top it up a little. Thatchers'll come in two to three weeks, gaffer?'

'Don't ye worry, Albert, I'll have a word with they,' said Tucker.

The boy helped his father groom the horses. Herbert lit the paraffin lamp and hung it on the wire above the stalls. The boy followed each brushstroke with his bare hand, as his father did, to rid the horses' shoulders of sweat marks where the heavy collars had been.

He walked home with his father and his brother. His mother gave them cold ham and eggs fried in pig fat, bread and butter. They ate in silence, then hauled their weary bodies up the stairs to bed.

July

Noble had gone to work each day but returned to the pasture in the evening and suckled her foal. Albert Sercombe took the foal, now a colt, from her one day in July. He led the colt out of the yard. The boy led old Pleasant after. He watched the colt yank and strain on the unfamiliar halter, saw the force his father was obliged to exert to restrain him.

They let them loose in the near paddock, climbed out between the fence poles and leaned upon the upper pole and watched Pleasant graze and the colt scurry and stop. He looked around, cantered to the far side of the paddock, returned to Pleasant, studied her.

'Her'll educate him,' Albert said.

They watched the colt gallop in one direction then stop, as if he had been ordered to, or so commanded himself. He stood still and they watched him, then he all of a sudden took off swerving somewhere else.

'Is he lookin for his dam?' Albert said. 'Is he forgettin, then rememberin? I don't know. No one knows how the brains of horses reason.'

Pleasant ignored the colt, and grazed.

'I like the look of him,' Albert Sercombe told his son. 'His testicles ain't fallen but when they do I'm not keen to geld him. I'll talk to the gaffer. See if the master'd care to come and take a look.' Albert filled his clay pipe, watching the colt. In due course he lit it. 'We've not had a stud go from Manor Farm since your grandfather's time.'

The boy felt his father grip his upper arm with one hand and his wrist with the other. 'How much muscle you got there, boy?'

The boy remembered one thing about his grandfather: he wore leather straps on his wrists, weakened by a lifetime of working the plough reins.

'You's strong enough, I reckon,' Albert Sercombe decided. 'How do you fancy bein the one to swing this colt? If you needs a hand, Dunstone will do your biddin. You seen me do it, boy. Don't touch him. Let the colt touch you.'

★ ★ ★

On the afternoon following the boy took a halter from the saddle room. He found the old lad walking between Manor Farm and the cross-roads, saw him walk along the lane then turn and walk twenty yards and turn again.

When he reached Dunstone the boy said, 'Will you help me?' The old lad followed him gladly. Dunstone walked in tiny steps, on his tiptoes, like one child creeping up on another. He spoke of what he had seen. 'I sin many things this day, Leo. I sin Isaac send his dog to fetch the cows for milkin and that dog he don't hurry them, you know, he brings em in slow with their full udders swayin, like. That's a clever dog.'

Dunstone trotted on his mincing feet. Leopold had heard his reports before, as had all who lived upon the estate, for Dunstone ranged across it when he was of a mood to. On rare occasions he witnessed something new and added the account to his repertoire.

They walked to the paddock. The boy bade Dunstone hold the long coiled rope and wait outside the fence. He tucked the halter inside the back of his trouser belt, under his jacket, climbed in and walked to Pleasant, and stroked the old mare, and spoke to her. The colt regarded him from a distance. The boy walked into the middle of the paddock and waited. The colt ignored him and moved away in a circuit, but his curiosity betrayed him and he kept coming nearer.

When the foal was not far away the boy took aniseed from his pocket and rubbed it between his fingers and the colt's head went up. His nostrils trembled. His head went down and he paced slowly, steadily, towards the boy. The boy spoke to the colt and then he reached behind him, released the halter, brought it round and slipped it over the colt's head. He waved to Dunstone to join him. The old lad scampered across the paddock. Leopold clipped the rope to the tie-ring on the halter, beneath the horse's head. He bade Dunstone hold the halter in a firm grip while he made his way slowly, inviting the colt to watch him, to the fence. There he took his time to remove his jacket and lay it over the upper pole, before ambling back across the paddock. He took over once again from the old lad.

Leopold walked backwards, letting the rope uncoil. When it had reached its full extent he bade Dunstone hold the end while he grasped the rope a little way along and they stepped back and took up the slack. The colt felt the pressure and backed away, pulling Leo and Dunstone forward. They dug their heels into the hard grassy ground and strained, and dragged the colt towards them. The colt set his hooves four-square upon the earth and held them. The boy and the old lad held their ground likewise. The young horse and the pair of diminutive humans were well matched. This tug-of-war continued, until the colt could bear the strain on his neck no longer, and jumped forward. The boy stepped back smartly, knocking into Dunstone, who staggered backward until the rope was taut once more.

And so they continued, moving by increments across and around the paddock, until the colt was weary. The boy thanked Dunstone for his help and said that mother would feed him should he care to go to their cottage. Dunstone nodded and turned and made off at his fast shuffling pace. The boy chewed aniseed and spoke to the colt and blew his breath into its nostrils. He removed the halter, and left the paddock.

★   ★   ★

'Avoid the soap, boy.'

Leo turned to his father, who never usually whispered in this manner. Ruth had left the kitchen, to fetch something from the garden or to visit the privy, and Albert kept an eye out for her return. He stirred sugar into his tea and sipped it.

'When mother heats the kettles tomorrow,' he said, indicating the zinc bath hung from a hook on the kitchen wall, 'you disappear.'

'How?' Leo asked.

His father shook his head. 'You'll think a somethin.'

The boy looked to his older brother Fred for guidance but he only shrugged. They heard voices outside approaching, Ruth and Kizzie.

'Why?' he whispered urgently.

His father looked at him as at a fool. 'A man should not wash,' he said, 'while breakin horses.'

★ ★ ★

On the second day swinging the colt Leo did not seek out Dunstone but went to the paddock on his own. He hung his jacket on a post and secured the halter inside his shirt, and walked to the centre of the field. He laid the coiled rope at his feet. The colt did not come at first but pranced here and there. The boy put his arms out to his sides horizontally and then he turned, slowly, and the colt stopped and watched him. The boy spun or pirouetted, then as if a spring inside him was unwinding he did so with less velocity and came slowly to a halt facing away from the colt. He lowered his arms. The colt watched and then took a step and walked forwards until he reached the boy and stood just behind him. The boy turned and put the halter upon the colt.

93

They played out their game. The boy pulled the rope, the colt tugged back, until it could take the strain no more and yielded. The boy was stronger than the day before and needed no help, he was not sure how. He took up the slack and they resumed. He knew he was being watched but did not look to see who it might be. His father valued this colt and if he had shared this assessment word would spread around the estate, for the carter was respected as his own father had been before him.

The boy finished as he had the afternoon before. He spoke to the colt and told him he was the finest young beast in God's creation, and that he, the boy, was his master. He inhaled the foal's lovely scent. A younger smell than that of the full-grown horses but Leo could not say how, exactly. He slipped the halter off the colt then walked back a few paces. The colt turned away in the manner of one insulted, holding himself stiffly, then he shook or sneezed himself loose and galloped away across the paddock bucking and kicking, as if some invisible simulacrum of his tormenter were being thrown off. The boy watched the colt, his young lean muscular beauty in motion, then turned and walked towards the fence. There was but one spectator there, sitting on the top pole, feet resting on the lower, a youth in Homburg hat, shirt, breeches, and riding boots of a sort worn by the master and his kind.

The boy walked slowly with his head down, coiling the loose rope elbow to thumb as he did so. The youth sat beside Leo's jacket where he'd left it draped over the post. When he reached the

94

fence he laid the halter and rope upon the ground and took his jacket and pulled it on, one arm and then the other. He did not look up but saw at the outermost of his vision the brown leather riding boots, diminutive in size.

'Are you not ashamed to treat a foal in so cruel a manner?' The youth spoke in a voice that was unbroken. 'Well, have you nothing to say for yourself?'

Leo reached down and picked up the halter and the coiled rope.

'I asked you a question, boy. Your silence is insolent.'

Leo bent and climbed out between the poles of the fence. His anger made him clumsy and he knocked his head upon the underside of the upper pole. He glanced up at the youth. The master's daughter looked down at him, her torso twisted, one arm gripping the upper pole for balance. Her hair was gathered up above and behind her head, inside the hat that was too large for her, but he glimpsed beneath its brim the same expression on her face as when her father had presumed that she would wish to fondle this foal new-born four months before.

He bent his head towards the ground.

'Are you shaking your head?' the girl asked. She raised her right hand from the pole and gripped it with the left instead and swung her legs over and jumped to the ground. The boy kept his head down and stepped aside.

'Are you walking away when I'm talking to you?' the girl said. 'How dare you?'

He heard her footsteps hurry after him. She

overtook and placed herself in his path. He stopped.

'Do you know who I am, boy?' she said. 'Of course you do. Shall I tell my father of the carter's boy's insolence?'

The boy shook his head. He kept his gaze on the finely tooled seams of the girl's brown riding boots. 'No,' he said. 'No. Tis not cruel, miss. Yon colt enjoys it.'

The girl released a laugh that held no trace of humour. 'Yes, of course, do you think I'm blind? Can I not see with my own eyes? He enjoys it . . . and the more fool him. He believes it is a joust, a bout between equals. He doesn't know it to be but the first stage of his submission, in a life of abject ceaseless slavery, does he?'

The boy looked up. Their eyes were level. Hers were brown, though not as dark as his own and those in his family. They were the colour of hazelnut shells. She had freckles too, much lighter brown. He looked back down before he spoke. 'No,' he said. 'I doubt he do.'

'Good,' she said. 'Good. You can speak, and you are not entirely stupid. How old are you, carter's boy?'

Her boots, though they had been polished recently, were dusty. 'I be twelve year old, miss. Last month.' He glanced up, long enough to see the girl smile.

'We are alike one year older than the century, you and I,' she said. 'Born in the last year of the old one. It is a strange privilege, I believe. What is your name?'

Her boots were relatively new. She must have

worn them often. 'It be Leopold, miss.' He looked up briefly to find her gazing directly at him, and looked back down.

'You have eyes the colour of blackberries, Leopold,' the girl said. She took a step to the side, and walked away, in the direction of the manor. After a while the boy raised his eyes. He watched, keeping his eyes upon her until, two hundred yards or further hence, the curve of the lane took her out of sight.

July

Ida Tucker the gaffer's wife was a musician. On Sunday afternoons she gathered her family around the piano and all manner of wailing could be heard faintly from the farmhouse. None of her daughters played their upright piano in time but she did not give up; there was surely an instrument to suit each one of them if they could but discover it. She asked Leo Sercombe to ride over to the village of Huish Champflower, where the Rector's wife would give him an oboe in a wooden case.

The boy did not hitch the cart but found panniers, which he secured with straps around the chest, buttocks and abdomen of the skewbald gelding. He attached bridle and reins and rode the pony bareback out of the estate, passing a wheat field in which his mother, sister and other women laboured. All wore bonnets to shield their faces from the rising sun. The wheat was seven or eight inches high. Each carried two implements, the length of walking sticks. One was forked, the other had a blade fixed at its end at right angles to the stick. With them the women and children worked slowly through the corn, cutting thistles.

★ ★ ★

It took Leo time to find the Rectory for unlike those he knew it stood some way from the church. A woman he took to be the housekeeper or cook answered the door. She was expecting him. She turned and picked up a flattish box from a table in the hallway. It was upholstered in scuffed and faded red leather, and was heavier than he expected. The woman told Leo to wait, and disappeared. She returned with a tall glass, which she handed to him. He rested the music case against the wall, raised the glass and drank in one long draught until the water was gone. It tasted faintly of metal. He gave her back the glass and she gave him a carrot. Then she stepped back inside and closed the door.

★   ★   ★

The boy rode back by a different route. Flies and gnats accompanied him. A swarm would leave him unmolested for a while, then another take its place. The cob swished his tail and twitched his ears to deter them. Red butterflies too shared Leo's journey for brief stretches. He had the impression they were inspecting him. Then, tired of his company, they fluttered off.

He became lost but not for long. The hills in the distance guided him in the approximate direction of home. He could not go far without seeing someone, in passage or at work, and would ask the way if he had to. Then he entered a wood he did not know. The cob followed a grassy path that was not overgrown at all yet held no foot or hoof prints. They walked through a stand of beech trees whose last year's brown leaves carpeted the ground. The thick, smooth trunks rose to canopies of green leaves.

They rode through the cool shade of the wood. Leo thought they would pass through soon but it seemed to be a forest. They came to a huge leafless oak tree. Branches sprouted from the trunk like great twisting knives. It was dead but looked permanent, as if it had stood there in that state for centuries, in some proud arboreal afterlife.

Leo dismounted and led the pony down towards a steep-sided creek, letting him drink. He mounted up and found a narrow path, branches of alder and birch brushing against them as they walked. He realised that he was hungry and took the carrot out of his pocket and crunched it as he rode. It must be well past noon. They came to another oak tree much like the earlier one, dead but apparently full of force, still. They passed red-barked conifers, their trunks at the base wide as windmills. He looked up and could not see how high they stood. The boy had never been in a wood like this before. Perhaps it was a part of the original forest of England, before the ships of Empire were built.

Leo found himself in another beech grove. It was strange how little undergrowth grew under beeches. Sweat ran in his eyes and soaked his shirt yet he could feel a chill down his spine. In his armpits. He rode another narrow path between overhanging branches. The sun flickered through the leaves and he tried to use it for direction and thought he had. He stopped the horse when he came to the great dead oak for a third, or maybe fourth, time. His heart was beating hard. What was this place? A maze? A trap?

Leo turned the cob in circles, scanning all around him. Children disappeared, did they not? And were never found again. Then the pony laid back his ears. A sign of aggression, even in a gelding. Could the cob see something that the boy could not? Leo pulled the reins up short and yelled at the cob to go and kicked him hard and rode as fast and as straight as he could, cantering out of the uncanny wood.

August

Amos Tucker rode by cart with Albert Sercombe at his side and the boy sitting cross-legged behind them, next to Tucker's dog. The boy and the dog sat gazing into the dust thrown up by the horse's hooves and the wheels of the cart. They rode from one cornfield to another. Oats, barley, wheat. In each one the men dismounted from the cart and walked into the field. They rubbed the ears of corn between their fingers and eased out grain and bit into it. The boy did likewise, analysing the texture and the nutty taste of each grain. Moisture or lack of it.

'Still taste green to me, gaffer,' his father said in a field of oats. The men's conversation was sparse. Sometimes they merely nodded to each other, or shook their heads, or made odd faces, like-minded connoisseurs of cereals. On these occasions the boy had little to help him interpret their opinion.

His father cracked a grain of barley between his teeth, chewed, and grimaced. Amos Tucker nodded gravely. The men studied the sky. White clouds floated in the west.

Tucker frowned. 'It won't start without us.'

There was wheat in the ten-acre twinned fields of Binnen, and more barley up in the Berry Fields. The men were determining the state of readiness of each crop and thus the order in which the harvest would take place this year. They wrote nothing down. Each time they reached a new field the dog jumped down from the cart and ran around with great purpose as though his canine reconnaissance were the true reason for this excursion and the human beings merely his chaperones or bodyguard.

In Dutch Barn Field the barley grew waist-high. 'It do receive a little wind up here,' Albert Sercombe said.

'One more day without rain,' said Amos Tucker. 'Dear Lord, one more day.'

'Tis a good bet that tomorrow's weather will be much like today's,' the boy's father said. 'But there be no one on this earth knows what the day after tomorrow will bring.'

The farmer sighed and looked heavenward, then shook his head. 'I hear you, Albert. Begin here tomorrow then, as you wish to.'

★ ★ ★

Leo Sercombe rose with his brother and his father in the dark. School holidays were timed to coincide with harvest and he could be paid a few coins for the work, his mother would allow it. At the farm his brother Fred put corn in the horses' cribs then gathered tools and disappeared. The boy watched his father cut five pieces of linseed cake from Isaac Wooland's cattle room. 'Fetch three halters,' he said.

The boy caught up with his father and they walked down to the pasture. His father called the

103

horses up out of the field. Noble and Red and Pleasant the old mare came on out of the gloom to the gate and the two black geldings followed them. Albert fed Noble and Red the cake and put halters on them, and led them out of the field and tied them to the fence.

'Us'll yoke them two to the pole,' he said. 'Which one will us put in the traces?' He fed the old mare a piece of cake and patted her rump and she turned and walked away. 'One a they two,' he said.

The boy studied the sibling pair. There was naught to choose between them.

'Ye'll be riding him all day,' his father prompted.

Coal was calm, stately, would do his bidding. Captain had energy, more life in his eyes. The boy made his choice. He approached Captain, fed the horse its piece of cake on his upturned palm and then, as the gelding munched the mouthful the boy reached up his full extent to slip the halter over Captain's nose and ears. Despite the bribe the horse lifted his head beyond the boy's reach. The linseed crackled in his mouth as he chewed the cake, regarding the world from the lofty height of his vision. Leo smiled. His father did not move to interfere but waited to see what would happen.

His son turned his gaze to the lower parts of the horse. He studied its anatomy, from one side to the other, up and down. Then he reached under its chest and felt its belly, searching for something there with the tips of his fingers. He looked away as he did so and closed his eyes.

104

Then he opened them and pinched the black gelding at a certain point on his belly or brisket; the horse looked down and the boy, standing up smartly, slipped the halter over Captain's nose and ears, this time all the way, and so secured him.

★　★　★

Fred and Herbert were in Dutch Barn Field with bagging-hooks and sticks, cutting an avenue round the outside of the field wide enough for the binder. Dunstone was with them, making corn bands and tying them round sheaves of barley, which he stacked upright against the hedgerow. The lads were working their way around the eight-acre field. They heard the binder come into the gateway for they looked up, then resumed their labour at a greater pace.

The boy helped his father unlock the iron wheels and pull the binder round. The horses were harnessed in a unicorn formation, Noble and Red hitched to the binder pole with Captain in the traces in front. Leo rode postilion on the leading horse. Albert sat on the iron seat of the Massey-Harris self-binder. The sun was up and the dew dried off the barley as they approached it. The boy rode Captain to the right and into the hedge-side avenue. His father pushed the small lever forward and engaged the main cog wheel. This was connected to the travelling wheels of the binder. The knife-bar agitated through the pointed sheath that protected it from stones. It agitated more slowly than the knife of the hay mower, for corn cut more easily than grass and the stubble was left much longer. All the interlocking cog wheels set themselves in motion.

The boy kept Captain in his place, following the line of the cereal. The cutting width was six feet. When he could, Leo twisted round and watched the fascinating contraption, its sails turning anti-clockwise, knocking the cut barley onto a canvas platform behind. The canvas looped over two wooden rollers, rotating in an endless circuit, moving the corn up over the machine to the far side, to the canvas packing table. Twine threaded out of a revolving tin box and knotted the corn in sheaves that were kicked off onto the stubble by a mechanical fork. The contraption rattled, the corn rustled, the sheaves swished as they were flung from the binder. His father had told him it was the wonder of the age. He confessed that his admiration for the engineers at Massey-Harris, who had devised this improvement on all the machines that had gone before, was exceeded only by his admiration for Arthur Richardson.

This soldier's praises his father sang many times. During the Second Boer War his company of forty men was engaged at close quarters by a force twice their number. When the order to retire was given, Sergeant Richardson rode back under heavy fire and picked up a trooper whose horse had been shot, and who was wounded in two places, and rode with him out of fire. Arthur Richardson was himself riding a wounded horse. He received the Victoria Cross. When the carter recounted this story to his sons or others it was as if he knew the man, and it never failed to move him.

Herbert and Fred worked behind the binder, lifting the discarded sheaves into stooks, eight sheaves in each, forming aisles of stacked barley. They were joined by Isaac Wooland the stockman. Kizzie brought food and drink at midday. The men ate the bread and cheese and drank the cold tea then lay on the stubble until Albert Sercombe rose and went to the horses. The others rose and followed him.

Leo approached the black gelding on its nearside. With his left hand he reached up and gripped the top of the hames of the collar. While they ate he had been envisioning the manoeuvre and calculated that he could accomplish it. He placed his right hand on the horse's withers and sprang up, twisting so that he might land in place, neatly side-saddle, but Captain was too tall and the boy merely belly flopped across the horse. He wriggled and scrambled to keep on top of the animal and to right himself. Before he could do so the gelding turned his head and promptly bit him on the arse. Leo found the strength to heave himself up and in a moment sat astride the horse, ready to chastise him, but to his dismay exactly that which he had hoped for had occurred. The spectacle was witnessed by all those in attendance. And they were laughing with a joyful incontinence.

Leo's cheeks burned. His brother Fred laughed as heartily as Herbert. Their sister Kizzie laughed, as did Isaac Wooland, so did his father.

Only Dunstone the old lad kept his dignity, frowning, for he had not seen what happened or did not understand it or failed to find it comical due merely to his witless condition.

'Should a given the beast summat to chew, afore he chew you,' Herbert called out for the company to extend their amusement.

Albert stood beside the horse, shaking his head, a man who should not wish to laugh at his son but could not help it. He had tears in his eyes, grinning still. 'Don't you worry, boy,' he said. 'Us have all been nipped on the backside by a horse in our time.'

★   ★   ★

In the afternoon Fred left to help his carter, Uncle Enoch, in the barley field on Great Eastern Hill, but he was not missed, for every time they brought the binder up the slope from the far western side it seemed there were more people in the field. Kizzie had stayed. Their mother was there, Ernest Cudmore the shepherd, Amos Tucker and his daughters. And as the irregular rectangle of uncut corn diminished to an acre, and less, so boys and girls of the estate and even from the village appeared. Some had their dogs with them, terriers quivering in anticipation as they watched the standing corn. Isaac, Herbert, Ernest, Kizzie, abandoned their sheaf stacking. They closed in, armed with cudgels and lash sticks cut from the hedgerow.

The horses pulled the binder, its blades cut the ripened barley, knotted sheaves were expelled

108

onto the stubble, and rabbits began to bolt from their precarious shelter. The dogs ran and caught them at their necks. Leo Sercombe watched the slaughter from his vantage point astride the black gelding. Men fell upon the rabbits. Both the laid sheaves and the raised stooks hindered the animals' escape. The boys and girls attacked them with their sticks and some threw stones.

★　★　★

Albert Sercombe finished cutting the corn in Dutch Barn Field before the dew began to fall in the evening. The children headed home with their plunder, for their mothers to make pies or stew for the meat-hungry labourers.

★　★　★

They unhitched the horses from the binder and left the machine in the field and walked the tired, sweating horses home. They led them to the yard, unyoked them from their harness and put halters over their heads. Albert led Noble to the stable, Herbert took Red, Leo led Captain.

They let the horses feed on vetches while they groomed them. When the horses' coats were dry, the lad Herbert and the boy led them from the yard and turned them out in the pasture.

August

The mornings were misty, and still, as they walked the horses to the binder waiting in the fields of oats and barley. Dew revealed cobwebs draped over hedgerows and over grass, the lacework of countless spiders on their farm, though the boy did not see a single insect. They must be resting after their intricate nocturnal labour. Each day the sun rose and burned away the mist and the horses pulled the binder through dry standing corn.

★　★　★

When the rain came, with just the wheat of Ferny Piece and Essythorn to reap, it came unannounced one night, with no warning in the dusk. By morning it had laid the crop. The wheat was spread in all directions. Albert Sercombe yoked his horses to the binder left in Ferny Piece the previous evening and set off, with the boy on the trace horse as the day before. Where the wheat had fallen with ears pointing towards the binder it could be cut, but otherwise Fred and Herbert walked before and lifted the corn with forks. Still the sheaves that came out were misshapen, and awkward to handle for Isaac Wooland and Kizzie Sercombe. They had to

110

disentangle the heavy sheaves, and manhandle them into stooks.

Soil stuck to the travelling wheel of the binder, which got bogged down. Twisted corn blocked the canvas elevator. Fred or Herbert removed such corn and threw it to the ground. Dunstone gathered it into odd sheaves and tied them by hand with corn bands he fashioned himself. He was the one person pleased with the direction events had taken.

When the binder was stopped it had to be reversed before moving forward once more. Albert ordered the horses back. They did so in the morning, Noble and Red, with old Pleasant now in the traces, obeying his commands. But it sapped their energy and midway through the working day, while others ate, he led Noble and Pleasant back to the stable and returned with the black geldings. He yoked them to the pole and put Red in the traces, and asked Leo if he would go to the stable to groom the two horses there and put them in the pasture when he was done.

August

One hot afternoon the boy crossed the estate. He went directly to the pheasant-rearing field and there found his brother Sid feeding the young birds in their runs. The brothers did not greet each other. Sid did not ask after their mother or others in the family, but said, 'Just in time to give me a hand, boy.'

There were forty coops in the rearing field, made by the estate carpenter. Each coop held twenty young pheasants. Sid fed these poults four times a day. The first feed was at six in the morning. Sid cooked the food in a four-gallon pot boiler in the rearing-field hut. Scalded biscuit meal and boiled rice. In between feeds he had to make his round checking the ginns. Small traps took the stoats and weasels, the six-inch ginns took foxes and the occasional badger.

Leo helped his brother with the last feed. Once the birds were all locked up Sid shot a few rabbits and Leo helped him gut and skin and butcher them. He dug a hole for the innards while Sid minced up the meat ready to add to the morning feed. Then Sid slept on a bench in the field hut, and Leo slept on the floor.

The door of the hut was opened in the dead of night. It was Aaron Budgell. Sid rose and went outside. Leo stood at the door and watched them in the moonlight. Sid and his gaffer slid a sack under a coop. They lifted the four corners and tied them, and loaded the coop onto the donkey cart. They walked the cart away. Leo followed them into the larch plantation. Pheasants liked to roost on their more or less horizontal branches. Aaron Budgell and Sid lifted the coop quietly and placed it on the ground.

The boys returned to the field hut and slept again.

In the morning they took four buckets, a shovel and a hole-ridden tray and set off. Sid knew where he was going for he had taken mental note of the anthills he had seen and remembered their locations. 'I should mark em on a map,' he said. 'Trouble is, if I write em down, I worry I'd forget where they is.'

Sid carried the long-handled shovel over his shoulder. Leo carried the buckets stacked inside one another and listened to his brother's gamekeeping tales.

'Last Tuesday, after the first feed, I went to the cottage where Mrs Budgell give me breakfast. Come back to the field and there they was. Seven poults I counted, dead in their run, all with a bite on the top of their heads. What do you think it was?'

Leo suggested weasel. 'No.' Stoat? 'No, not that neither.' Leo said he did not know. 'Fox? Badger?'

Sid shook his head. 'Next mornin I did everythin the same only I didn't, I doubled back quiet, like, with my gun. Waited and watched, till I saw summat movin. There he was and I shot him.'

Leo asked him what it was.

Sid grimaced, and turned his head to the side to spit as he walked. 'A flea-ridden bloody hedgehog,' he said. 'Folk don't believe you but tis true. Mister Budgell said one time one of they buggers went for the broody hens. Went for their rear ends, tore em up summat rotten. Before he helped hisself to the eggs.'

The first anthill was at the edge of a grove of conifers, a mound amidst the pine needles. Sid explained that the anthill was composed of rubble from the subterranean colonies. The insects excavated tunnels and chambers and brought the grains of soil up to the top of the hill. He had watched them, Sid said, and Leo should do the same. A person could learn a great deal from ants. He said that in hot weather like this the workers moved their larvae up towards the top of the anthill. He handed his brother the shovel. Leo dug into the mound and turned over the load to reveal hundreds of white eggs amongst the dry sandy soil. Sid held the tray and nodded in such a way as to indicate that his brother should transfer a shovelful to it. Leo did so. Sid shook the griddle until all the soil had fallen through the holes, leaving only the eggs. Ants that were caught up in these machinations struggled furiously to retrieve the eggs and return them to where they should be. Sid poured the eggs into one of the buckets, and thus the Sercombe boys continued. They filled the buckets and walked back towards the rearing field.

Leo asked his brother if he did not feel sorry

114

for the insects, that their labours which he so admired should be for naught. Sid shook his head and told Leo that he would never make a gamekeeper, he had not the stomach for it. Nor had he the interest in all of God's creation. He should stick to his horses, his jades and screws and suchlike pad-nags, to whose limited array of behaviours he was better suited. Leo told him quietly that he intended to.

August

Albert Sercombe oiled the waggon wheels and greased the turn-tables. He tied a pair of ropes to the back of his waggon, coiled them and dropped them into the bed. Herbert did likewise to the second waggon. Albert laid two-tined forks of varying length against the outside wall of the barn in the stack yard. He called his son over and pointed to the longest one. 'Do you remember what this one's for?'

Leo nodded. His father was a tall man and Leo estimated that the fork was as long as him and half as long again. Amos Tucker measured by paces the size of the base of a stack and Isaac Wooland the stockman laid old straw upon the ground where so directed.

Uncle Enoch and the boy's brother Fred prepared their waggons. All the horses save for Pleasant were hitched. Dunstone was in the middle of the yard though no one had seen him come. He might have emerged from beneath a cart or a nest in the dung-heap. The spinster Mildred Daw studied the two-tined forks against the wall. She selected two and held them together up against her, the tines on the ground. One came up to her nose, the other to her forehead. She replaced the latter and went over to Albert and climbed up on to the waggon.

116

Isaiah Vagges greeted Amos Tucker loudly. 'Sap's dried out a the stalks?' he yelled.

'Good to see you, Isaiah,' the farmer said. 'Glad you got my message.'

Isaiah Vagges slapped Isaac Wooland on the back as Isaac bent, continuing to place straw as the foundation of a stack, and said, 'Still followin them cows around?'

Isaac lost his balance and stumbled but regained it. Before he could remonstrate with Isaiah the old farmhand had moved on. He was full of good cheer and regaled each person in the yard, coming in time to Leo and saying, 'Not yet decided to grow, boy?' He came close and put an arm on Leo's shoulder. He smelled of turpentine and linseed oil, and something else the boy could not identify, components of some home-made embrocation for his rheumatism. 'Don't worry, boy, once ye start ye'll grow tall as yon old man there.'

He greeted Mildred Daw with some witticism the boy could not make out, and which she ignored entirely. Seeing that she had nabbed by choice or by appointment the job of Albert's forker, Isaiah chose a fork for himself and joined Herbert.

★   ★   ★

The boy lay in the waggon behind his father and Mildred Daw, bumping and rattling over the dry ground. The sky was white and empty. He saw but one bird. It flew like an arrow overhead, aiming for its destination. When they reached the far end of Dutch Barn Field Albert called out,

117

'Whoa,' and the waggon came to a leisurely halt. Mildred Daw climbed down, clutching the fork she'd chosen, and speared two sheaves from the nearest stook so swiftly that the boy had to clamber over the far side of the waggon to avoid being hit as she swung her fork and with a jerk of the wrist flipped the sheaves into the bed of the waggon. Albert climbed in. He had his own, shorter fork and shifted the sheaves into the position he desired.

The boy took his place beside Captain, the nearside horse. He watched Mildred Daw fork the sheaves of barley and his father loading the waggon. Each sheaf as he laid it bound the one before. He packed the body of the waggon, then placed sheaves on the sloping sides and across each end. It did not seem that every sheaf overlapped the one below but the boy surmised that it must have for the load became gradually longer and wider than the waggon as it rose.

He watched his father and Mildred Daw. Neither spoke to the other, nor could he see any wave of hand or nod of head that might indicate a request for where to hurl the next sheaf. He found he could not tell which of the two of them decided the manner in which the waggon was loaded. Albert worked from the front to the back, then vice versa, placing the sheaves lengthways. The ears of barley always pointed inwards, yet the boy could not see his father turning sheaves on the waggon, so it seemed that Mildred tossed them to him facing the way he required. The only commands his father gave were to his son, for the boy to move the horses

118

forward. They made their way across the great field back towards the gate.

When the load was as tall as he was, Albert began to build the ends higher than the middle and the whole load narrower. They had almost reached the gate when, with a single row of sheaves, Albert completed the load. 'That should do it,' he called down.

Mildred Daw took the ropes they'd let fall behind the waggon and threw them up to Albert. She walked round to the front and he dropped them to her and she secured them to the hooks below.

The carter slid and clambered to the ground. Mildred walked around the waggon, prodding her fork into a corner, pushing the barley a little tighter.

'How many sheaves you reckon's on?' Albert asked. Mildred pondered. Albert said, 'Three hundred?'

She nodded. 'I reckon.'

He smiled. 'Gaffer'll count em.'

Albert climbed onto Captain and rode him side-saddle out of the field, watching the load behind him shake and sway with every irregularity in the ground and the rutted tracks along the lane. The boy rode on Coal beside him. Mildred waited in the field. The waggon creaked and rolled.

★ ★ ★

In the yard Albert Sercombe untied the ropes. Leo pulled them over the top of the load. They fell upon him and he coiled one and then the other. Isaac Wooland rested a ladder against the waggon and climbed onto the load, and straightaway tossed sheaves down to the base of old straw he had recently laid. Amos Tucker laid the sheaves around the outside of his stack.

Albert took the ladder and placed it against the wall where some forks yet unused still rested. Amos Tucker defined the shape of the stack with the first row of sheaves. It was a little wider than the base of old straw. The second row half overlapped the first, moving inward. He continued stacking around until the centre was reached. Then he returned to the outside and worked around it, this time overlapping outwards. Each sheaf he stepped on as he placed it, firming it down with his considerable weight. Suddenly the waggon was empty, and Isaac Wooland was standing in the empty bed. He climbed out. Albert was already sitting on Captain. He did not wait but commanded the horses forward. The boy followed behind, and climbed up into the empty waggon.

★ ★ ★

They returned to the field. Mildred Daw was waiting for them on the far side. Herbert meanwhile had plotted his own course from one stook to the next and had almost reached the gate. The boy judged that Herbert's load was not as high as his father's but Herbert tied it down.

'Don't worry, lad,' they heard Isaiah Vagges call to him. ''Tis tight's a gnat's arse. This load would carry clear to Taunton.'

Amos Tucker's daughters brought food and drink to the field and the harvesters stopped to rest in the shadows of hedgerow trees. Albert slaked his thirst with cold tea but Isaiah Vagges guddled cider and Herbert copied him until his carter said, 'Steady, lad.' Isaiah was known as the architect of his own downfall, a fine worker whose weakness for all forms of alcohol had rendered him unreliable. When sober he was such a grafter and an optimist that he'd been given second chances on every farm on the estate, and beyond, by men and women each one of whom he'd let down. He would be lured by wastrels and by his own nature into drinking bouts and be incapacitated at crucial times. He would disappear for days or weeks on end. His wife took their child and returned to her family in Minehead. He would pick fights when drunk and suffered dreadful injuries. All this Leo had heard when his parents gossiped with each other of a winter evening. There'd been reports of Isaiah Vagges as a young man in the inns of Exeter and of Barnstaple. He was jailed in Okehampton. Whenever he returned all were glad to see him, save for those few who found his friendliness an intrusion. Now he was old.

'I swear,' Isaiah said, as they lay digesting their morning bait, 'every time I see thee, Mildred Daw, ye wears more items a men's clothing than before.'

The spinster turned away, as if to study the far hedge.

'I mean not to offend thee,' Isaiah said.

Albert rose to his feet. 'Well, them waggons won't load their selves,' he said. 'You can sweat some a that cider out.'

★ ★ ★

Each time the boy returned with his father with a new load to the yard, Amos Tucker had built the stack higher with Herbert's intervening waggonload of barley. Albert fetched a barrow of vetches and placed it for the horses to help themselves. On occasion he brought in buckets of water for them to drink. Amos Tucker built his stacks in the oblong shape of a house, with walls rising at an outward slant. At times Isaac Wooland threw sheaves down to him, at others he tossed them up, and for brief periods the waggonload and the rising stack were at the same height and the two men could have stepped across and swapped position if they had a mind to.

Amos Tucker removed his jacket. His waistcoat bulged like some odd men's corset, his white shirt was wet with sweat and his face some colour midway between a radish and a beetroot, yet he worked with a calm authority. He built the house, then he built the roof, now stacking sheaves in a ridge along the centre of the stack and laying others out at an angle like the tiles of a house, the last overlapping the stack below.

Returning to the field, Albert spoke to his son. 'Impressive, the gaffer, eh?' The boy nodded. 'He can build a stack and not come down all day.

Has his bait thrown up to him. Answers the call a nature with a piss over the side. When I've to build one, I'm up and down that ladder to make sure it's not leanin, I don't mind tellin you nor no one. And barley what he's workin with now's more inclined to slip than wheat. No, boy, I'm glad I'm not doin it. Leave me with the horses.'

They worked until it was too dark to see. The last load they brought to the yard beside the stack and covered with sheets. Amos Tucker felt his way down the ladder to the ground. The boy lit a paraffin stable lamp and held it for his father to unyoke the horses. The work was not arduous for the beasts. They had spent much of the day at ease. As soon as they were stripped of their harness the carters turned them into the pasture for they had no sweat on their bodies and there was plentiful grass to graze on.

Albert and his sons Fred and Leo walked home. Ruth had a meal of vegetable stew enlivened by bacon fat awaiting them. Albert told his wife how the day had gone. He told her Mildred Daw was steady as ever, and that Isaiah Vagges was still a bibbling fool. He told her Pleasant would soon be of little use and that the filly would before too long be ready to replace her. The boys ate in silence and climbed the stairs to their bedroom and slept.

August

Ruth Sercombe spoke of her dowry only if another commented upon it. This had happened just once to the boy's knowledge, for visitors rarely entered the parlour. Leo studied the china. 'Staffordshire blue and white,' his mother had named it to the vicar in a tone that assumed he could not fail to be impressed. The boy scrutinised the blue pictures. Of ancient cities or parts thereof, pillars and entranceways to huge buildings that would make the Manor House seem tiny. People outside were pouring water into baths or courting. He put the plate down carefully, muting china on china.

There was a case of books, leather- or board-bound. A Holy Bible with pages made of thin crisp paper. Ruth's husband could not read and her older children had not wished to. Kizzie did everything well at school. Perhaps she would be a teacher. Leo looked through one of his favourites, *Everyman's Handbook*. It was inscribed: *To Ruth Penhaligon from Miss Hare, Penzance Church of England High School, 1889.* He opened it at random and learned that apples are preserved by packing them in sawdust. He read a list of winners of the Derby. A proverb taught that *it is better to ride on an ass that carries me, than on a horse that throws me.*

124

Leo heard the back door open and his father enter the kitchen next door, greeting Ruth and being greeted by her. The boy breathed silently. He knew the scene so well he could almost see it through the wall. They had a wooden table, four chairs and one wooden armchair. His father's. Mother used it if he was out. Now she rose, relinquished the chair to him, shifted the kettle to the hotplate. He was back for breakfast. Fred would soon follow. Leo could hear the sounds of preparation.

'Seen the boy?' Albert asked.

'Is he not with you?' Ruth said. 'Must be still abed.'

His father said no more. His mother said, 'What troubles you, man?'

There was a long pause. Then, 'He never asks nothin.'

The sounds Leo's mother made ceased. He pictured her leaning back against the rail of the stove.

'I want to learn him what I know,' the carter said. 'Horses trust him, see?'

'He watches,' Ruth told him. 'All the time. Didn't you tell me you picked it up off of your father the same way?'

The kettle whistled. Leo heard his mother remove it and pour water into the teapot.

'I want him to have the best job on this estate one day,' his father said. 'On the stud farm or in the master's stable. I don't want no other bastard's son to come before ours.'

'The master won't live for ever.'

'Aye, the poor master.'

125

'Left with just that headstrong girl a his. What'll happen when the master's gone?'

'It's naught to do with us, mother. Things'll carry on one way or another. Naught for us to worry over.'

★ ★ ★

The boy bent and untied the laces of his boots and removed them. Scarcely breathing, holding a boot in each hand, he climbed the stairs in his socks, step by step. In the room he shared with Fred he sat on his bed and pulled the boots back on. He tied the laces as before, then rose and clumped downstairs to breakfast.

September

The poorest of the village came to the estate at certain times. One was harvest. As the first field of corn was being carted so they came. Mothers pushing children in prams, widows, spinsters. One of the old women wore a granny bonnet tied beneath her chin. As the last load left the first field of wheat those who had gathered at the gate went on to the stubble. They walked the sun-burned ground picking up single ears of corn. Bent over, they picked with one hand and passed the ears to the other. When each bunch was too large to carry they tied it with straw and put it aside. How each woman knew which bunch was hers Leo did not know. Perhaps the gleaners each twisted their tie of straw such as to scrawl their signature. The old woman in the bonnet said that gleaning was not what it was since the new-fangled binders came and her friend said new horse-rakes cleaned up all but the last few ears of corn. The bunches were gathered in the evening, or when the field had been scoured, into large sheaves in the shape of rosettes of wheat, which they carried home to their cottages.

The boy's mother said it would be good to turn their poultry out in the stubble for the corn. Amos Tucker said his pigs would benefit the more. But neither dared raise it with the master. Albert Sercombe told them both the gleaners had the right to the leftover corn, it was the only right he knew of that had survived the enclosures. The cottagers would rub the corn out from the ears by hand in the evenings and on wet winter days, and the miller would give them one day of his time to grind their corn to flour.

★ ★ ★

Rain interrupted the harvest. On wet days, while Amos Tucker fretted, the carters and their lads drew straw for thatching the stacks, stripping lengths of wheat of its foliage and tying them in bundles. This year Leopold joined them. The work was unending for if all went well the yard would be full with ten or more stacks of wheat or oats or barley to be given a rain-proof roof. And it was dreary, for though it required little exertion the discomfort of sitting or standing in the same posture for hour upon hour had a more demoralising effect than hard labour to which their bodies and minds were accustomed.

'If I were the gaffer,' Herbert said, 'I'd ask the master to build a couple or three big Dutch barns for storin my corn.'

'If you was the gaffer,' Albert told him, 'you'd last no longer than the bad steward in the Good Book. It'd be slapdash here and bodge it there.'

Dunstone joined them in the barn for it was work that he could do, if at a slow pace for he measured each strand of wheat and cut it precisely with his knife so that he produced one

128

bundle for another's ten but each was perfect.

They grew irritable and bored, and welcomed Isaiah Vagges, who like Mildred Daw was paid half his daily wage when it rained if he so wished to help with this chore.

'I'll be thatchin,' he told them, 'so's I best keep an eye on you sluggards. Lost in reveries and dreamin a fair women. I don't want my bundles all a mish-mash. Here, lad,' he said, addressing Fred Sercombe. 'Ave you heard of the manner in which Mildred here dealt with her suitor back when us was young? I'll tell thee.' He turned to the subject of the story. 'I'll tell them, Mildred, for it casts but a fond light upon thee. But do not interrupt me if ye think the details wrong, I beg ye.'

Mildred ignored Isaiah entirely as she bundled the wheat straw. Perhaps she was deaf or had become so.

Isaiah turned to the others. 'Ye'll like this one too, lad,' he said to Herbert. 'It happened in the summer of 'eighty-eight. Mildred got took to the flower show in Watchet, the evenin grew cool, her friends set off for home, but Mildred stayed drinkin cider with a silk-tongued ruffian by the name a Jasper Huxtable. I knew his brother, a good pal a mine. All ruffians and rogues, the ole family. Look at her now ye might doubt me, but then Mildred Daw was a right comely maid, sixteen year old, fair-complexioned. Were ye not, Mildred? Bowerly, she was.

'This rogue spoke to her of the great ships he'd seen in Avonmouth and the factories big as villages in Bristol, though I doubt he'd ever bin as far as Weston-Super-bloody-Mare. Excuse my language, Albert. He offered to walk Mildred ome. They dawdled back in the moonlight. A tawny owl called from above them as they walked through Raven's Wood. Back in a field Jasper suggested they rest a moment on a stook a sheaves that'd fallen over. He laid is and upon her in a place that made her understand what e was up to. Do you know what she did, lads, have you eard the tale?'

Fred and Herbert shook their heads. Leo did not move.

'Your fathers know it. Dunstone too, though he may not remember. Well, here it is. First she disabused him of his intentions in no uncertain manner. Jasper lay on the stubble, clutchin his manhood, groanin to himself. But that weren't all. Mildred intended to leave. She did not plan it, how could she, but some fool loader had left his two-tined fork in the field. It was only when she saw the implement layin there that the idea come to mind. She took it up, went back to her suitor, turned him with her dainty foot over on to his front, and pinned him to the ground with the two tines of the fork either side of his neck. Is that not exactly as it happened, Mildred? She then stood upon the fork and pressed it deep into the earth, leavin scarce enough slack for the lad to breathe.'

Albert and Enoch Sercombe, chuckling, nodded their approval, of the act or perhaps of Isaiah's telling of the story or of both. Fred and Herbert looked from Isaiah to the spinster and back to Isaiah in consternation.

'And there was Jasper Huxtable found the mornin following by the harvestin team.'

The boy looked at Mildred Daw. He could imagine her doing such a thing to someone who displeased her. He thought that Isaiah should be careful.

'They found this poor lad but how did they know what happened?' Herbert demanded. 'How do you know, old man?' He gestured to Mildred. 'Did she go round tellin all and sundry what she done?'

'That, lads, is the best thing about it,' Isaiah said. 'T'was Jasper himself who sang, so outraged was he by her treatment of him. So used was he to havin is way with the maids of our district. He made imself a laughin stock.'

'Should a kept his peasel to his self,' said Fred.

'So long as Jasper lives, and for a further generation now that I've told thee, tis what e'll be known for. His bastard children too.'

131

September

Ruth Sercombe gathered all the eggs that she could find. She inscribed the date 13.9.11 in pencil upon the shells as was her habit, and added them to those laid on previous days. She counted the eggs. There were forty-three in shades of white and brown, and she packed them with straw in two willow-rod baskets. These she asked Leo to carry with great care to the manor. He wondered why she did not ask Kizzie. Was it not girls' or women's work? Though he did not articulate his grievance aloud his countenance perhaps betrayed it. His mother said, 'Your sister is liable to forget what her is carryin, start thinkin silly thoughts and swingin the baskets.'

'I am not, mother,' Kizzie said. 'How can you say such a thing and sully my reputation in my own home?' Her indignation was well acted.

'Would you prefer to carry the eggs?' Ruth asked her daughter.

Leo looked at his sister. Kizzie narrowed her eyes. She saw she could not win, only choose the lesser of twin defeats. 'I concede the eggs' journey might be less perilous in my dull brother's care, mother.'

★   ★   ★

The boy walked away from the cottage. A pair of crows sidled along his mother's washing line like tight-rope walkers, of a kind he had seen at Minehead Fair, a family of tumblers and acrobats who carried in their blood some odd immunity to the pull of gravity.

He walked along the lanes across the estate. Stones beneath his boots clattered as if hollow. Each basket was covered with a white linen cloth to keep the full glare of the morning sun from the eggs. The distance was two miles, give or take some yards, and three times on the journey he laid the baskets gently upon the ground and waited for the ache in his upper arms to fade away, then picked up the baskets and resumed walking.

The closer he came to the big house the more people he saw. Gardeners, coachmen, stable boys. He did not study what they did but kept his eyes down. A butcher's covered cart was leaving, a grocer's arrived. He followed it around to the back of the house. The grocer passed over wooden boxes full of produce, which two maids conveyed through the wide back door. Leo placed his baskets upon the ground and waited. The grocer kept on passing boxes to the maids. They began bringing empty ones upon their return, which he took from them into his waggon.

One of the maids had red hair poking out from beneath her cap, of a redness the boy had not seen before. The other had black hair, dark eyes, and she assessed him as she passed. Eventually she addressed him. 'What is you, a beggar boy? If you is, you'd best scat. Full house this weekend. Cook's in no mood for charity. Er'll box yer ears.'

The maid hoisted an empty box to the grocer. He installed it behind him and passed her a full one, which she carried inside. When she next emerged she spoke to Leo again. 'Still here?'

The girls carried many loads. The red-haired one was taller. There was sweat on her forehead along the line of the white cap, and with each full box whose bulk she heaved so she gasped a little more. The dark, shorter one showed no strain and could, it seemed, have performed the task all day. When the delivery was complete the grocer waited. He stood by his cart. He said nothing to Leo, but gazed towards the door. The darker girl came out bearing an armful of empty boxes. The grocer took these and stacked them in his waggon. He walked around to the front and climbed up onto the seat. He clicked his teeth and the vanner set off towing the cart across the gravel.

The maid stood before Leo and looked down at the baskets. He lifted them and passed them to her. 'I know you,' the girl said. 'I knew I did. Aunt Ruth's boy. Don't you recognise me?'

Leo looked at her. He neither nodded nor shook his head.

'You're Fred's little brother,' the maid said. 'We was in school together. You and me is cousins.' She waited for some seconds, then shrugged her shoulders. 'Tell Fred hello from Gladys.' The maid turned and carried the baskets into the house. She left the door open,

134

whether for a breeze or because she intended to return shortly with the empty baskets Leo did not know. His mother surely needed them. He stood waiting. Occasionally someone came in or out of the door. A man, a lad, a girl, each in the uniform of their station. All ignored him. He did not budge. When he'd arrived the back yard was in shade but the sun rose over the top of the house and now he stood beneath its glare. The red-haired maid emerged. She walked away from the house towards one of the buildings in the yard. He could hear her rummaging amongst whatever objects existed therein. She reappeared carrying some kind of wooden bat, or paddle. Tool or toy. As she walked past she made to strike him, and giggled. The boy did not flinch.

Shortly the dark-haired girl stood in the doorway, carrying the willow baskets. 'Meg said you was still here,' she said. There was a note of complaint in her voice, as if she had been blamed for the boy's presence. 'You should a said.' She waited in the doorway for Leo to come to her.

Leo took the baskets from his cousin, and nodded, and turned and walked out of the yard. He knew where the stables were and made his way to them. He loved the Shire horses that he would work with in his life to come but all horses intrigued him. As well as motley cobs and hacks the master kept half a dozen hunters, for himself and those he invited to ride with him. They were half- and three-quarter bred, with Irish Draught. The master liked to travel to Ireland to buy them. He hunted with the foxhounds from

135

Dulverton and on Exmoor with the staghounds. He also hunted elsewhere and had his horses transported by train. The grooms and stable lads exercised them daily. By now they'd have been returned to their pasture. One, though, was tethered by its halter to a ring on the wall in the yard and was being studied by two men.

The horse was a chestnut mare. Her hair had been clipped all over save for the shape of a saddle, which remained a darker colour upon her hide.

The older man picked up the mare's off-hind leg and bent it slowly. The mare raised her head and her ears went back. The man lowered her leg and spoke to the lad and walked away. The lad fetched a hose-pipe that was curled up beside a tap. He unwound the pipe towards the horse. Leo walked along the wall of stable doors until he was close enough to see the swelling at the mare's hind hock. The lad went to the tap and turned it on. Water emerged from the end of the pipe and brought it to life like a black snake. The lad was dark and lanky. He trotted over and picked up the spout and directed the water at the swelling on the mare's leg.

Leo watched the mare accept the stable lad's aquatic ministrations, her ears forward, her head bent. She appeared to enjoy the jet of cool water. Perhaps it numbed the pain of the sprained muscles in her leg. She was a fine creature, neither the fastest nor the strongest animal but a combination of the two as was required for a day chasing a pack of dogs. He had seen them. Farm workers stopped and watched when they passed

136

near or distant, a horn blowing, hounds speaking, nobles and gentry galloping like some red chaotic cavalry charging. His father hated it for his carthorses were seized by the urge to join them. Some memory awoken of when they were ridden by giants hunting on the old moors. The memory of an earlier or perhaps an alternative life. 'Hold em,' his father would yell, and all the carters hung grimly on to their Shires until the urge subsided. But once Herbert let go and Red raced away towing a harrow. The horse galloped through a gateway that was too narrow. The gateposts stopped the harrow, and all the harness was torn asunder. The tackle shattered. The horse continued for a few yards then came to a halt, confused by his own excitement.

Some hunters were thoroughbreds, racehorses retired or failed. His father said the master preferred them tough, with a fine, sloping shoulder and good feet. 'No hoof, no horse,' he said, though whether it was his own maxim or the master's or someone else's entirely Leo did not know.

He moved closer and studied the mare's small almost dainty hooves, the elegant fetlock joints that seemed too frail to carry that weight of beast and rider landing from a vaulted fence or hedge.

The stable lad looked lazily about him then. He glanced over his shoulder and leaped and cursed this boy who'd come silently up behind him. He sprayed water over the mare and all around her.

'Who the fuck is you?' the lad demanded. 'And what the ell's you doin creepin up on me?'

Leo did not answer. The lad resumed directing the water at the hunter's hock. 'Get lost,' he said over his shoulder.

Leo did not move, but continued studying the horse's feet.

The stable lad glanced back at him. 'And why the fuck is you shakin your head?'

'You shouldn't do that,' Leo said.

'Speak up, you little squirt,' the lad said.

Leo did not know how to raise his voice. He had tried before but couldn't find the mechanism within his mouth or throat. 'You shouldn't put cold water on her leg.'

He thought the stable lad would strike him then, but instead he grinned suddenly and turned the hose-pipe upon Leo, directing it around his body until his clothes were soaked. Leo did not move. 'I should put it on you instead, is that it?' the lad yelled. 'You little twat.' He directed the water at Leo's head. Leo closed his eyes. He felt his hair lifting and falling from his skull under the pressure of the water. He did not believe in the efficacy of such treatment for this horse but it might be good for others. The water ceased beating upon his face. He opened his eyes. The lad was once more hosing the chestnut mare. The groom stood beside him.

'You'd better ave a good reason for wastin my water,' he said.

'This clod come up behind me, gaffer,' the lad said, petulant. 'Scared me alf out a my wits. Then he tells me I shouldn't be a-hosin her hock. Who the little toe rag thinks he is I couldn't tell ee.'

The groom was halfway in height between the boy and the spindly lad, and was soundly built, beefy. He turned to Leo. 'We are very busy, boy, and I have no time for pranks nor foolishness, so tell me now why he should not hose the mare and her swollen hock.'

Leo looked up at the groom. He opened his mouth to speak but could not. His jaw trembled, knocking his upper and lower teeth against one another. Cold water dripped from him. He swallowed, clenched his jaw, squeezed a breath through his teeth and said, 'Her heel is cracked.'

The groom looked at him a moment longer, then looked at the lad and said, 'Turn it off.' He stepped towards the horse and lifted her back-right leg as he had before but this time he ignored her knee and studied her foot instead. The lad returned.

'Look at this,' the groom told him, pointing to the fine cracks in the mare's heel. 'How did we not spot that?' He told the stable lad to pack the heel with Vaseline once he'd dried it off, and that tomorrow they should apply a paste of Epsom salts and glycerine to the swelling on the mare's hock and make a poultice. The lad nodded. 'And you can apologise to the boy here.'

The stable lad frowned. 'He crept up behind me, gaffer,' he whined. 'Give me one ell of a fright.'

The groom said nothing. The lad sighed, and said, 'Sorry, nipper. You does look like a drowned rat.' He grinned then, as he had before, but this time the groom turned towards him and as he turned he raised his hand and also swung his shoulder so that with little effort he put some weight behind his fist, which he swung upwards and punched the lad on the ear. The lad staggered sideways, yelping and putting his hand to the side of his head. The groom paid him no heed.

'He didn't mean no harm,' the man told Leo. 'I believe I knows who you might be,' he said. 'Is you the carter Sercombe's boy?'

Leo nodded, glancing briefly at the groom.

'I've heard about you,' the groom continued. 'Another Sercombe with equine blood in his bones, so they say.'

Leo did not know whether he should mention that he had an older brother, also a carter. Whether not to do so amounted to disloyalty. He glanced around. The stable lad still grimaced, and held a hand to his ear as if trying to listen to the sound of his pain.

'Come another time, boy, when tis less busy. You'd best get walkin home now, dry out on the move.'

The boy walked away from the stables. He figured to take a shorter route home, over stiles and brooks that might have put his earlier fragile cargo in jeopardy. Within moments his teeth ceased chattering. In the midday sun the water in his hair was warm as sweat. He circled one paddock and walked through a glade of poplars to another, and stopped dead. He stepped to his left behind a tree trunk so that part at least of his body was hid.

Though she wore boy's clothes as before and a gentleman's tweed cap he knew at once it was the master's daughter. Perhaps by her posture. She rode a blue roan pony. The horse trotted, then slowed down. It looked as if it was going to settle into a walk, but just before it did so it began instead to trot again. After some yards the pony slowed once more, and just before it walked it sped up again. Thus the horse and rider crossed the paddock. They did so along a line directly across the boy's line of vision, as if on display for him. Leo stepped around the trunk of the tree in order to follow them, and stepped back as they came the other way.

When they reached the fence the girl turned the horse and came back in the opposite direction in like manner. It was not easy to see how she asked or ordered her pony to do as she wished. There was no movement of her hands on the reins, or the reins upon the bit, that he could see. With her legs she squeezed the pony's belly but she did not kick him. Again she turned the horse and took him across the paddock. The boy watched. The girl's posture was upright and unvarying, but he saw that as the horse slowed down and the rider stopped rising off the saddle, so she exerted some downward pressure with her back and her seat and that this too communicated some request the pony understood.

The girl did not speak at any time during these manoeuvres, until she allowed the pony to come to a halt in the middle of the paddock, and then she leaned forward and patted his neck and spoke to him in effusive tones, telling him what a fine boy he was, how clever, how obedient, how marvellous.

After the girl had made much of her horse she raised herself up once more and set off across the paddock. Leo did not know whether she would wish to be observed by the son of a carter as she trained her pony. He did not believe she would appreciate being viewed from the shadows behind a tree. He could walk backwards into the glade and skirt around the paddock in a wide arc, with little loss of time. Instead he walked forward down the slope from the glade, into the late-morning sun. At the fence he placed the empty willow baskets on the ground and watched.

The girl did not see him or else took no notice. She continued suppleing the roan. Having done so from front to rear, now she did so laterally. Moving from the centre of the paddock she took up position on the far side, close to the fence, with the fence on her and the pony's left-hand side. She walked the horse forward some paces, and brought it to the right. But then rather than keep it coming round, in a curve or a circle, she used her right leg to push the pony's forehead to the left, so that he walked forward along a straightish line beside the fence but with his head and neck and spine following a curve centred around the girl's right leg. She walked the horse all the way around the paddock twice and then stopped and congratulated him, once more leaning forward to stroke him. Then she repeated the routine but this time at a trot.

The boy had never seen this exercise performed yet he understood it. The pony's fore-legs followed one line, his hind-legs another parallel to it. The girl kept the roan's hind-legs on the correct line, and his hind-quarters from veering to the left as if to make a circle, by bringing his left leg back behind the girth with her own left leg. The roan's head and neck remained still. Leo judged the two of them had practised this exercise many times. He did not know whose patience he admired more, the girl's or the pony's.

When they had trotted four times around the paddock the girl once more embraced her pony and told him of his unequalled virtuosity, then she turned him and walked him in the opposite direction along the fence, shouldering him this time to the left. Once more she walked him then she trotted him. Leo studied them carefully. So far as he could tell she used so little force as to be insignificant, yet the roan did as she intended. When they passed in front of him he saw the horse was sweating and the girl too.

The girl rode to the gate. She brought the roan beside it. Leo wondered whether he should stay where he was or run the yards along the fence and open the gate for her. He did not know which she would prefer, but he knew that if she chose to remain mounted then he wished to see how she negotiated the obstacle.

The pony was beside the gate, facing away from the post upon which the gate was hinged. The girl leaned forward and lifted the loop of rope off the fence post. She let go of the rope and grasped the top bar of the gate, and heeled the pony's girth. The pony stepped away from the gate and stepped backwards at the same time, enabling the girl to pull the gate open. When the gap was sufficiently wide she let go of the gate and walked the horse through, then turned him round and brought him back and closed the gate in the same way as she had opened it but in reverse.

She looped the rope over the post and walked the horse along the fence to the boy. She looked down at him. He did not look up at her but kept his gaze upon the fetlocks of the roan, and upon his hair, whose colour he had never seen before. Close to, the hairs were a mixture of black and white. Yet from a distance the gelding's coat appeared to have a tinge of blue. The boy could not quite understand it.

'Is it the purpose of a gentleman's daughter,' he heard the girl ask, 'to provide entertainment for some idling servant boy?'

Leo wished to ask the girl if she spoke to all in this manner. He said nothing.

'Do you not have something better to do with your time?' she asked. 'Leopold, is it not? Did my riding amuse you?'

'No, miss,' Leo answered.

'I doubt you have any idea what we were doing, Embarr and I.'

Leo glanced up, then down. 'You was bendin his spine, miss. It seemed to me he had to flex his hocks, and bring em underneath him. If I may say so . . . '

'You may say what so?'

' . . . most horses would wish to bend their neck only, miss, but this roan a yours put all the parts a his frame at your disposal. He is a rare

144

beast, I believe. I know I have not seen so many horses, but this one is mightily responsive.'

Leo closed his mouth to stop himself from saying more. He could have. He understood how odd it was that he should be able to speak with such garrulity to this girl of all people, even if it was of horses.

'Do you give the rider no credit?' she asked.

Leo frowned. 'You are as fine a rider as I have seen,' he said.

'Of the many riders you have seen.' He glanced up for long enough to see the girl's smile. 'It must be strange for you, attached like most to cruelty, to see a horse trained with gentleness.'

'It is strange to me, Miss Prideaux,' the boy agreed. 'I am much taken with it.'

'My father does not approve,' the girl said. 'He likes the way your father and those on the stud farm break their horses.' Leo could tell from a change in her voice that she was no longer facing him but had raised her head. 'Daddy is old-fashioned in his thinking,' she said quietly, as if to herself. Then she turned back to the boy and said, 'I saw what that idiotic stable lad did to you. If I had a whip I would have applied it to him. But you appear quite dry now.'

Leo said, 'The Lord did guide me, miss, to a scorched place, and He makes my bones strong.'

The girl did not say anything to this. Perhaps she was smiling again. Leo said nothing more, but studied the horse. When she brought him out of the paddock he was breathing hard from the exercise, but already he was calm, his lungs

145

easing in and out, barely registering.

'When you speak, Leopold,' the girl said, 'it sounds as if there is grit caught in your larynx. Perhaps the stable lad should have stuck the hose-pipe down your throat and flushed it out. Indeed, I am thirsty myself.'

The girl turned the roan away from Leo. He knew he should not speak what was on his mind, but if he did not do so now the chance may never come again. 'Miss Prideaux,' he called.

The pony had taken a few steps away from him. The girl brought it to a halt. She did not turn him. Leo walked past her and turned and looked up at her. 'Miss,' he said, 'I should love to ride him.'

The girl parted her lips and made a sound at the back of her mouth, a gasp of surprise or indignation, or the performance of such. 'You would, would you?' she said.

Leo swallowed and blinked, his eyes watering in the bright sun. 'More than anythin in this world,' he said.

The girl nodded. 'Then one day perhaps you shall, Leopold Sercombe,' she said. She kicked the horse's girth with her heels, and rode away into the shimmering noon, until the two became indistinguishable from each other, before they turned into the stable yard and disappeared.

October

The boy passed through the orchard. There was a buzzing all around, he walked through the sound. Wasps gorged themselves on windfall pears, damsons, plums. He prodded apples with the tip of his boot to see if any wasps lurked before picking them up. At other times he picked cob nuts, acorns. They called their pig the Pharoah. Each one was so christened. They called his sty and yard the palace.

Leo tossed the apples into the pig's sty and the animal grunted his approval. His sty was a lean-to against the wall of the cottage. Albert Sercombe had renewed it two years previously. Its walls were thick slabs sawn off the outside of elm butts he'd collected in a cart from the sawmill. The slabs were convex on the outside, flat inside. Their edges abutted one to another unevenly, allowing the draughts Leo's mother believed were necessary for the pig's wellbeing.

When the pig had eaten all the apples he could find in his little yard he came up to the fence. Leo scratched his hairy spine. The pig stood still. It was hard to believe it was the same creature he had carried over his shoulder in a hessian sack less than six months before. They called him the Pharoah because he was a king of sorts and they his servants whose only duty was to feed him.

147

Waste from the vegetable garden and scraps from the kitchen went into the stock-pot where they simmered to a pulpy mash. Cabbage leaves, potato peelings, greasy plates, any remnant of cooking or eating, Ruth poured it all into a wooden trough the pig cleaned so well he polished it with his tongue, enough to raise the grain. Leo's father gave the pig cinders or nuggets of coal to crunch, to stimulate his saliva and so aid digestion. Fred cleared away the shit, shook up the straw, added more when necessary. Two weeks ago Ruth announced that the Pharoah was matured, his metabolism was changing and he could now put on the fat the men needed to sustain them working their long hard days. The Pharoah was ready to be fed extra and so Kizzie brought him barley, and potatoes.

Pigs were less complicated or interesting in their thinking than horses, yet the boy had a fondness for them. He scratched the Pharoah behind his bristly ears.

October

Sid Sercombe took the doe from its bag and held it as Leo attached the muzzle to her head according to his brother's instruction. It was like a tiny bridle whose foremost part kept her jaws clamped shut. The rear strapped around her neck, and was tightened with a buckle. Sid checked it was secure, then he carried the ferret to one of the holes and presented her to it. She sniffed the hole, then looked back around her as if to say goodbye, farewell, to this world of light and space. Her posture was dramatic and comical. Sid told his brother not to laugh as it would put her off, but it did not seem to for she put her muzzled snout once more to the hole, and slithered in.

The second doe the boy held as Sid put on the muzzle, the third likewise, and these too disappeared into the warren. The ferrets' strong musky smell remained on the boy's fingers. They stepped back to where Aaron Budgell stood loading the guns. He gave the boy a small old single-barrel gun fired by external hammer, and placed him between himself at one side and Sid the other. Their wait was brief. The first rabbit bolted out in front of Sid. Leo saw him swing the gun and squeeze the trigger. The rabbit appeared to run smack into an invisible wall. It fell back as if stunned.

So they worked for some time, shooting the vermin as they came out of the burrows. When it had gone quiet for a while Mister Budgell said that would do it and the boy put down his gun and collected the rabbits. He counted twenty-three. He did not know why they used guns rather than nets. For Aaron Budgell's sport, perhaps. Sid meanwhile took a dog ferret from its bag. He clipped to a collar round its neck a length of cord marked with knots spaced equidistantly along its length. He put the ferret to a hole as he had the muzzled does, and it entered the darkness. Two more he despatched likewise. He tied the ends of their lines to stakes he hammered into the ground by each entrance.

The boy helped Aaron Budgell tie the dead rabbits by their front paws to a pole lodged in the forks of the branches of two adjacent trees.

Before long, the first of the loose-muzzled ferrets emerged, sniffing the air. Sid lifted her, removed the muzzle and returned her to her bag. The other two does soon followed. They each came into the light slowly, imperiously, as if upon a whim, though Sid assured his brother that the dog ferrets had driven them out.

Aaron Budgell said there was no hurry. 'They line ferrets won't be goin nowhere,' he said, and it was a good time for lunch. Mrs Budgell had provided a cottage loaf, which Mister Budgell cut into three with his ancient knife, and a lump of cheese he divided likewise. He and Sid drank mild, from earthenware bottles. Leo drank cold tea, but Sid allowed him some sips of his beer. Mister Budgell said he didn't mind ferreting in much colder weather than this for then at lunch they would drink old beer, dark and thick, which always warmed him up lovely.

They ate and drank. 'I reckon, gaffer,' Sid said, 'that I likes ferrets as much as any creature.'

The head keeper agreed that as well as being ferocious killers, ferrets were curious and quaint animals who seemed to treasure their relationship with man. In contrast to donkeys, he said, nodding towards the cart they had left standing some way off. 'I do believe,' he said, 'that certain species improve in time, like they say. But if you studies the Bible at all you has to conclude that some, such as asses, do deteriorate in their character and their behaviour. They are nothing like they used to be in the Holy Land.' Aaron Budgell sat up and raised his great chest. He opened his mouth as if to speak but let out instead a long and fruitful burp. Then he said, 'Let's get ourselves to diggin.'

★ ★ ★

The head keeper explained to the boy that his dog ferrets had sought the rabbits backed-up in chambers and dead-ends of their burrows and killed them. The ferrets would not now come out voluntarily until they were starving. 'If a man could train ferrets to come to his call,' Aaron Budgell said, 'he'd be as popular as he was rich.'

Sid put his ear to the hole by which one of the ferrets had entered the warren. He pulled taut the line that had been tied to its collar. The knots on the string enabled him to measure how far in

151

it had gone, allowing for unknown twists and turns in the tunnels. Aaron Budgell climbed on top of the bank. Sid gave him the figure of twelve or thirteen feet. The keeper judged it and dug the spade into the earth and heeled it in as far as it would go. The spade was an implement of elegance. It was spoon-shaped, and had a long handle made of beech. Inserted into the end of the wooden handle was a metal hook. He bent forward and put his ear to the long handle and listened. He stood back up to his full height and shivered the spade, then pulled it loose with ease, and repeated the procedure. And a third time. 'Ah,' he exclaimed. 'I believe us can hear them scrabblin about.' He began to dig. Sid fetched a second shovel. He told his brother to stay by the hole.

Leo asked why they did not pull the ferret out. Sid shook his head. 'He'd rather let hisself be throttled than be dragged out. I loves ferrets, but I ain't sayin they's the brightest animals in Creation.'

★   ★   ★

When they'd dug the last of the ferrets and the dead rabbits out, and returned the dog ferrets to their bags, Aaron Budgell opened his old knife again. The blade had been sharpened so many times it was half the width it must have been when new. He sharpened it again on a stone and paunched the rabbits. Leo told him there were thirty-six. Some had bare patches on their backs. Mister Budgell said it was where a muzzled

152

ferret had kept scratching the hind-quarters of a cornered rabbit when she couldn't kill it. Sid gave his brother a shovel and gestured hence, and Leo dug a hole. He buried the guts while the keepers loaded the donkey cart.

'See her now, how impatient with us her is,' Aaron Budgell said. 'Can't wait to get back home.' At that moment the donkey arched her neck forward and let out a long braying lament. '"Get a bloody move on,' er's tellin us.'

'Er's a contrary beast,' Sid agreed.

'Aye, lad,' his gaffer said. 'What you have to admit is, what er's got is character.'

As they walked back beside the cart to the keeper's cottage Aaron Budgell told the boy that a dealer from Taunton called on a Monday and paid cash for the rabbits, and that Leo would receive his share for a good day's work. He told the boy he was a fine little worker and that he had a calmness that was welcome. He said he'd been considering asking the master if he might wish to raise more birds, in which case he would need a new boy keeper. 'Your brother unfortunately tells me,' Aaron Budgell said, 'that we's lost you already to horses. Is that right?'

The boy looked up at the big keeper, and nodded.

'Yes,' Budgell said. 'I've heard that they does that to a man.'

November

The boy was given a message to convey to the head sawyer. His father kept it terse. Leo walked away from Manor Farm in the hot afternoon sun. He took the track across the valley, down past the high elms. Rooks in the upper branches cackled their disapproval or ridicule of him.

In the bed of the valley the track ran straight as a furrow ploughed by his father. Ploughmen, perhaps, once carved the lanes. He heard Isaac Wooland's bullocks before he saw them. Then he saw them, gathered by the fence on the right-hand side of the track, jostling, pressing against the wooden poles. Heifers grazed across the track and over the brook, half-hidden by a scrawny hedge. The bullocks moaned and lowed and groaned to their female brethren. Leo passed between them. The heifers appeared to ignore the bullocks, or to be deaf to the noise they made.

It reminded the boy of the German brass band who'd toured the villages the previous Christmas, tuning up their windy instruments. Loud farting bleats, trumpet blasts, pipe-clearing coughs of sound. Odd notes. It wasn't music. But then after a pause their leader announced that they would play a Christmas carol. He named the title of it in German. He uttered

154

some further words in their language, nodding his head, and then the band blew in unison. The audience of all ages listened to 'Silent Night' in rapt wonder.

But the bullocks could not pause, and play together, they could only continue each his own lonely tuneless racket.

★ ★ ★

The estate sawmill was on Warren Farm. A man stood with one foot on a huge log, the other on a length of wood placed upon the log and running from it to the ground outside the sawpit. He pulled the handle of the saw up and let it go back down, pulled it up, each time to the same height. Let it fall to the same depth. The boy watched the slow creeping forward of the cut. The sawyer eyed his chalk-line the whole way. Sweat dripped from his chin. Leo stepped forward until he could see the lad below, sawdust spraying upon his head and face and shoulders. The bottom dog.

Leo walked away, to the second sawpit. It was empty. He jumped down, out of the heat suddenly into a moist, cool tank. The odour of sawdust here. Tangy, sappy. From chinks in the pit's slab-lined walls, yellow frogs peered out at him. He jumped and, scrabbling, hauled himself out.

The top dog called down to the apprentice, 'Yep,' and stopped. He stepped from the pit and bent and picked up a hammer from the ground. He leaned over and from underneath tapped the plank on which he'd been standing. On the second tap it came loose. He shifted it two feet or maybe three along the log and knocked in the nail with a single tap. He dropped the hammer to the ground and stepped back onto the plank, and placed his left foot back upon the log. He grasped the handle of the saw and then, about to resume his labour, looked about him, his eyes darting and head jerking in the manner of a hen or some such creature that is prey to larger ones. Perhaps he had registered Leo's presence at the edge of his vision, or heard him.

The sawyer beheld the boy and raised his chin and eyebrows both. 'Do for you?' he said.

'Father says he'll bring his team tomorrow,' Leo said.

The sawyer stared at him. Working out who this boy was, whose son, to which team he was referring. He blinked slowly. 'Gaffer's up in Hangman's Wood,' he said. 'Go tell him.'

Now it was Leo's turn to stare back at the sawyer. Why could he not tell his own boss later? Did it please him to send this boy on an errand that was not required?

Leo swallowed. ''Tis a simple message,' he said.

The sawyer made a strange movement with his lips. It appeared that he was working something out of the depths of his mouth to the front. A shard of timber, perhaps. He spat it to the ground. 'It's takin us about a week to cut coffin boards from this tree,' he said. 'I'm lookin out for nails, bullets, wire. Keepin the line.' He tapped his skull, to indicate perhaps that it was full. 'Hangman's Wood. Go tell im yourself.'

156

The boy glanced into the pit. The apprentice peered up at him. His eyes, encircled by sawdust that sweat had stuck to his skin, were round like those of an owl.

★　★　★

The boy walked up from Warren Farm to the wood on the hill in the middle of the estate. Four of the six farms abutted its circumference. He passed a gang of men coppicing, cutting shoots with their bill hooks from the stumps of trees. From hardy birch a man was making broomsticks. From willow stools they cut rods for baskets. A lad built stacks of them. A boy collected the remnant twigs and smaller branches and tied them into bundles for fuel. Leo wondered if any of them saw him. He thought they must but none acknowledged him.

He walked through the wood. He had in his time climbed many of the trees. He passed an oak he'd not noticed before. The vertical wrinkles in its bark were spiralled, as if its roots were the handle of a carpenter's brace and some sleepy giant of the soil turned the trunk from below, screwing it as it grew, over years, decades, centuries, rotating slowly up towards the light.

★　★　★

He found the sawyers. A pair of men attacked the base of a great oak with their long-bladed felling axes.

From the trunk of one already felled three

men severed the limbs with axes and saws.

Over the trunk of another barkers teemed. One man cut lines through the bark, around the circumference of the tree, every couple of feet. The trunk had been brought down upon another, lying crosswise so that it was raised above the ground along its length. A second man used his light axe to make one longitudinal cut. A third and a fourth inserted heart-shaped barking irons, worked the wooden handles to and fro like the boy's mother paddling bread in and out of the oven, and lifted sections of bark. The men stripped the trees like teams of insects. A fifth man took the shells of bark as they were passed to him and a sixth stacked them in shocks to dry before they'd be sent to the tan yard. This last man was the oldest. Leo approached and when the man came to him he gave his message.

The man nodded. 'Albert Sercombe and his timber waggon and his horses. Tell im us'll be ready. Six trunks to haul to the yard, and a couple a loads a good branches.'

Leo turned to go.

'Wait.'

Leo turned back to the sawyer.

'Do me a favour, boy? Go back by the manor. Find the head groom. Herb Shattock. No one else. Tell him us is in for the meetin. Got it?'

Leo nodded.

'Tell me.'

The boy gazed up at the man. He had grey curly hair and red-rimmed eyes. Perhaps over time tiny specks of sawdust sneaked inside the lids.

'Sawyers is in for the meetin.'

'Good. Here, boy.'

The red-eyed sawyer put his right hand into his trouser pocket and withdrew it in the shape of a fist. He flicked his thumb and a coin spun into the air towards the boy. Leo caught it in his own fist, then opened his hand so that the farthing lay on his palm. Her old Majesty's bun-head gazed towards the west of her Empire, in the year 1893. The boy looked up to thank the sawyer, but he was already on his way back to the job he'd briefly abdicated.

★ ★ ★

The boy walked through the wood, seeing no one, and walked out of it across fields of sheep towards the big house. In one field crows grubbed the animals' dung for worms and suchlike savoury morsels. The boy counted precisely as many crows as sheep, for each white ewe one black bird, small avian familiars of the beasts, feeding from their excrement. Black hooded goblins. As he walked through the field, sheep bleated and parted for him and crows minced away. Some gave a hop and were airborne, witchlike, in taking to the air, doing what their woolly ovine acquaintances could not.

★ ★ ★

Leo approached the stables cautiously. He did not wish to meet the lad who would blame him for the thick ear the groom had inflicted two

159

months earlier, and would surely give Leo one the same or worse. He estimated that the lad was both a bully and a coward, and according to his father there were none so dangerous. He wished indeed to avoid all but Herb Shattock.

The boy walked through the back yards of the big house and past outbuildings whose purpose or function he did not know. There were people but he kept his head down and they were no more than figures briefly seen, when he glanced this way or that. One addressed him with a brief — 'All right?' — but the boy ignored everyone and walked on. As he approached the stable yard there was a great clattering of hooves. Sticking close by the wall he entered the yard and saw the master's half dozen hunters being ridden away by lads and grooms.

They disappeared and the sounds of the horses faded. Leo stood still and listened. The yard was empty but not deserted. He knew there was a horse or horses here for he could sense them, he did not know how exactly. Whether he could smell their rich odour or hear their calm deep breathing. He walked along one side of the yard, looking into the half-open boxes. All were vacant. He came to the tack room and glanced through the open door and stepped back. Two men stood close to one another. Neither spoke. The master, and the groom he had encountered before. Leo took another step back and watched them through the window. They seemed to be pondering some question, perhaps mathematical, as if doing so at the same time in the same vicinity might improve the working of their brains.

The master shook his head. The groom said, 'I'm sorry, sir. He was rollin in the pasture and he wouldn't stop. That's why I brought im in.'

'You cannot keep them all immune from such catastrophe, Shattock,' the master said. 'I don't expect you to.'

'All I can tell you is, whenever I seen a horse in pain like this, tis no helpin im.'

'I hear you.'

'To put im out of is misery, sir, tis the kindest — '

'I said, I hear you, man,' the master said.

The two men might have been brothers so alike were they in colouring, and in their mid-size height and stout frame. Leo heard a horse stamping in one of the loose boxes across the yard.

The master stepped out of the door of the tack room and stood there gazing ahead of him. There was perhaps a yard between him and Leo but the boy did not breathe or shift or twitch, so still was he. He did not look at the master and the master surely did not see him. The master spoke to the groom behind him. 'If I allow you to, I worry that I shall not be forgiven, you see. I would rather the animal suffered than that should happen.'

Leo watched the groom through the window. The groom said nothing. The master waited but the groom would not or was not able to help him. So the two men stood in this manner, facing the same way, Mister Shattock behind the master, each waiting for the other to speak. Leo could not restrain himself. With the slightest

161

movement of his head and the utmost swivel of his eyeballs he saw the master. Lord Prideaux's face was set hard but whether in an expression of anger or pain or fear the boy could not tell.

The master took a deep breath and sighed. 'Destroy him,' he said, and turned away from Leo and walked out of the yard.

The groom did not move. He appeared to be contemplating the empty space that Lord Prideaux had recently occupied, as if it took time for the master's absence to sink in. Then he turned around and, pulling from a pocket a ring of keys on a chain whose other end was attached to his waistcoat, he selected one key and unlocked a tall cupboard. The groom lifted a rifle from a rack within the cupboard and a box of bullets. He took a single bullet from the box and put it in a pocket of his jacket. He paused, then took a second bullet and put it in the same pocket.

Leo heard the sound again of a horse kicking its feet against the ground or perhaps the walls of its box. He walked briskly across the yard towards it. The upper door of the box was open. The blue roan was inside. He stood still, grinding his teeth. Then he pawed at the ground.

The groom came across the yard with the rifle over his shoulder, holding it by the barrel. 'Albert Sercombe's son,' he said. 'You times yer visits to moments of commotion, boy.'

He stood beside Leo. They looked at the pony. 'You ever see a horse shot?' the groom asked.

Leo shook his head.

'Do you wish to?'

The boy began to shake his head again for he had no desire to see any horse killed. Not ever. But if a horse had to be put down it would be an education to see how it was done. This man would do it properly. He nodded.

The groom handed the boy the rifle and, hissing between his teeth, opened the door of the box and stepped inside. It was a similar whistling sound to the one the boy's father made when working close by the horses, though each man had his own particular tone. The roan had on a halter. The groom tied a rope to the halter and patted the pony's head and led it out of the box. The boy, carrying the rifle as the groom had, over his shoulder, followed behind. They walked out of the yard and around a paddock and into the glade from which Leo had seen the girl riding the roan. The groom must be taking them to some quiet peaceful spot on which to execute the animal. Perhaps also with soft soil to dig a grave. Or perhaps they would butcher the carcase and boil the meat for the master's dogs. There was so much he did not know.

They had entered the glade when he heard a scream behind him and rapid footsteps and, turning, saw the girl dash towards them. There was a figure running behind her whom he could not identify. The girl in a long white skirt, the other in black. He stood still. The girl ran past him and he turned. The groom had not stopped but carried on walking, a further ten or twelve yards. The girl ran alongside the pony and flung her arms around his neck. The groom stopped walking.

'No,' the girl yelled.

'Miss Charlotte,' the groom said.

'No,' she cried again. Then, looking wildly towards Leo, she ordered, 'Take the gun.'

Leo felt the rifle yanked away from him. As he was spun round he grasped tight hold of the barrel with both hands. The maid who had revealed herself to be his cousin had hold of the stock with one hand and the barrel around the trigger with the other and was pulling it. The two of them conducted a fierce tug-of-war. The maid was the weight of the boy and half again and dragged him backwards with her, but he would not let go. The rifle bucked this way and that in crazy ways as if it had its own vitality and the boy and maid were merely holding on. Leo reckoned that he could keep his fingered grip upon the barrel indefinitely, but that his shoulders and upper arms might not last. He crept forward, allowing the barrel of the gun to point towards the ground, bending his knees and crouching to keep hold of it as he advanced. Coming almost alongside the maid, he swung his foot around and kicked her with all his might at the back of her left knee. She squawked. Her leg gave way and as she sat upon the ground she let go of the gun. Leo walked away with it to a spot some yards distant from the scene and turned and watched.

The groom said, 'Miss Charlotte, please.' The girl would not let go of the blue roan but clung tightly to his neck. The groom could have prised her loose but did not have the will or perhaps the authority to do so. He turned to the maid and

164

said, 'Gladys, fetch Lord Prideaux.'

The maid Gladys sat weeping. She hauled herself to her feet and limped away from them back towards the big house.

'Here, Miss Charlotte,' the groom said, stepping towards the girl and handing her the halter rope. 'Let's us take him back to the yard.'

The boy did not believe the girl would budge, but to his surprise she took the rope from the groom and, holding the rope where it was tied to the halter, turned the roan and walked him out of the glade. The groom followed. As he passed close to Leo he held out his hand and the boy stepped forward and gave him the rifle, then he walked after them.

★ ★ ★

The master came to the loose box and explained to his daughter that her pony was in great pain and should be released, but she would have none of it. 'He might recover, Daddy, he could, you don't know,' she said. 'We must give him a chance.'

The boy stood in the background and either no one saw him or all accepted his presence, for not a word was said to him.

The groom told the girl that the roan had a twisted gut. Torsion or strangulation of the intestine. It could happen to any horse, it was the physical flaw endured by their species just as certain dogs had back legs that gave out before the rest of their frames and the hips of female humans were barely fit for childbirth. The girl said that if they shot the horse they might as well shoot her for she should wish to die and would otherwise kill herself somehow.

The master left the yard. The groom put the rifle back in his cupboard and the bullets in his pocket back in the box they came from. The stable lads returned from exercising the hunters. The groom sent one of them off to fetch the man on Home Farm who was the castrator of horses on the estate, another to seek a certain old man in the village, a quack who possessed knowledge of horse anatomy that he the groom did not.

Leo explored the stable yard. Lads were grooming the hunters and the other horses. When they passed close to one another they whispered the news of what was happening. Leo kept well clear of the lanky one. He found a stairway to the hayloft above the stables. He took off his boots and carried them, tiptoeing across the rough boards, and lay down looking through the opening into the box below where the girl stood stroking her pony and speaking to him, too quietly for the boy to make out the words. He heard the door open and a man's voice. The master told his daughter how disgraceful it was that even in this day and age a telephone could not be connected to a place like this in the godforsaken back of beyond. They reaped the rewards of their obtuse ancestors for settling here when there were doubtless a hundred places closer to civilisation there for the taking. Be that as it may, he'd had a telegram sent to the veterinary surgeon in Taunton.

The girl said nothing. Her father asked her to

166

come to the house shortly for supper but she refused. He told her he was her father and commanded her to obey him. When she replied, it sounded as if she spoke through tears but the boy could not tell for sure from his hiding place.

'I won't leave, Daddy,' she said, sniffing. 'How do I know they won't take Embarr out again and murder him?'

'I will tell Shattock not to,' her father said. 'I promise.'

'I don't care,' the girl said. 'I have to stay anyway, Daddy. I'm not leaving Embarr.'

No one spoke for some time. Leo inched his body forward until he could lean over the edge of the opening and see the scene below. The master stood in the doorway. Asking himself what a father was supposed to do. Or wondering how much obstinacy or mettle his daughter possessed.

'Very well,' he said. 'I'll have food sent over.'

No sooner had the master left than the horse castrator was brought to the box by the groom. He said there were many kinds of colic, caused by many things. The horse could be constipated and be suffering grass sickness. Or he could have eaten his straw bedding which had impacted in the gut. These were only examples. He said that probably the pony would die but that they could give it liquid paraffin and salt water and this might clear the blockage, he could not say. 'Tidn't my area of expertise, Mister Shattock.'

After he had gone the boy heard horses being led out of the yard to pasture. He wondered where the stable lads went for their tea if they lived in. He thought they would be considered too dirt-ridden to sit in the kitchen of the big house. Light began to seep out of the hayloft and the loose box below. Suddenly the girl spoke. 'Leopold Sercombe,' she said.

He was stunned by what he heard, and did not move. He felt his heart beating against the floorboards where he lay.

'I know you're there.'

Leo raised himself up on his elbows, releasing his lungs that he might speak. 'T'wasn't my idea,' he said.

'Of course it wasn't,' she replied. 'I know that.'

Leo squirmed around half a circle and let his legs drop through the opening and lowered himself into the wooden crib. To his surprise he saw the horse was now lying on his side on the straw. He seemed to be trying to paw or kick at his own belly.

⋆ ⋆ ⋆

In time two maids appeared, one bearing a tray of food, another flasks and cups. The groom lit a paraffin lamp which he hung on a nail protruding from a rafter. The first maid laid the tray on the straw. The second looked up and saw the boy crouching in the manger like some strange stable sprite, and gasped. The first maid, his cousin, turned. She said, 'You wait, boy, you just wait. When I catch you, I'm goin to give you such a hammerin.'

The maids left and the girl said, 'Do you have

many friends, Leopold Sercombe? You make them so easily.'

'Every time I come here, miss, I makes another enemy,' he told her. 'I don't intend to.'

The girl told him that she wasn't hungry. 'Come here and help yourself.'

Leo climbed down. The girl lifted the muslin veils from the tray of food. There was a plate of meat and vegetables, a jug of gravy, a bowl of some kind of pudding and another of various fruits, only one of which, an apple, he recognised. What occasion warranted such a feast? The master's birthday, perhaps, or that of the master's grandmother, the dowager countess, who lived still in the house, or indeed the girl herself? The boy had not eaten for many hours and had a keen hunger. As he ate, the girl recovered her appetite somewhat and joined him. Between them they cleaned the plates.

'Embarr won't eat a thing,' the girl said. 'Whatever he's offered, he turns away from.'

'Just as well, miss,' Leo told her. 'The last thing he want's a ruptured gut.'

'Why can't he just be sick? Why doesn't the groom give him salted water?'

'Do you not know?' Leo asked. 'Horses cannot vomit. Any food has to pass right through em.'

★   ★   ★

Some time in the evening an old man was brought into the box. Leo recognised him from church. He was one of those Leo's father would speak with afterwards, outside the lych-gate. The

169

groom told the girl this man's name was Moses Pincombe and that he had helped bring many foals into the world upon the estate during her father and her grandfather's time. The roan lay on the straw. The old man asked the groom to boil some pints of linseed oil and to bring him pure lard. He removed his cap, nodded to the girl, folded the cap and put it in his pocket. He had a walking stick which he leaned against the wall and then with some difficulty lowered himself to his knees by the pony's head. He had some white-ish hairs scattered around the sides of his skull but otherwise was bald. He pulled back the pony's eyelids and examined his eyes.

The old man struggled to raise himself up. Leo helped him as best he could. 'I's awful sorry, miss,' the old man said, leaning a hand still on the boy's shoulder even though he was now standing. 'Herb's told me. I's afeared his eyes is dulled. See how he sweats. He's on the way out.'

While they waited for the groom to return, the roan became animated, rolling in the straw from side to side as if trying to rid himself of a terrible itch within the bones of his spine. Then he ceased just as suddenly and lay still once more upon the floor.

A lad appeared with a pan of lard he said the cook had given him. The old man asked the lad to put the pan upon the straw. Still leaning on Leo with one hand he reached the other towards the lad, who took it, and between them they helped the old man kneel beside the horse's rump. He pulled up the sleeve of the right arm of his jacket and folded it over. He did the same with his shirt. Then he put his right hand into the pan and slathered his fingers with the lard. With his left hand he lifted aside the roan's tail, then inserted the tips of his fingers into the pony's arse. He worked them in further and then his hand followed, and his wrist. The old man lay on his left side, his right arm deep inside the pony's rectum, delving into his insides. The roan did not object. The old man said nothing, either to the horse or to the people there. The groom entered the box and joined the girl and the boy and the lad watching, by the dim yellow light of the paraffin lamp, the ancient quack immersed in his intimate diagnosis.

At length the old man withdrew his arm and hand and fingers with a sticky sound. Leo thought his hand would be filthy with shit but it was not. The groom handed the old man a towel and he wiped the lard off himself. The lad and the boy helped the old man to his feet.

'Can't be sure, Herb,' he said. 'I would think his guts is twisted but it could be a section is ridden over a length behind or before it. Either way amounts to the same thing.' He turned to the girl who still sat beside the pony's head, stroking him. 'I's awful sorry, miss.'

★ ★ ★

The old man left, as did the lad, and finally the groom. The girl poured liquid from the flask into a cup and drank it. Then she refilled the cup and passed it to the boy. Leo sniffed it. It had a subtle aroma of something that made saliva

171

materialise in his mouth. He took a sip. He felt its taste on his tongue, and threw back his neck and emptied the cup, savouring it as it washed through his mouth. He gasped, and asked the girl if what he had just drunk was nectar. She asked him what on earth he meant and he said nectar was mentioned in the Good Book and in other ancient tales. He didn't know it still existed. She told him he was talking nonsense, that he had merely drunk a cup of lemon barley water.

★   ★   ★

A maid brought blankets. Leo climbed up into the hayloft and slept. He woke occasionally. The pony rolled as it had before. Leo went outside to piss. The moon was only just on the wane from being full and cast a silver tinge upon all it illuminated. He knew that he would work with horses all his life but understood as he had not before that there were different ways and places to do so. He doubted whether one life was long enough to know all there was to know of horses. Perhaps that was why the Good Lord gave us many lives. And he understood that as the girl would not forsake her roan, so he would not leave her.

★   ★   ★

In the morning when the boy awoke and crawled over the floorboards to see into the box below he saw the blue roan was now standing. The girl stood beside him, scratching his withers. Leo clambered down into the manger and then over it to the ground.

'He's better, look, do you see?' the girl said. 'I think he's better, don't you, Leopold?'

Leo said nothing, and the girl said, 'He's standing, can't you see? On his own legs. He has risen from the dead like an equine Lazarus, don't you see, Leopold Sercombe?'

The boy said nothing but stood on the other side of the pony's head and stroked his flank.

★ ★ ★

A servant maid brought a silver tray of food for the girl's breakfast. The girl carried the tray into the yard where lads saddled hunters and brushed down trap-carting cobs, and flung the tray as far as she could, scattering its contents. Plates snapped into shards of pottery. Food was strewn upon the ground. Bacon. Sausages. Egg yolk. Slices of toast. Silver cutlery lay amongst the debris. The girl returned to the loose box. The maid began picking up what she could.

The girl wept for a time then stopped. The horse tried to kick himself where he stood. He began to breathe rapidly and to expel air through his nostrils, snorting loudly. He did this until the girl implored him to stop, but he continued. The girl cried to the roan and begged him to cease. It was no use. The pony inhaled and exhaled like some furious child engrossed in a tantrum. Eventually he slumped, standing, exhausted, and looked like an old nag, all worn out.

The groom entered the box with a man the girl greeted with great enthusiasm. 'You'll save him, Mister Herle, won't you?'

'Let us see what we can do,' the man said.

The groom brought four stable lads in. They surrounded the horse, two on each side, and stood firm against him. The surgeon took the roan's pulse. He attached the listening pieces of a stethoscope to his ears and placed the other end upon one part and then another of the pony's body, as if roaming around in search of some quiet thing inside. Some other tiny creature hiding there, subtle and malign, causing the roan all this distress.

'Dear girl,' the surgeon said. 'It would be kinder, dear Charlotte . . . ' He looked at the girl but did not finish what he'd begun to say. He looked to the door, where the boy saw the master standing, just outside. The surgeon shrugged. 'I shall give him morphia and chloral. It will help to ease his pain.'

The surgeon opened his bag of medicines and filled a syringe with liquid. He attached a long needle. 'Hold him steady,' he ordered. 'I need to hit the vein.' The stable lads pressed upon the roan, but he trembled and shook. The surgeon took aim at the pony's neck, and slid the needle in. He withdrew the plunger of the syringe an inch, or less, then cursed and pulled the long needle out from the pony's flesh. 'Hold him,' he said again, and made a second attempt to find the jugular. Again he failed. The girl shivered,

174

and squeezed her eyes shut each time the surgeon missed. Eventually he drew a little venous blood into the syringe and then he pressed the plunger slowly down and sent the medicine into the pony's bloodstream.

★　★　★

The vet Herle promised to return that afternoon or evening. The pony spent the morning standing gazing at the wall in front of him. He looked like some strange monk-like version of his species who had taken a vow of silence and stood in contemplation of mortality. Of eternal life in the Elysian fields. Or the American plains. Was it not true that horses ran free there? Droves of wild mustang. Following a proud stallion leader. Perhaps he imagined himself allowed to remain entire and be that stallion. Was it not true that an Indian brave chose a wild horse, lassoed it, handled it? He mounted the horse and they rode out on the prairie together. Of such a rider the roan dreamed.

★　★　★

Lunch was brought for the girl. She did not throw this meal away. Again she shared it with Leo. In the afternoon a young woman visited. 'I thought I should see the poor creature responsible for my inactivity, Lottie,' she said. She spoke with an odd accent. Whether from another country or some far distant part of Britain the boy did not know for sure. 'I have a

175

translation for you. Goethe.' She leaned on the lower door of the box. 'Everyone in the house talks of your vigil. They talk of nothing else.'

The girl asked what they said.

The woman removed her spectacles and cleaned them with a handkerchief she pulled from a pocket in her skirt. 'Some say you are foolish and your father he is indulgent. That this here is only a pony while the world goes to hell in a hand-cart. The miners and dockers and railwaymen of your North strike and riot and hold this nation, if not your Empire, to ransom. The suffragettes wish us women to become Vandals and Goths and destroy all in our way. Half the Irish threaten you with civil war unless they receive Home Rule, the other half threaten civil war if it is given. You know nothing of such matters, Lottie, why should you? But this is what they say. At such a time, a child clinging to her dying pony is unseemly.'

The woman asked if it was safe to come in. The girl said it was so she entered the box. Leo saw her limp, though not, it appeared, with pain. One leg looked shorter than the other. Her white shirt was sewn with ruffles down its front. She stood just inside the door.

'What do others say?' the girl asked.

'They say your love for this horse is something rare, Lottie,' the woman told her. 'There are not so many of them. Dear child, I came to see if there is any point in bringing books down here. Clearly there is none. I suppose we could practise some German conversation?'

The girl shook her head.

176

The governess smiled. Her teeth were discoloured. 'I look forward to resuming our lessons in due course,' she said, and left.

* * *

The roan lay in the straw. The girl and the boy lay down too. 'You smell of horse,' the girl said.

Leo sat up. 'I beg your pardon, miss,' he said. 'But if I does, don't you too?'

'Yes, but you can't smell it on me,' she told him. 'I can on you and on myself. And I will change these clothes and bathe and then I will no longer.'

Leo did not know what he was permitted to say. He said what came to mind. 'You are most fortunate, miss.'

'No, I am not,' she said. 'Don't you understand? I am forced to wash some kind of truth or knowledge from myself.'

They spoke no more, and lay there in the straw.

* * *

Some time later Leo sat bolt upright from a nap. He did not know the reason only that there was one. The girl dozed. The roan lay quiet. Leo rose and walked to the door of the loose box and opened it a fraction and slipped out. He walked across the yard. It was something he had heard. Or someone.

The tack-room door was open. He stood against the wall outside and eavesdropped on his mother speaking with the groom. She had traced Leo's steps here, she said, via the sawyers. The groom said her son had given him no message so Ruth gave it to him. He addressed her as Mrs Sercombe, she him as Mister Shattock. The groom explained what had happened to the pony of the master's daughter. That she would not leave it, and neither it seemed would the boy. He said that Ruth could take her son home, or try to, but that he the groom would not send the boy away. No, he was sorry, but he would not do that.

Ruth said her son could come home when he was hungry. Herb Shattock agreed. Leo walked back to the loose box.

★ ★ ★

The veterinary surgeon did not return that day, or evening. The pony rolled and twisted in the straw. He tried to kick his own belly as he lay. Not once did he neigh, or whinny. Leo climbed into the hayloft to sleep. He woke and thought that the hunters had come in from the pasture and all were stampeding in the loose box below. Somehow. He woke fully. The girl's voice cried out in the dark. She called to him for help. She was climbing into the hay manger. Leo crouched on the boards and leaned down towards her. She grasped his hands and he pulled and helped her climb up. They lay side by side and watched the roan jump and kick, contorting himself in pain and rage.

Moonlight spilled into the loose box as the

groom opened the upper door. 'Are you all right, Miss Charlotte?' he called. 'Are you safe?'

She called out that she was, but perhaps he could not hear her above the cacophony of the dying horse's frenzy, for he yelled louder, 'Are you safe?'

This time he did hear her reply.

The roan jerked and reared, bucked and kicked for longer than seemed possible. Leo held the girl's hand, trembling. Eventually the roan ceased and lay down in the straw. The girl and the boy climbed down. The pony was covered in sweat and panting, his flanks heaving. His mouth was surrounded by bubbly foam. His eyes were no longer dull but open wide, inflamed with some frantic understanding of his plight. The girl lay beside him stroking his damp neck and talking to him. The boy stood above her. Herb Shattock watched from the doorway, his head and torso casting moon shadow across the pony's rump.

The roan calmed. He kicked his legs once behind him. He closed his eyes. He let out an exhalation and the pause before he inhaled grew longer than before. Leo waited for him to breathe. The wait continued until the boy understood that it was over for the roan's heart had finally given out. The girl wept as she spoke to the dead horse. The boy walked past her to the door. Herb Shattock opened the door and let him out. The groom walked across the yard. The boy followed him.

In the tack room was a cot, where the groom must have slept. It explained how he'd reached

179

the box so swiftly when the roan went berserk. 'I've a stove in here,' he said. 'We'll make Miss Charlotte a mug a tea.'

'Do you wish me to fetch her father?' Leo asked.

The groom shook his head. ''Tis only three o clock in the mornin,' he said. 'We can send word once folk stirs.' He opened the baffle on the little stove. The black coals glowed orange. He filled the kettle from a brass tap above the sink. The room was unlike Albert Sercombe's tack room. It was as tidy as the Sercombes' parlour. As if Herb Shattock expected important visitors. It was not a tack room at all, but the groom's bothy. The cooking grate shone with black lead. An iron saucepan stood on the second hob. On the mantelpiece above were a tea caddy and a jar of tobacco. On the wall hung pictures of horses.

'I do not like that surgeon,' the groom said. 'I never have, to tell the truth. That Mister Herle. He could a come back to give the poor beast another shot. To help out Lord Prideaux. He said he would. He must a took hisself off elsewhere.'

The boy asked the groom if he could ask him something. The groom nodded and the boy said he had tried to work it out but could not. He did not know if what he had witnessed was cruel or kind. Which was it?

The groom shook his head. 'I do not know either,' he said. 'All I know is she went with her horse right up to the gates. The pearly gates or whatever portal our horses go through. She went all the way to the threshold with im. That is what you just seen there, boy.'

180

Christmas

It was the custom to give the teachers in the village school some gift at Christmas. This year one of the Haswell boys came up with a plan with which most agreed. On the last day of term the children got to school early. Miss Pugsley could not believe one single child was there before her, yet this day all were. They would not let her in, but said they must wait for Miss Pine too and so kept her talking in the yard.

When the junior teacher arrived Kizzie Sercombe as the eldest girl told the women that their presents were in the classroom. Miss Pugsley thanked the children. It was Miss Pine's first Christmas and it appeared that Miss Pugsley had not told her to expect anything and she was clearly delighted. The children made way for the teachers and ushered them in. Then they closed the door, tied the handle to the drainpipe, and ran to the windows to watch.

They had given Miss Pugsley a Christmas goose, Miss Pine a duck. Each was still alive. It would have been churlish to refuse the gifts. The teachers chased them around the classroom. Neither had been brought up with animals, and looked as terrified as their prey if not more so. Miss Pugsley cornered her goose but it hissed and flapped its wings and rushed past her. Miss

181

Pine ran to the door but the children there would not open it. In the end she sat upon a bench and wept, and the Haswell boys went in and caught the birds and wrung their necks for the teachers, and the last day of term resumed.

★ ★ ★

At the end of the day Miss Pugsley informed the class that she was off to spend the festive season on the far side of Taunton with her sister's family, whom she was sure would appreciate the goose. She wished them all a Merry Christmas. Then she asked Leo Sercombe please to stay behind.

He stood before her desk. She picked up off the surface a postcard, and studied the double portrait of the King and Queen, George and Mary, on its face. A souvenir of their Coronation. Miss Pugsley turned the card over. She examined what was written thereon then turned it for the boy to see. The card was scribed with fine, consistent copperplate.

'Who else,' she asked, 'would have written this?' She turned it back so she could see the words and read aloud, '*Then I saw heaven opened, and behold, a white horse! He who sat upon it was called Faithful and True, and in righteousness he doth judge and make war.*'

Miss Pugsley lowered the card and looked Leo in the eye. 'It is such beautiful script,' she said.

He shifted his gaze. The floor was dirty. It would surely be cleaned while the school was closed. 'It is from the *Book of Revelations*, miss,' he said.

182

'Thank you, Leo,' Miss Pugsley told him. 'Thank you very much. Enjoy your Christmas.'

The boy smiled and turned and walked out of the room.

He walked home as night came down like cold, early darkness clamped upon the earth. He bent low to the ground along the avenue and gathered acorns. There was just sufficient light by which to do so. It was his habit to fill his pockets, for not only were acorns a piquant delicacy for the pig but they were poisonous to horses, and if he could he would have cleared them from the ground every autumn all across the county and beyond.

The pig snaffled the acorns. He was grown tremendously obese and could barely move but dragged himself in and out of the shed of his sty and into its tiny yard.

The pig shit the boy's brother Fred piled in a heap at the end of their mother's kitchen garden, with all manner of other waste added to it: soot, ashes, each family member's hair cut by Ruth including her own, their night soil, rotten fruit, mouldy bread, fish waste, seaweed, bloody rags, woollen scraps, residue of Albert's pipe tobacco he tapped onto the heap, human piss, pigeon shit, weeds. Any vegetable matter the Pharoah disdained . . . All was thrown on the heap and turned into black compost to be dug into the garden soil, as manure on the farm would be dug into the fields.

January 1912

The wheelwright's shop was next-door to the smithy. His name was Hector Merry. The boy watched as he walked from the smithy to his shop, from his shop to the waggon outside. Merry's right foot hit the ground pointing outwards, as if he were planning to veer off at a diagonal. But then his left foot did likewise: now he appeared about to strike out leftward. His torso too shifted, following each foot's lead. Yet each time he came back on course, and despite his corporeal burlesque Hector Merry marched straight ahead. He might have given the impression of a vacillating man, one undecided about which direction to take along the village road, along the path ahead of him, changing his mind from one footstep to the next. Yet he did not. Shoulders back, spine straight, Hector Merry looked like a man of purpose and conviction.

After the iron tyres had been heated in the forge and put onto the new wheels, the wheels were rolled into the wheelwright's shop and attached to the new waggon. Then Hector Merry's lads and the Crocker sons pushed the waggon outside.

A number of old men and some women had gathered by now. A new waggon from Hector

184

Merry was something to see. Amos Tucker was there too, it was his waggon, but he stood among the old men in the road, sucking on their pipes, appraising the workmanship, while Albert Sercombe studied it up close, moving slowly around the vehicle. The great rear wheels were as high as his chest, and he was a tall man. He kept one hand upon the wood, assessing it by touch as well as sight, or getting the feel of it, or simply out of pleasure. All seasoned ash, it was a cock-raved waggon with strouters. The boy kept close to him. Albert ran his hands along the curved timber, the chamfered spindle sides.

Hector Merry followed Albert at a few yards' distance, reliving the glide and flow of his plane, perhaps. Or recalling the knotty struggle of this stock, that joint of spoke and felloe. Jacob Crocker too was a keen spectator for the waggon was a collaboration, not only in the tyres but the iron axles too and other smaller parts for which the boy knew not the name. It was a thing of wonder. Put together like some intricate puzzle, yet the wheels and the body of the waggon would have also to bear great weight and to withstand shocks and jolts of uneven roads and frozen rutted tracks.

When Albert had finished his circular inspection he climbed up into the bed of the waggon and walked around, stamping his boots. Then he jumped down and walked over to the smithy, where Noble and Red were tied up. He brought one and Leo the other to the waggon. The horses already wore their harness. He backed them into the curved shafts and hitched

185

them up. He took longer than usual, as if there were some ceremony to the ritual in this public place.

Albert gave his son a knee-up to Noble on the nearside and he rode her side-on. Albert walked beside them, and they headed back to the estate. Old folks waved them off. The tall hunched Crocker son came out, swinging a dirty empty bottle tied to a length of cord. He swung it against the side of the waggon. It looked as if he wished to play some strange variant of the game of conkers, glass versus wood. But on the second swing the bottle smashed and the spectators cheered for the Crocker lad had launched their waggon on its maiden voyage as was done for boats built in the yard at the Port of Bridgwater.

As they walked out of the village Leo looked back. Hector Merry was following them, with that distinctive gait of his. Perhaps he could not bear to let his waggon go. He did not close the gap but kept a consistent distance of some twenty yards between them. Perhaps it was required for a wheelwright to follow his conveyance to its farm. Would he seek payment from the master, not Amos Tucker?

Leo watched the wheelwright walk along. Sometimes he lowered his head to his chest. At other times he looked away, off to one side or the other, as if something had diverted his attention. Then he would look back at the waggon, pondering it afresh.

Albert Sercombe glanced up at his son. He saw the boy turn and followed his gaze. He watched a while himself, looking over his shoulder as he led the horse. 'If it makes a bad noise,' he said, 'he'll have us take it back to the shop to fix it.'

The boy watched again. Hector Merry kept turning his head so that one ear was cocked forward as he walked, listening to the wheels turning and the waggon creaking as the joints settled into one another on the move.

'You're more 'n likely thinkin what a fine craftsman that Mister Merry is. And you'd be right, boy. But they say he's nowhere near as good's his father Josh Merry was. That's what they old folks will have been whisperin. Take these wheels.' Albert gestured behind him. 'Beautiful four-inch wheels. In the days before roads was paved with stone the heavy waggons had wheel-rims nine inches wide. They was so wide the tracks they made formed footpaths in the mud. Think of the skill it took to make them.'

Leo glanced back. Hector Merry was diminishing behind them. The wheelwright waved. 'Father,' Leo said.

Albert looked over his shoulder. 'Reckon us ave got the nod,' he said, and waved in reply.

February

James Sparke's wife wrote out his itinerary then copied it, each assignation on a separate strip of paper. A name, a place, the date. These she delivered to the farms and cottages upon the estate to which he had sold one of his fattening pigs, plus one or two others who had bought elsewhere. There was a reason the job was done here in the unusual month of February, though none could tell Leo what it was. On the Tuesday allotted to Ruth Sercombe, Leo and his sister Kizzie stayed home from school. Albert and Fred returned from Manor Farm once they'd fed the horses. Fred carried a rough bench borrowed from the gaffer Amos Tucker upside down on his shoulder.

Ruth gathered necessary implements in her kitchen. Kizzie swilled the yard by the back door of the cottage and brushed it down. Drops of water froze instantly and became beads of ice she brushed away. Fred laid a bed of wheat straw in the yard. Leo helped his father fill kettles and pans of water heating on the stove. They conducted their preparations quietly, calmly, for Ruth told them that the righteous have regard for the life of their beast. She told them also that the bacon would cure better if the Pharoah were neither fretful nor fierce at the hour of his death but content as he had been all his life in the palace.

★ ★ ★

They heard James Sparke approaching. In one hand he carried a wicker basket of knives, hooks, ropes, steelyard weighing tackle, the iron and metal scraping and clanking. His nose was red. He bore his pole-axe on his shoulder. 'It wants to rain,' he said. 'But it's too cold to, no?' Ruth whispered to him, her breath smoking, asking him to set his basket on the ground. He sharpened his knife while she spoke in his ear.

Leo followed his father round the corner to the sty. There was barely room for the Pharoah to turn around in his tiny compound. The boy believed the pig did not feel the cold as they did. Albert talked to him as he climbed over the fence. He slipped a length of plough-string into the pig's mouth and pulled it tight around his upper jaw. There was no gate for they had no need of one save for this moment. Fred had joined them and he and Leo twisted and heaved a side section of fence loose and removed it.

Albert led the Pharoah out of his compound for the first time since he was dropped into it when they brought him home. He led him round the corner of the cottage and into the yard. Ruth requested of the members of her family that they look away, that they pretend to be involved in other activities, but they could not. Fred dropped some meal onto the straw. The Pharoah ignored it. Perhaps he could eat no more, this day was so timed that such a creature was full and could be made no fatter. Instead he squealed as he had when they took him from his sow and began to pull against the taut string.

'Steady,' James Sparke said. 'Hold him steady.' He raised the pole-axe up over and behind him, then brought the flat head down on the Pharoah's forehead. The animal ceased squealing and staggered, but did not fall. Sparke cursed and raised the axe and struck the pig a second time. The Pharoah keeled over. Sparke laid the head of the axe on the ground and took the knife he had sharpened from his basket and slit the pig's throat. Ruth held a bowl and collected the blood as it poured out, bright red. Kizzie stood by, and when the bowl was full she passed her mother a fresh one and took the full bowl and poured the blood into a bucket. Fred stirred the blood in the bucket with a long spoon so that it would not thicken and clot.

When the blood flow slowed Albert forked straw over the dead pig. James Sparke inserted a bunt into the pig's mouth and another into his arse. He stood and sniffed at the wind. 'Westerly, yes?' he asked Albert, and lit the straw at one end of the pig. The flames hissed and crackled as they travelled along the carcase. Sparke forked loose straw onto the pig. Smoke blew this way and that. The boy ran around as it engulfed him and made his eyes water. The pig was a burnt offering, the straw and the singeing bristles were fragrant incense, James Sparke the ritual slaughterer consecrating their sacrifice. All was as it had ever been or would be.

'Let's turn him,' James Sparke said. Kizzie had taken over stirring the blood. Fred helped his father roll the pig over to his other side. Sparke covered the corpse with fresh straw using his fork then delicately lifted a wisp that was still alight and set it to the pyre. He never left the fire alone but constantly agitated the burning straw with his fork. Twice more they turned the pig, to burn off the hairs upon his back and belly, then Sparke took a broom Ruth gave him and brushed the blackened corpse.

'On the bench now, yes?' James Sparke said. He laid aside the broom. The bench that Fred had borrowed was a form of thick elm plank into which strong oak legs were tenoned. Along the middle of it ran a V-shaped channel, joined by further channels running into it on either side.

James Sparke and Albert took hold of the pig's front trotters, Fred and Ruth the hind. At a word from Sparke they lifted the carcase. They carried it a few steps, staggering with its weight, to the foot of the bench. There they swung it forwards and backwards. 'Count a three,' Sparke said, and on the third swing ordered, 'Yup!' He and Albert lifted the pig's head and trotted along either side of the bench, and at the end of the swing Ruth and Fred set the dead pig's rump on the bench and the rest of his body was lowered along it.

Albert and Fred carried out buckets of hot and boiling water and threw them over the pig's inert steaming body. Leo stirred the bucket of blood. Ruth and Kizzie scraped off any bristles that had escaped the flames. It was known that James Sparke would not scrape a pig. A strange squeamishness considering all else he did. He did not like it. He said it gave him the crinkum-crankums.

Their black pig the Pharoah became a hairless, mottled brown carcase. James Sparke pulled the horns from off the toes with surprising ease and threw them away. The boy picked one up. It was warm, and had a bowl like a cup. Sparke cut the tongue from out of the pig's mouth and handed it to Ruth. Then he made a cut to the middle joint of one leg after another and turned each hock backward. He opened up the belly with one longitudinal cut of his sharp knife. Delving into the pig's innards, Sparke separated and removed the organs and entrails and put them on plates Ruth held out for him. Liver, lights, heart, chitterlings. They steamed in the cold morning. Some she put in bowls of clean cold water.

Kizzie stirred the bucket of blood. Sparke removed the Pharoah's bladder and passed it to Albert, who drained it and inserted the broken stem of one of his clay pipes. He held the bladder with one hand and the pipe stem with the other for Fred to blow into. Albert told Leo to take a length of string from his left-hand jacket pocket, nodding towards it. Fred blew into the pipe stem, his cheeks reddening. Albert kept saying, 'A little more.' They inflated the bladder to a size it was not possible to believe had ever been done while it was inside the animal. Albert claimed that it would be easier to clean the bladder now, ready to hold the rendered fat, but Leo reckoned that this was not so, that in truth his father found some boyish pleasure in producing this strange balloon.

'Should do us,' said Albert. He took the bladder and, pinching it with his fingers, held it while Fred tied up the tube.

James Sparke inserted a hook into each of the pig's hind-legs, and tied a length of rope between them, then the men lifted the pig and hoisted it onto a spike sticking out of the wall of the cottage. With a hazel stick James Sparke propped the pig's belly open to the frosty air. Then without a further word he picked up his pole-axe and, leaving the basket of other tools in Albert's shed, walked away. Albert and Fred returned directly to the farm. The boy swept the yard, and poured water onto the bloody surface of the bench and brushed it down. Ruth cut and cleaned the entrails of the pig. Her hands were pink. When she was ready she called Kizzie inside and mother and daughter cooked the first dish from the Pharoah, a Bloody Pie of heart, liver, chitterlings, groats and blood.

★　★　★

In the afternoon the boy harnessed their pony to the small cart and took it to the village. At the shop he handed Alf Blackmore a piece of paper with his mother's order. Three oblong lumps of salt. The boy was not big enough to carry one unaided so Alf Blackmore's lad put them in the cart and Leo brought them home.

★　★　★

On the day following James Sparke returned. First he weighed the pig. While it hung from the spike, members of the family had estimated its weight. So too had other cottagers. None were quite accurate, though Fred was closest. The pig weighed fourteen stone and seven and one half pounds. 'Heavier than any man you'll be familiar with, no?' James Sparke told Leo. 'Save Amos Tucker, I suppose.' Why they measured it the boy did not know, other than to play this game. To see if James Sparke's fattening pigs were improving or in decline? To assess the diet that the family had given the Pharoah?

They lifted the carcase from the scales and laid it on the elm bench, then as before Albert and Fred, the carters, went back to work on the farm.

James Sparke cut off the pig's head. He divided the head into two halves. He severed the ears, and extracted the eyes. The boy held out a saucer Ruth had given him. James Sparke lifted out the brains and put them in the saucer and Leo carried it inside to his mother. Ruth took the saucer and asked her son if the cold had got to him for he looked wobbly on his feet. He said it was not the cold. He told her he could not believe the Pharaoh, who had been grunting and snuffling in his customary, comical manner the day before, was now no more than this gross profusion of meat.

'He lived that we could eat him,' Ruth said. 'That we can live. Who ordained it? None but the Lord.' She added that it was a mystery and Leo was right to ponder it. He nodded, and went back outside.

James Sparke cut the carcase into halves. He cut the hams, gammons, spare ribs, hazeletts, griskins and rearings. All this he explained to the boy and girl as he did it. They ferried the parts inside.

It was not the boy who noticed Lottie but his sister. Kizzie nudged Leo and whispered in his ear, 'The master's daughter.' Leo looked up and saw her standing a few yards away, watching the butcher at work. Kizzie fetched her mother. Ruth came out, wiping her hands and forearms with a cloth, and asked if the young mistress wanted something or if there was anything they could do for her. The girl said she wished only to stand and watch this dissection, for it interested her, if the carter's wife wouldn't mind. Ruth said she would not and returned inside.

When all the bony parts had been cut there remained only the two great flitches. James Sparke took payment from Ruth and left with his basket of tools. The boy saw that Lottie had vanished as ghostly as she'd come. He and his sister crushed the salt from the blocks he'd fetched the day before and helped Ruth rub it into the hams and flitches and all the rest until they had a good covering to soak in over the months to come. As each was completed Ruth hung it from a hook in the kitchen or the parlour.

March

The boy went with his father to his uncle Enoch the under carter's stable and brought out the two five-year-old bay geldings. Herbert emptied Albert's stables of his horses. Father and son led the geldings to two adjacent stalls and worked on them. They groomed the horses as every day, then wet their hooves and scrubbed them. Albert twisted hay into a wisp and dried his horse's legs, and the boy did likewise. They sponged under their cruppers and when the feather hair dried below the fetlocks they combed it until it hung over the great hooves like silk.

Albert came into the boy's stall. 'You should know this,' he said. 'See how his brown coat shines.' He took a small linen bag from his pocket and untied the string and loosened it. The boy imbued a strong, unfamiliar aroma. Something like rosemary. 'Tansy,' his father said. 'I bakes the leaves dry then rub em between my ands into powder. Sprinkles a little into their meal.' Albert looked over his shoulder. 'Your uncle has no need to know. Your brother neither. My father told me, and I tell you.' He looked around him again, for fear that someone might be lurking in the shadows. 'Don't put too much in, else they'll sweat it out and all the world'll smell it.'

Albert pulled tight the drawstring and returned the bag to his pocket. He said that at a summer show he might rub a horse down lightly with a rag dipped in paraffin, for not only would it bring up a quick shine but it would also keep flies off and help the horse stand steady in the ring. 'Wet their chaff with a little piss now and again,' he said. 'Keep a good bloom on their hide.'

'Whose?' the boy asked.

Albert frowned. 'Your own, a course.'

Leo shook his head. 'I never seen you do it.'

Albert grinned. 'Never will. Not you nor no one. Let's plait em.'

Albert returned to the other stall. They plaited the black manes and tails of the bay geldings, keeping the twisted patterns in place with straw, tying ribbons into the hair. The horses ate an extra portion of oats, chaff and mangel in their mangers. By the light of the lanterns they checked the horses' feet, poking the last bits of reddish mud from around the frog with picks. When they were done they put on new halters Amos Tucker had bought for the purpose and led them out of the stalls.

The farmer had by now appeared and he told Albert that he would see them in town. 'Keep an eye out,' Amos said. 'We don't want some crooked horse coper spoilin or spookin em.'

Albert tied the halter rope of one horse to the tail of the other. He led the foremost gelding out of the yard. The boy walked behind. His uncle Enoch and brother Fred watched their horses leave the farm.

They walked the dark lanes. Others would be going but perhaps they were the first. They heard sounds from neighbouring farms. Whether those carters too were preparing to take their animals was speculation. As a grey and streaky sky became visible above them Albert called his son forward beside him. Leo had been to the town, twice, but never yet to the Fair. His father told him that one hundred years before, fifteen thousand sheep were sold there. But the wool trade died. Now the numbers were pitiful. Carthorses were sold instead, and wild Exmoor ponies herded and driven on the hoof. Others, too. Dulverton Fair had folded when he was a youngster, then Tiverton Fair too, and now all the horses came here. He said that the first horse the old gaffer had asked him to sell was one he had watched being born, broken himself and worked behind the plough for two years. He would not do that again. 'I'll break em and work em but I won't sell em.' He had spoken of this problem with Amos Tucker's father and they had resolved it. He only sold the under carter, Enoch's, horses. His own were not sold until they were too old to work, and then not for serious profit.

They led the two bay geldings into Bampton. Others were on the road. The boy had imagined there would be one large sale ring, like the show

198

ring at the village fête, when his father competed with other carters roundabout in classes for the best-decorated horse in cart harness or in a pair of plough gears, and the master gave out shining trophies. There were a number of these at home in the parlour.

Instead, the High Street was unrecognisable. It was aswarm with livestock. Cattle roamed, sheep and horses, seemingly unattached to each other or anyone. Moorland ponies and carthorses and also young, unbroken colts and Welsh cobs. The boy stuck close to his father, who led their geldings slowly through the crowd. He stared glassily ahead to demonstrate that he had no concern for the behaviour of his own beasts while all around him was a pandemonium of cattle lowing and sheep bleating, of horses backing up and kicking. Collie dogs slunk around small flocks or else cowered, defeated by the impossibility of herding their charges in this chaos. Farmers shouted at their lads. Lads yelled at their beasts. The High Street reeked of ammonia.

★   ★   ★

Past the Taunton Hotel Albert Sercombe turned off and they walked through a yard of parked carts and waggons, all unyoked. Behind the hotel was an orchard. In amongst the yet leafless fruit trees, horses stood like a troop of cavalry mounts waiting patiently for battle. They found a vacant tree and tied their horses' halter ropes to another cord that Albert slung around its trunk.

Albert Sercombe filled his pipe with his old black shag and lit it, and watched the horses that passed them by. Shires in ones and twos like theirs but also droves of others. He pointed out purebred Exmoor ponies to his son. They stood eleven or twelve hands high. He said that Exmoor ponies were superior to those of Dartmoor. The biggest could carry a man of thirteen stone in weight. The boy asked his father how much he weighed. Albert said it must be many years since he had stood on a pair of scales, though he had grown neither heavier nor lighter as far as he knew and so he supposed he weighed twelve stone as he had before. He allowed that he might be surprised. He pointed out a packet of half-bred colts. He reckoned they might fetch thirty guineas each and the moorland ponies half that.

There was a sudden distant whistle and the geldings startled. Albert hushed them and made soothing noises, stroking the more nervous of the two. The boy reached up and did likewise to the other. A breeze blew through the orchard and he smelled the coal-burning smoke of the train.

'Now you'll see it busy,' his father said.

★　★　★

They came into the orchard on a spree. Auctioneers had their own sites and set up. His father pointed out dealers, Exeter buyers of dray horses for the railway and breweries and mills. There were farmers, farm suppliers, veterinary surgeons, gentry, town dandies. Men wore tight

200

breeches, cloth leggings, coloured waistcoats. Bowler hats, flat caps, some straw boaters as if it were a summer's day and not a grey March morning. One or two carried long whips, perhaps for the horse they intended to buy. There were no women present, none at all.

'Here he comes,' Albert said.

They saw Amos Tucker barrelling his way through the crowded orchard towards them. It was as if he knew which tree was theirs.

'How's it lookin?' Amos said.

'Ripe, gaffer,' Albert replied.

They untied the halters of the geldings and led them to an open field beyond the orchard. Two long lines of men three deep faced each other across an avenue. Behind those standing, others sat in crowded waggons. Albert Sercombe joined a queue of men with carthorses. When their turn came Amos held the less nervous gelding while Albert ran the other up and down the avenue. Then they swapped the animals and he ran the second horse. Red-faced and blowing hard, Albert took some time to get his breath back. 'Ain't used to runnin,' he gasped. The gaffer and the boy held the horses until he had recovered, then they led them back to their tree.

Now spectators from the field came over to inspect the geldings. They opened the horses' mouths, rolled back their eyelids. Felt their forelegs, pulled at their hides. The boy wondered that the animals did not jib at these intrusions, but even the anxious one seemed to enjoy them.

Some knew Amos Tucker, some his father. They asked questions of the geldings' characters

201

or qualities. The answers were not exactly lies but close enough. Both horses were amenable to all work and had no weaknesses. Amos Tucker was very solemn and said that, to be fair, he would rather not sell them but would do so out of foolish generosity only if a fine judge of equine flesh were desperate to have them. The boy's father said the animals' condition spoke for itself and all but a blind dawcock could see it; he would not demean a man by describing what he could make out plain for himself, only he did feel obliged to point out this. And mention that.

They led the geldings to a spot which belonged, said Amos Tucker, to his auctioneer. This man stood upon a wooden rostrum, with a counter across in front of him on which he had papers and a hammer. It did not look either permanent or stable. The ring had no fence but was formed by the bodies of those in attendance. Albert led one of the horses inside it. The auctioneer said, 'Now, gentlemen, the first of Mister Amos Tucker's geldings. Warranted sound in wind and limb, a good worker in all gears. Free from vice.'

The auctioneer spoke yet his voice had the volume of someone shouting. The boy did not know how he did it. It was as if he had an affliction the opposite of Leo's own, and had found a use for it.

'You couldn't buy from a better farm nor buy animals broken in by a better carter.'

Albert led the gelding around the ring. A man in a velour hat with a blue and black jay's feather in its broad band stepped forward to feel the horse but Albert told him to back off. He'd had his chance. The crowd nodded and tutted their approval of the carter who would not tolerate this breach of local custom or manners.

'Gentlemen. Who will start me at forty guineas?'

A man nodded and the auctioneer spoke suddenly in some breathless hiccupping language the boy could not understand. The men around the ring seemed to, for one would raise a finger, another lift his hat, and each time the auctioneer nodded back at them. Then abruptly he lifted the wooden gavel and banged it upon his counter and announced that the gelding was sold for fifty-two guineas to an Exeter man.

The second, less nervous, gelding was auctioned likewise and sold for fifty-five guineas to a man who knew the gaffer, for he came up to them.

'Good horse, Jack.'

'Better be, Amos.'

They did not shake hands but each struck the palm of his right hand against the other's and both shouted, 'Sold,' for all to hear.

'Luck money, Amos?'

The gaffer extracted from his leather purse a half-sovereign and gave it to the man. This buyer was another farmer, from a village close to theirs. He and the dealer took the geldings, and the men from Manor Farm found themselves unencumbered. Amos Tucker could not stop smiling. He gave Albert five shillings beer money and the boy a shilling too.

'Don't get lost,' Albert told his son. He and

Amos walked off talking to each other, the gaffer with his hand on the taller man's shoulder. The boy looked around the orchard, teeming with horses and men. His father and the gaffer had disappeared into the crowd. The boy turned and made his way back towards the open field. All had changed. There was no longer the wide avenue through the middle of two banks of spectators but knots of men, and horses being run haphazardly. Some being ridden. He joined a group and realised that it contained the master and his groom Herb Shattock. The boy eased his way between the closely jostling bodies of men.

One man spoke to the master. Others listened. 'A good warmblood horse, sir. She'll yoke up in anything you put her in, sir. A lovely mane. She's good to shoe, easy to catch. Nothin bothers this mare, sir. And will you look at the colour of her! Strawberry red she is and with one lucky white ear.'

The gypsy horse dealer sang the praises of what looked to the boy like an ordinary cob. He could not believe the master would wish to buy her.

'Or this one comin here, sir, I know this one. He doesn't hot up or get fizzy on you. A huntin man like yourself, you could take him huntin, sir, he doesn't kick hounds. Lovely stable manners. Sixteen hands high if he's a foot and he's Hungarian blood in him, I swear to God on that.'

The groom looked down and saw the boy and said, 'It's you, laddie, are you here with your father?'

Leo nodded. 'Sold two Shire geldings for Mister Tucker.'

'I hope he got a good price.' The dealer had stopped speaking and Herb Shattock added, 'Not from one a these diddy thieves here.'

The gypsy said he would overlook the offence as it came from one so uncouth. Herb Shattock asked the master if he remembered the carter Sercombe's son and the master said of course he did. The gypsy said they should look at this one now and all turned to watch a gypsy lad run a beautiful white horse.

'Now has he got good bone, sir?' the dealer asked. 'Behold him.' They watched. The lad ran around the field in figures of eight or perhaps randomly, and the group of men shifted round to follow them. 'Three-year-old colt, never been raced but he's all ready to, sir. You could bring him on yourself if you've a mind to.'

The lad sprinted across the field. The horse cantered gently behind him, rather as if he were not being led but was shadowing this spindly youth in mockery of his species' inferior condition.

'How tall do you think he is?' Lord Prideaux asked.

'Fourteen hands, master,' his groom answered. 'A little more, possibly.'

'I should like to see him ridden.'

'I'll tell the lad to hop aboard, sir,' the dealer said. 'Right away.'

'No.' The master turned to Leo. 'How would you like to ride this fine colt?'

Leo opened his mouth to speak but could not.

He nodded. The master asked Herb Shattock if he thought it was a good idea. The groom said it was. The boy would probably be thrown but he was light and might escape injury. The master said he would enjoy seeing the colt ridden by one other than its owner. The gypsy raised his arm straight up and made a gesture with his hand and the lad brought the horse to them. The other men in their loose group fell back.

'Help the nipper aboard,' said the dealer. The lad tied the end of the long rope to the ring on the other side of the halter then looped what were now rudimentary reins over the colt's head. He cupped his hands. Leo put his left boot into them and stepped up. The lad tossed him more forcefully than he needed to, perhaps he misjudged his weight, and the boy had to grab the horse's mane to save himself from sailing clear over the colt's body.

'Have you ridden bareback before?' Herb Shattock asked.

The boy nodded for he had, many times. Their cob. The geldings when they'd been half-grown. None though like this white colt.

The boy held the rope rein and turned the colt towards the open field. He saw a way clear to the far fence a hundred yards away, and dug his heels into the horse's flanks. The horse loped slowly forward. Leo did the same again. Still the colt only walked. Leo heard footsteps behind him. He turned and saw the gypsy lad running after them. 'Kick the fucker hard,' the lad yelled, and as he drew alongside he gave the colt an almighty slap upon his rump. 'Git on,' he yelled.

Leo kicked with all his strength and the colt leaped forward. He accelerated from walking pace to a canter to full gallop in the space of a breath and they flew.

The boy thought he would be hanging on in desperation to the reins, the horse's mane, anything he could get hold of. It was not like that. He found himself hugging the horse with his whole body from his face upon the mane, his torso on the horse's neck, his crotch on its spine, his thighs and knees and feet pressing upon the horse's muscular hurtling form. He was less hanging on than moulding his body to that of the galloping animal. He thought it was a most interesting phenomenon and he wanted to laugh even as he knew that he was terrified. The grass sped by beneath him. He had no control over the horse. It was as if the colt had been told where he should go and the boy was merely following, yet the horse went where the boy wished him to. As if by coincidence. It was inexplicable.

As they neared the fence the colt slowed. He turned to the right and cantered along the fence to the corner of the field, then back again. As he reached the point he had come from so he turned back to the distant knot of interested men, the boy kicked him hard and he accelerated in their direction. He raced towards and then away from the group. He saw space between others and the pair of them made for it at full pelt. It seemed that people were yelling to them, but out of some other realm of existence which he and the colt had left and were no longer attached to. They raced from one point to another in the field as if other men and horses had been placed in position for just this spectacle. Nothing could stop them. The boy did not know that such exhilaration existed, save for in the last days when young men shall see visions, all see wonders in the heaven above and signs on the earth beneath, blood, and fire, and vapour of smoke.

They turned once more from the fence. The boy aimed for the right-hand side of the men. Whether the colt read his mind or had received some other twitching communication from his limbs the boy was not sure but they galloped past the group and slowed down, turned and came back around the other side.

The gypsy lad stepped forward and took the rope from the boy. Leo could feel the colt breathing hard beneath him. Lifting his right leg, he swung around and slid off the colt to the ground. He realised that despite the cool temperature he was drenched in sweat, as was the horse. When he stood upon the grass he did not know what to do. There were men around him talking but he could not hear them. The master's tweed coat or jacket was made of a thousand brown twists of living breathing thread. The gypsy dealer's fingers were stained with a nicotine of the same intense brown colour precisely as the new halters the geldings had worn this morning. How could that be? He looked up. The sky was no longer grey and streaked but clear and the deep pale blue of a hedge sparrow's eggs, then all went dark as he heard the words, 'Catch him, man.'

When Leo came round, the master told the boy that he could ride. He really could ride a horse. The dealer said the boy had gypsy blood for sure, look at those dark brown eyes, too dark for a gentile. 'You'll surely wish to buy the colt now, sir,' he said. 'I'll find out how much they want for him but I'll beat em down for you, don't worry about that.'

The master said that he was not in the market for such a beast, fine as he was, but that he had enjoyed the demonstration. He gave the gypsy lad a shilling, and Leo the same. The dealer was about to speak but the master promised that he would not insult him with such a gratuity, and looked forward to doing business with him another time. The dealer said his lordship might not be here again but the master assured him that he came every year. The dealer said that he himself might not come again. The master smiled and said that would be a shame and wished him good fortune. He turned and walked out of the field into the orchard.

The groom said to Leo, 'You should eat, boy. Come with us.'

The High Street was awash with men and horses. The boy saw as he had not before that shops and dwellings were boarded up for the day. They walked past public houses from which the windows had been removed, not merely their

209

glass panes but the entire frames, and through one the boy glimpsed his father's head and that of Amos Tucker amidst the throng. The master took them to one of the tea rooms. Leo thought he could recall being brought here with his sister by their aunts, but he remembered being impressed by brightly patterned carpets and today the wooden floor was covered with straw.

The master asked the boy what he would like to eat but the boy could not say, so the master ordered for him. Then he lit a cigar. The smoke unlike that from a clay pipe was pungent and nauseating. The master repeated to the groom that the carter's son could ride a horse. He truly could. Leo wondered if he should tell the master that his own daughter was a finer rider, though he was not sure that fine as she was she could have ridden that colt as fast as he had. The boy said that he thought there were ten thousand horses in the town but Herb Shattock said it was more like two, and the master nodded. Leo asked why the shops were boarded up. The groom told him that ten or fifteen years past a cow walked into a tailor's shop through the plate-glass window. He said the pub windows were removed as a precaution for when the brawling started later.

When the food came the boy ate in silence. Hot mutton stew, warm bread and butter. Cold pork pies. Greengages preserved in sweet syrup, and shortbread. The master and his groom spoke but Leo did not listen. The food took all his attention. The men drank beer and ginger wine. The boy drank lemonade.

⋆　⋆　⋆

When they rose Leo thanked the master for his food. Herb Shattock asked the boy if he would find his father and he said that he would. He did not go straight to the pub where he had seen Albert but wandered, replete and dozy. The streets were emptying finally of horses as men who'd purchased them took them home. Those who had failed to sell the horses they'd brought did likewise. Pedlars set up their stalls where auctioneers had been. A few women appeared, here and there. A bearded man walked dolefully up the High Street bearing a sandwich-board that proclaimed the end of the world was nigh. It was time to repent. Now or never. Maids strolled in twos and threes. From a covered waggon a quack doctor extolled the virtues of his liniment. Carters and farmers with their rheumatics or lumbago heard him out. A diminutive man with a thin moustache set up a three-legged table and on it placed three cards. Two numbers and the Queen of Hearts. He turned the cards over and asked for someone to tell him where the queen was. A young man told him and the card sharp asked if he would put money on it. The youth said he would and placed a sixpence on the card. All those watching agreed. The sharp turned it over. The five of clubs. The crowd laughed in wonder. The sixpence disappeared.

The boards came off the fronts of shops, their interiors lit up with lanterns, and the boy realised it was dusk. He heard music. A harmonium. Fiddles. He saw Herbert with some

211

other lads he recognised. He followed them into the orchard where a ring had been set up with wooden stakes and rope. In the ring stood a giant. A gypsy shouted out that Gentle George here would take on all-comers in bare-fist boxing. When the boy looked closely at the giant he saw that he might be a gypsy but a freak one. Herbert and his mates challenged each other to enter the ring, each offering to pay another to risk it. Leo thought that none would do so. He sought the music and saw his brother Fred holding the hand of a maid Leo had never seen before.

He made his way to the pub. On the way a hawker tried to sell him a penknife. 'Here, boy, does your father smoke a pipe? This one's got a pick to clean it.' The boy ignored him but then he remembered the coins in his pocket and went back. The knife had a bone handle and did not look the most robust tool he had ever seen, but he had none of his own, and he thought that the pick might have other uses. The blade could be sharpened. With one of the coins he bought the knife.

★   ★   ★

In the pub Leo found his father, standing in a corner speaking to no one. Amos Tucker had disappeared. Albert did not see his son until Leo had been in front of him for some while. 'There you are,' Albert said eventually. 'Let me empty this mug and we can go.' The boy did not know if his father had been waiting impatiently for him, so as to depart this place, or on the contrary was sorry to be obliged to leave so soon. Albert sipped his beer. Leo closed his eyes. There was something he had always wondered. A bird sang for a reason. To alert kith or kin to danger. To warn an enemy off. To woo. Why then did they make their noises when in a flock such that each was indistinguishable from another? Roosting in a tree or in flight. He had often pondered this. Now with his eyes closed he heard the sound of men talking. It was a kind of human song. Men spoke because they enjoyed doing so and so did birds. What they said had little meaning.

'I'm talkin to you.'

The boy opened his eyes. There stood a man he recognised. The one with the jay's feather in the band of his black hat, who had wished to inspect the first gelding in the auction ring.

'Back off,' his father said, just as he had earlier.

The man made to swing a punch. As he did so Albert Sercombe chucked the remains of his pewter mug of beer in the man's face. As the man hesitated Albert let go of the empty mug and threw a straight arm at his chin. To the boy's astonishment it missed and pawed the air beside him. The man tried again. He landed a punch on Albert's left ear. Albert did not seem to feel it but swung his fist again. The man appeared to stand stock still and wait for it. The boy did not know whether the cracking sound he heard came from the man's jaw or his father's knuckles. There was no space to flounder in the crowded room. Instead the man crumpled boneless where he stood and collapsed unconscious to the floor. Albert stepped over him and men parted to let him through. The boy followed. They climbed out of the empty window space and into the High Street, and walked out of the town.

March

In the evening of the day Albert Sercombe and his lad Herbert took their two teams of horses to the forge and fetched the steam engine and the threshing drum. These belonged to the blacksmith Jacob Crocker, who hired them out along with himself and his crooked-backed son. It was dark when they hauled them to Manor Farm, a noisy caravan with their iron-tyred wheels approaching along the pot-holed road, metalwork rattling, wood creaking. Leo could see the faint glow of his father's pipe when he inhaled. He helped Amos Tucker light stable lamps and hang them in the yard.

They brought the engine with its chimney stack up beyond the last rick in the yard. Albert told Noble to hold up. Tension was released from the traces and the collar relaxed on her sweaty shoulders. Behind her, Red stood back half a pace to rest in his breeching strap between the shafts. Herbert brought up the drum behind the engine, beside the rick. It was covered in a great canvas sheet like some mysterious statuary ferried in secrecy, to be revealed with a flourish on the morrow. The men unharnessed the horses and tended to them.

★ ★ ★

215

In the morning the boy accompanied his father and brother back to the farm. The earth was covered with a light frost and their boots rang over the hard ground. While they fed and groomed the horses, Jacob Crocker and his son arrived. They unsheeted the threshing drum and uncoiled the huge leather driving-belt. Young Crocker slipped it over the large driving-wheel of the engine and onto the smaller pulley-wheel of the thresher. Jacob Crocker took a pair of steel-rimmed glasses out of his red waistcoat pocket and peered at the spirit level embedded in the wall of the thresher. 'That'un,' he said. His tall son laid a wooden chock under one of the wheels and stood and kicked it in with his heel. Jacob Crocker studied the level once more. 'That 'un.'

When he was satisfied that it was true his son broke up hard steam coal with his hammer from a pile the farmer had placed beside the engine. Leo felt the fire box. It was still warm from the day before. Young Crocker shovelled in shining cobbles of coal.

Amos Tucker rolled half a hogshead barrel alongside the steam engine. 'You'll find yokes an buckets in yon tool shed,' he told the boy. 'Fill em up from the pond.'

★   ★   ★

Others congregated in the yard. Ernest Cudmore the shepherd and Isaac Wooland the stockman found the long ladder and carried it to the corn rick. They laid it on the ground, its end abutting the bottom of the rick. Ernest walked back along

216

beside the ladder and joined Isaac at the far end. They picked it up one either side, hoisted it aloft and stepped underneath, Isaac holding the end rung just above his head. The stockman was not a particularly tall man but still Ernest Cudmore was six inches shorter and held the third or fourth rung in, his arms fully extended. Together they walked towards the rick, passing the ladder over their heads one rung at a time, thus raising it in the air. The effect of their different heights made the sight comical. Young Crocker looked down at Leo when he heard him chuckling and frowned in disapproval or lack of understanding. Then he turned to the spectacle himself and Leo heard a kind of snickering issue from him.

The higher the two men raised the ladder, the closer Isaac came upon the shorter man in front of him until, as the ladder approached the vertical, it looked as if Isaac meant to crush the shepherd between his body and the ladder. Ernest struggled aside out of the squeeze he found himself in and for a moment the ladder tottered. Isaac floundered, his hands holding a rung far above his head. It looked like if he took one arm off he would stagger backwards. But then he seemed to summon some burst of power from somewhere and stepped forward with great purpose and flung the ladder hard against the corn rick. He and Ernest pulled the bottom of the ladder away from the rick and now it leaned secure against it. Ernest climbed up and Isaac followed. They stepped off onto the roof and began drawing out the pegs from the thatch, still white with frost.

Young Crocker turned to Leo, grinning, and shook his head. Leo carried buckets to the pond. He broke the thin ice there and scooped cold water into the buckets. He put the yoke across his shoulders and attached one bucket to the left-hand hook and the other to the right, and brought them both up. He bent forward under the yoke and set them down. Then he lifted one and poured the water into the barrel. Young Crocker dropped a hose-pipe from the boiler into the tub. He stared at the pressure gauge. When Leo returned with another load he was still peering at it.

Albert and Herbert finished with their horses, Enoch and Fred likewise. Isaiah Vagges the old waggoner appeared, and Mildred Daw the spinster too. The congregants greeted one another and Amos Tucker directed them to their stations. Mildred rubbed linseed oil into the larch handle of her fork. Isaiah massaged a small lump of grease or lard into his hands. Fred laid a net around the corn rick. Herbert passed round lengths of string, which men tied around their trouser legs, just below the knees. The boy copied them. All of a sudden a shrill whistle blew and all turned to young Crocker on the steam engine. He opened the regulator and set the wheels in motion. The leather belt began to turn the drum. Brass knobs rose and fell. Puffs of smoke belched out of the chimney.

Leo delivered more water. The barrel was almost full and he watched the workers take up their positions. His father laid a pile of four-bushel sacks upon the ground and Enoch

218

hooked one under the grain chutes. Fred and Herbert dragged sheets of hessian and set them beneath the threshing drum. Isaiah Vagges and Mildred Daw stood to one side.

Jacob Crocker climbed up to a platform by the drum. He held out a hand and pulled Amos Tucker up easily beside him as if the corpulent farmer were some slender girl and the blacksmith a young gallant. He nodded to his son, who knocked open the engine's throttle with the palm of his hand. The drum rotated faster now and Leo could hear it moaning as it turned, a metal gut calling to be filled. Then Jacob looked up to Ernest Cudmore and Isaac Wooland atop the rick above them and nodded to them too. Straight away the shepherd tossed wheat sheaves down to the platform. Amos Tucker cut their straw bands. Jacob lifted the loose wheat and fed it ears first into the hungry drum.

The first corn went through the empty drum. Its moaning rotation was interspersed by the chattering sound of grain being separated, like hail on a corrugated-iron roof. Riddles separated the grain into two grades. As more sheaves were thrown in the sound of separate grains was lost in a low and constant growl. The grain ran from the drum into the sacks hung there. Leo saw that two of the farmer's daughters had appeared beside his father and uncle. When the first sack was full they sewed it up with long needles and twine in swift crude strokes.

The sheaves of wheat had gone through the drum and came out denuded of their grain and changed thereby into straw. This Isaiah and Mildred forked over to a spot across the yard where a man Leo recognised as one of the other estate farmers, a friend of Amos Tucker, began to lay a new rick.

The chaff flew out from under the centre of the drum and settled more or less in a cloud of dust on the hessian sacks laid there. Herbert and Fred brought up the four corners. These Herbert held in his fists and Fred helped him lift the gathered sheet over his shoulder and set off for the chaff barn.

Leo looked into the barrel and saw it was already half-empty. He resumed his water carrying. When it was once more almost brim-full he studied the threshing machine. Its engine was an impossible chaos of pistons, cranks, rods and wheels, juddering and wheezing. If anyone spoke he could not hear them above the noise. He could smell the coal in the steam that gulped out of the chimney. The great belt circulated endlessly on the wooden wheels. How it stayed in place was not clear for there were no restraints to its sliding off. It never did. Smaller belts drove smaller pulleys that shook the riddles.

'You dreamin, boy?' Leo looked up. Young Crocker, his face and hands already filthy with black oil, pointed with the long spout of his oil can to the barrel. Leo picked up the yoke and the buckets and trotted out of the yard and down to the pond.

★　★　★

The boy's father and uncle Enoch had the most arduous task, lifting the great sacks of wheat grain. They carried a sack across their shoulders so that the entire eighteen-stone weight was not directly on their backs. Herbert was eighteen and allowed to carry barley sacks of sixteen stone and oats of twelve. The following year he would carry wheat. Fred at seventeen could carry none. Their father had told them of men whose spines were ruined from carrying the sacks when their bones were too young. He and Enoch took them in turn across the yard and up the dozen stone steps to the granary. Each struggling tread of his father those of a farmer up his hill of Golgotha.

They and others too at intervals made brief excursions to the tool shed, to fill their mugs from the nine-gallon barrel of cider Amos Tucker had placed there for them.

★ ★ ★

By ten o'clock the top of the rick had been pitched through the thresher, and the new straw rick stood waist-high. At a signal from Amos Tucker, young Crocker blew the steam whistle. He turned the regulator to a gradual stop. The driving belt wound down. The sound of the drum ceased. The yard was quiet again but the noise of the machines rang in their ears like the sound of something there still all around them yet invisible.

Fred and Herbert walked across the yard, fidgeting and stretching and running their fingers in under their collars where the chaff and

221

the whirling dust had infiltrated. It stuck to the sweat of their backs, between the shoulder blades, in their armpits.

'I fuckin hates this job,' Herbert said.

* * *

They ate their lunch in the tool shed, sat on the benches and any bucket or drum that might provide a seat. They ate bread and cheese and drank the cloudy rough cider. Amos Tucker's daughters sat next to each other on a single barrel, like a pair of Siamese twins, their dust-besmirched white dresses a single garment.

Isaiah Vagges told Jacob Crocker that his son seemed to know how to run the machine.

'Aye,' Jacob said. 'He's no smith but he can work that engine. He'd like to work on the trains if I let im, I reckon.'

'That's not bad pay, that,' Herbert said.

Young Crocker listened as they spoke of him, head bowed.

'Aye,' said Jacob Crocker. 'He's an engineer, but he's no smith.'

'Useful machine, though,' Isaiah said. 'We used to have to thresh the corn with flails.' He looked around the room. 'You young gentlemen think this is hard work, you should a been here thirty year ago.'

Amos Tucker and the other farmer spoke quietly to one another in a corner. When they were silent, Enoch said, 'Reckon tis time ye got one a them barrows, gaffer? In time for next year?'

Amos Tucker looked blankly at the under

carter. 'Ye puts the sack on its platform,' Enoch said. He laid his lump of cheese in his lap and used his hands to illustrate what he described. 'Winds a handle to raise it. The platform keeps in place with a ratchet. When tis the height you wants ye can roll the sack onto your shoulders.'

Amos Tucker nodded slowly. 'What do you reckon, Albert?' he asked his carter. 'Could we do with such a barrow?'

Albert chewed his bread. 'Some might,' he said. 'My brother is gettin old, a course. But not to worry, my lad'll soon be of an age to carry his father's corn.'

'Yes, and I'll be bloody glad to,' Herbert said. 'Let some other sod carry the chaff. I hates it.'

'Careful what ye wish for, lad,' Enoch said.

'Aye, and careful with your language,' Amos Tucker told him.

Enoch shook his head. 'Others use a barrow. Ask yon Crockers while you've got em here.'

Amos said nothing. No one spoke, but waited for what might happen, for all knew of the brothers' mutual animosity.

'A further device we could do with,' Enoch persisted. 'An elevator what takes straw from the thresher to the rick. All the time Isaiah and Mildred there waste walkin across the yard with them forkfuls a straw over their shoulders, they could lift it easy onto an elevator.'

'He's tryin to do us out of a job, gaffer,' Isaiah said. 'He'll ave you pay us to be a sleepin.'

No one else joined Isaiah in making light of the matter.

'Ask Mister Doddridge,' Enoch said. 'I believe

223

he's got one a they on Wood Farm.'

The other farmer, Doddridge, looked towards Amos Tucker and said nothing. 'We can think on this and talk of it another time,' Amos said, rising to his feet.

'Tis a pity to waste the opportunity to ask yon Crockers' opinion.'

'Someone might wish to tell my brother,' Albert said, 'to shut his rattle.'

Enoch made his hand into a fist and rapped the knuckles against his own skull loudly. 'Like fuckin iron,' he said. 'Nothin can get in through it. No ideas. No nothin.'

'Enough,' Amos said.

'That is if he don't wish me to shut it for him,' Albert said.

The boy walked to the door of the shed and looked out on to the yard. The farmer's chickens had come in number and were gleaning the rickyard of loose grain. They pecked at the ground with swift efficiency. Their strutting posture gave the impression they were helping themselves to what was theirs by right, even as they couldn't believe their luck, and must take what they could before their luck ran out. Above them, sparrows snaffled what they could find on the ledges and in the crevices of the machines. Leo ran out of the shed, and the rooster and hens scattered in great and noisy affront.

★ ★ ★

In the afternoon Dunstone the old lad appeared. 'What can I do?' he asked. 'What can I do?'

224

Amos Tucker told him he could help the boy carry water. Leo found him another bucket and they worked in tandem, Dunstone following close after him and telling him of all he had seen in his peregrinations about the estate that morning. 'I seen horses on Home Farm bigger an your'n here,' he said. 'Bigger an I ever seen. I seen one a the gardeners up at the big house sneakin a fag in the glass-house. With one a they maids. Smokin away they was. Wouldn't give me one neither.'

★ ★ ★

Late in the afternoon Amos Tucker's two younger daughters came into the yard with the farmer's terriers. As the corn rick grew smaller so rats began to rush out, into the net Fred had secured there. The terriers caught most of them. Others the girls clubbed with wooden cudgels. One small pink rat Nellie Tucker held by its tail and brought over to Leo. 'Here,' she said. 'Would you like me to put this feller down your shirt?'

Leo looked at her, neither advancing nor retreating, neither smiling nor grimacing, nor saying a word. Then Dunstone saw the baby rat squirming as if a puppet hung from a string. A brief squeak issued from him. He turned around and scuttled off, and Nellie ran after him, caterwauling.

March

The boy walked home from school. He slowed, let the others carry on ahead, chattering, bickering. None looked back.

A pair of geese came flying low, over the hedge, landing in the meadow by the river. He'd noted a couple there this morning. There were many more now, standing in pairs apart from each other. Waiting. Like celebrants gathering for some country baptism, or mass wedding. Perhaps when the priest of their kind and his cackling acolytes and the matronly geese with the food arrived, the shy creatures would begin to mingle.

He passed Sedge Field with Isaac Wooland's dairy herd of Ruby Reds. Red Rubies. He stopped. The cows, some twenty or twenty-five of them, stood close to one another, jostling, by the hedge where it curved some thirty yards along from the gate. He climbed up on to the second rung and leaned over and watched. They might have been a crowd penned in, yet the whole of the field around them was empty. The cows were silent. Their udders were full. They chewed the cud. Leo climbed over the gate. One of the cows looked at him then looked away but did not move. He squatted and peered in amongst their legs. There was something there,

226

he was unsure what. Some shapeless entity. He stared, waiting for his brain to come to an interpretation, even if erroneous. A conjecture. There were two cylindrical shapes, close together. It dawned on him that he was gazing at the soles of a pair of boots.

Leo rose up off his lean haunches and walked slowly forward. He did not know cows, or have any feeling for their actions or their characters. He couldn't talk to them. As he reached the herd one of them let out a long mewling groan. He had no idea of its meaning. Threat. Lament. They were blank animals to him.

'Git on,' he said. 'Shift it.'

They took no notice. Perhaps they couldn't hear his voice. They smelled of soft bovine ordure and herbage and something sour. He had no stick with him, to beat them on their rumps and force a way through. Then the one that had lowed did so again, and she walked lazily away, past the boy towards the middle of the empty field, her udders swaying. Another followed her example, and a third, and a fourth. Gradually the whole herd dispersed from this odd spot. Leo waited for them to depart. None of them stepped on Isaac Wooland but walked delicately around his prone figure. The last one left stood above him, leaning her long neck down and licking his face of its sweat. She looked up, abruptly startled to find herself alone, faced by this son of man who stood erect, and stumbled away after her brethren.

Leo kneeled down beside the stockman. A strange choice of place to sleep in the middle of the afternoon. He prodded Isaac's shoulder. He lifted the man's hand but when he let it go it fell back limply. Isaac's jaw was half-covered in greyish bristles, inexpertly shaven. The flesh of Isaac Wooland's dead body was still soft and warm. He must have died minutes before. Perhaps he was still dying when Kizzie and the others passed by on the other side of the hedge, all children's gibberish and blether.

★   ★   ★

They fetched a cart and the boy brought them to the spot. They stood considering Isaac's body. Albert lit his pipe. Enoch looked at the herd of cows who had moved to the far side of the field, and shook his head. They were like a gang of criminals who would protect the guilty one amongst them. Amos Tucker stood by the body and, putting his hands on his knees for support, leaned forward and studied Isaac's face. Leo could see plainly now where he had been kicked on the left side of his head, for in death a bruise was spreading, yellow, purplish, around his eye and cheek.

April

The day was unseasonably warm and all life girded and roused its sleeping self. On haw and wild fruit trees blossom sprayed, countless posies offered to the boy's passing sight. The wind brought petals down upon him. On an empty pasture the dew had identified spider webs laid across the grass, an incredible multitude of them, closely packed, each trap its own discrete squarish parcel of territory. Without the dew he would not have seen them. One phenomenon of nature had made another visible. For whom? The passing boy. What if he had not passed but taken a different route across the estate? What then? He did not know. Would the webs not have lain clear but unobserved by man? Birds looked down from on high but he did not believe it interested them unless they wished to swoop low and nick an insect struggling in a web for themselves.

The birds were swallows. They came to and from a barn over to the side of the track. They must be nest-building in the eaves yet they did not all fly off to the woods or down to earth for materials. No, many rose up into the sky. Some he eyed and tried to keep in sight but they grew minute and then were lost to him. Perhaps there existed some other realm up there in the heavens. A mirrored image of this one, with gravity working the other way, and the swallows by going up from this world came down in that one and gathered beakfuls of mud and brought them back again to make nests on earth. Why? He pondered the matter and in time decided that there were no humans in that otherworld, and so no buildings with their overhanging roofs and jutting timbers creating the places for their habitations such birds preferred. That was why they returned. So Leo amused himself.

They flew too high and fast for swallows. It was too early in the year for swifts yet that they were. Here already. He stopped. They beat their wings in hectic blurs then let them rest, arching out from their bodies like scything blades, and sliced through the invisible wind. They were black in the sky though he knew their feathers were brown. They veered and wove at such speed it took concentration just to watch them. Their brains were minuscule yet they avoided collisions. It was not possible to understand how. They lived their frantic lives and soon were spent. They were no doubt devouring insects but were they also playing, cavorting together in the air at their insane speed? He watched one chase another and to his surprise alight upon it. For some seconds the two became a single four-winged bird gliding. Then they decoupled and with their madly flurried wings were parted and went their separate ways. Would the two of them know each other again? What had he just seen?

★ ★ ★

At the gamekeeper's cottage Mrs Budgell said his brother was not there but that Sid had left something for him. He stayed by the back door while she fetched it. The chains by which Aaron Budgell's spaniels were tethered lay unused upon the ground like the rusty skins of metallic snakes. Mrs Budgell came back bearing a tray made of short lengths of hazel switch interwoven and tied with string. She walked one careful step at a time, eyes on the precious cargo. Upon the rustic tray was the small, delicate skeleton of some unknown creature. She handed the tray to Leo, who took it with equal anxious care.

'What is it?' he asked.

Mrs Budgell frowned. 'Bones,' she said.

'Does thou know what creature owned them?' he asked.

She regarded the fragile skeleton as if for the first time, tilting her head this way and that. 'It don't look like nothin I seen.' She shook her head. 'I don't know nothin about animals,' she said. 'Don't wish to neither. My old man knows moren enough about em for the two of us. I don't bother him about is animals and he don't bother me about my ouse.' Mrs Budgell turned and stepped inside and half-turned back again, closing the door behind her. Leo set off, carrying the tray with its delicate cargo. He heard the door open and Mrs Budgell's voice call to him. 'Sid,' she yelled. She must have known he did not carry the same name as his brother but could not remember his and made do with the closest

231

to hand. Leo turned.

'It come back to me,' she said. 'Yon brother said to tell you tis a weasel.'

Leo thanked her. She returned inside once more.

★ ★ ★

As he walked along the track through the wood Leo studied the skeleton. The leg-bones were bent in a crouch all ready to spring upon its prey, as if animals continued their savage choreography of hunter and hunted in a spectral limbo after death. The weasel's long spine continued past its pelvis for ten or more vertebrae, diminishing in size into its tail. The rib-cage was long and voluminous, slung from the spine. Perhaps weasels had long, thin hearts. The feet, upon which the skeleton stood squarely, were built of thin bones that looked as if they could snap like brittle stalks of straw. The head too was long, the skull moulded back far from the sharp-toothed mouth, as if the brain though small was longer, the creature cleverer, than one would have thought.

If he could draw, Leo thought, he should like to sketch this entity. He wondered whether, before God made the creeping things and the beasts of the earth for Adam and Eve on the sixth day, He had spent much of the eternity preceding this world in idle sketching. Designing the animals that would be there on that day as well as all those to come.

* * *

To his relief the boy found Herb Shattock in his tack room. The groom sat at his desk, writing in a small book. He must have been scribbling much faster than he appeared to be for he filled two pages and turned them, and did the same again. The boy stood in the doorway. He recalled the tea room at Bampton Fair to which the master had invited him. A waiting woman had brought them a tray with bowls of stew on it. He felt like a parody of such a waiter, bearing this home-made tray and the bones of an animal with no meat upon it.

Herb Shattock's pencil scraped faintly across the pages of his notebook. As the sun moved the boy watched the silhouette of himself enter the room and sidle along the wall. Shattock turned, pencil in hand. He stared at Leo and blinked, then broke into a smile. 'Come on in there, boy,' he said.

Leo came forward and placed the tray upon the desk. The groom stared at it. 'What's this, then?' he said. 'Pole cat?'

'Weasel,' Leo said.

'Aye,' the groom said, studying the extraordinary bones. 'And what do you wish me to do with it?'

'I'd be might grateful if you could give it to the young mistress, Mister Shattock.'

Herb Shattock frowned. He blinked again. Leo looked at the notebook. The words written in pencil were uncommonly large on the page. PRIDE OF GALWAY. HALF HOUR ON THE

GALLOP. LINSEED OIL IN CHAFF filled one side.

'Miss Charlotte?' the groom said. 'What's er want with this?'

'I'm not rightly sure, Mister Shattock.'

The groom put the pencil down beside the notebook. 'Did er ask you for it?'

The boy shook his head.

'I'm not a postman, boy.'

'I don't know no one else,' Leo said. 'Well, I do, but they don't like me. I believe her might have an interest in the anatomy of animals.'

Herb Shattock gazed at the boy. 'I seems to remember bein told that time was, weasels were brung up tame. Kept in the granaries to fend off mice. Don't know when that stopped.' He rubbed his eyes. 'Yes, boy, I'll do that for you.'

'You don't ave to say tis from me,' Leo said.

The groom nodded. 'Do us a favour in turn.' He rose. 'Come with me, boy.' The chair scraped back on the stone-flagged floor. Herb Shattock walked over to the far wall and lifted a bridle off its hook. 'Take this,' he said. He himself carried a small saddle.

Leo followed the groom into the yard and along the block. A lad brushed a horse down yonder, another carried buckets of water. Leo took them in at a glance and kept his head down. The top half of a stable door was open. Herb Shattock half-opened the bottom half and rested the saddle upon it. He entered the box and spoke to the young horse therein. A filly. He reached behind him. The boy passed him the bridle and watched as Herb Shattock fed the bit

234

into the pony's mouth and passed the bridle over her head and tied the straps, talking all the while in a litany of odd noises, a language issued through his teeth, akin to that of the boy's father but distinct from it. To each horseman his own voice. He placed the saddle upon her back, crouched down and reached for the girth straps, and tightened them. The pony stood docile and compliant.

Herb Shattock led her out of the yard and down through the trees to the paddock where Leo had watched the girl suppling her roan. This pony was entirely black save for a white blaze upon her forehead. She was similar in stature to the blue roan. Perhaps a little taller, slighter, more elegant.

In the paddock the groom came to a halt. Holding the bridle with his left hand, he reached for the stirrup with his right and turned it away from the saddle flap. The boy stepped with his left foot into a stirrup for the first time in his life and, reaching for the front and back of the saddle, kicked up from the ground, flexed his left thigh muscles and pulled himself up. He swung his right leg over the saddle and sat upon it. He leaned over to his right and turned the right-hand stirrup as Herb Shattock had and pushed his right boot into it, then sat up and took hold of the reins lying loose upon the pony's neck.

The groom still held the bridle. He rested his other hand upon the boy's knee. 'Lord Prideaux reckons his daughter's done grievin,' he said. 'I've examined this mare. Her's no defects of sight nor wind that I can see, her ain't lame. Her knees is good. I don't think er's a crib-biter nor a windsucker. Not a weaver, neither. I've had one a the lads ride her but my smallest lad's twice the size a Miss Charlotte. You're a sight lighter an her, I should say, you don't weigh much moren your own bones, boy, but you's closer. Would you ride her for me? Take her round, nothin spectacular.'

Leo nodded. Herb Shattock let go of the bridle and walked to the fence. The boy took up the reins and made a clicking sound with his teeth and heeled the pony's flanks. It felt odd to sit upon the saddle and to feel his feet enclosed in the iron stirrups, yet he liked it. The pony walked forward. He trotted her around the perimeter, then when he asked her to speed up she did so instantly and cantered. She was exceedingly obedient. It occurred to him that if he did not give her an order she would stand all day awaiting one. He stopped her and turned her in circles, then figures of eight, one way then the other. When he galloped her it was apparent that she did not have the fearful speed of the colt he'd ridden at Bampton Fair.

Leo brought the mare over to the fence. She stood, blowing hard. Herb Shattock put his ear to her nostrils and listened. Then he studied them closely. The boy asked him what he was looking for.

'Blood,' the groom said. 'If there's bleedin into the lung. But I can't see none.' He stood back. 'What do you think? Is her as accommodatin as her looks?'

Leo nodded. 'I believe so.' He shook his head.

236

'She does not have the character of the blue roan.'

'That's what I reckoned,' Mister Shattock agreed. 'Tis no bad thing.'

The boy dislodged his feet from the stirrups and dismounted from the horse as if there were no saddle, pivoting from his belly and sliding to the ground. He watched the groom lead the pony back through the trees, then turned and walked homeward under the noonday sun.

April

The wheelwright Hector Merry came to the farm to measure Isaac Wooland's body. A bachelor, Isaac had slept in a room in the attic of the farmhouse but his body was laid out in a shed off the dairy. The wheelwright came back out into the yard and conferred with Amos Tucker. The boy could not forget him walking behind his new-wrought waggon, listening to it. Hector asked Amos what kind of timber he wished for the box, they had all sorts down at the sawmill. Oak was the most expensive, of course, and then there was . . . The farmer interrupted him.

'We'll not have oak for old Isaac, no chance,' he said. 'When we had that landslip as I was a boy, I seen a body barely altered from when it were buried eighty year afore.' Amos grew annoyed. 'I heard a one yard where bodies buried in the reign a George the third was in the same condition. It ain't right, Hector.'

The wheelwright nodded. 'I'll get you the softest, cheapest planks they got.'

The farmer grew red-faced. 'It's not the bloody money and you knows it.' The boy had never heard him curse before. ''Tis what is Christian. Earth to earth. Wrap him in a shroud like what they used to and let him return to the soil.'

'You'll not want a stone coffin then, Amos, like the master's family?'

Amos Tucker looked for a moment like he would get angrier still. But then as if the fire within him had been abruptly dowsed he smiled. 'Let they rich folk dishonour their dead as they wish,' he said.

'Lined with lead and all,' said Hector Merry.

'Aye, a slow and sorry putrefaction.'

★ ★ ★

The coffin carrying Isaac Wooland's body was borne into the church by four Sercombes: Albert and Fred, Enoch and Herbert. It was customary for six men to bear the box but in such case Ernest Cudmore would perforce be one of them and the little shepherd would have to take the weight not on his shoulders but holding it high above his head. Amos Tucker declared that he'd not have people laughing at the sight nor trying all too clearly not to at his stockman's funeral.

Behind the coffin, the priest led his curate and servers. They followed as for every service in their customary order up the aisle and walked solemnly to their places like horses into the stables.

The master and his daughter sat in their pew at the front. Her dowager ladyship no longer attended church nor was known to leave the big house. Amos Tucker sat beside his shepherd. Leo sat between his mother and his sister Kizzie. His father and brother joined them.

The priest was a man of ill humour, cranky like a prophet of the Old Book, grimly disposed

239

towards the dim and recalcitrant members of his flock, the villagers' own Ezekiel. His voice was mesmerising. The boy was obliged to listen. There was no choice. He spoke in his priestly voice. He read from the Good Book: ''I said, I will take heed to my ways, that I offend thee not in my tongue. I will keep my mouth as it were with a bridle, while the ungodly is in my sight.

''I held my tongue, and spake nothing. I kept silence, yea, even from good words, but it was pain and grief to me.

''My heart was hot within me, and while I was thus musing the fire kindled. And at the last I spake with my tongue.

''Lord let me know mine end, and the number of my days.''

They kneeled down to pray, and rose to sing a hymn.

Lord of all hopefulness, Lord of all joy,
Whose trust, ever childlike, no cares could destroy,
Be there at our waking, and give us, we pray,
Your bliss in our hearts, Lord,
At the break of the day.

The boy listened to the voices around him. His father sang loud and out of tune. Fred trailed off at the end of every line. Their mother sang quietly and sweetly. Only Kizzie sang well, her voice soaring over the heads of those in the pew in front of them, towards the altar.

Lord of all gentleness, Lord of all calm,
Whose voice is contentment, whose presence

is balm,
Be there at our sleeping, and give us, we pray,
Your peace in our hearts, Lord,
At the end of the day.

They buried the box in the graveyard and Ernest Cudmore threw down the first handful of soil upon it. They committed the stockman's body to the ground.

''In sure and certain hope of the Resurrection to eternal life, through our Lord Jesus Christ,'' the vicar proclaimed. His voice broadcast across the yard and brooked no argument. ''Who shall change our vile body, that it may be like unto his glorious body, according to the mighty working, whereby he is able to subdue all things to himself.''

★ ★ ★

Many repaired to the estate and Manor Farm. Amos Tucker's wife and daughters had prepared a feast. Men spoke of the departed. Amos said that when he was a boy Isaac told him how he hated hedgehogs, or fuzz pigs as he called them, for they sucked the milk from cows resting in a field. Isaiah Vagges asked if they minded the time when Isaac kept a billy goat with the herd, to keep illness from attacking the cows. Ernest Cudmore said that must have been long ago, before his time. He said that when he first tended sheep as a lad, the master and his brother and sister were sent of a morning, before their breakfast, to walk amongst the flock, for sheep's

241

breath was known to ward off consumption.

Amos said that in the past there had been many strange beliefs, for men were credulous. Ernest Cudmore said he still believed it. Amos asked if anyone recalled when the cows got into a field of kale and they had to tip the milk into the river for it was tainted.

'I thought he fed them cattle on kale?' Fred said.

'Aye, and mangels too, in moderate amounts. But the best food turns to poison. Too much of anythin's no good.'

'Don't tell the ladies that, gaffer, for pity's sake,' Herbert said, and the first laughter of the day was heard.

⋆ ⋆ ⋆

The boy found his father outside, by the wall of Mrs Tucker's garden, conversing with Moses Pincombe, the horse quack or obstetrician, who had attended Miss Charlotte's dying roan. He was the only man outside the farm his father spoke to beyond the briefest repartee demanded by human society. They spoke of Jonas Sercombe, Albert's father, with whom Moses Pincombe had been friends from boyhood. They spoke of horses, of their characters or odd things they had done.

Herb Shattock the master's groom came out and joined them. Each man wore his good black suit. Albert smoked his pipe. Herb rolled a cigarette. He said he'd a horse, a hunter the master had had sent over from Ireland, but it was a bad one. He did not want to tell Lord Prideaux that he'd been had, but he could see no alternative if the horse could not be domineered. Unless Albert would care to take a look, and perhaps Moses too?

The boy saw his father raise an eyebrow and the old man nod, then without a word the men turned and walked out of the garden and onto the track across the estate towards the stables of the big house. Moses Pincombe limped along with the aid of a stick, and the other two took their pace from his. Albert, the tallest, walked with a rolling gait, swaying all the way up from his ploughman's half-ruined ankles. The boy's father was a broad-shouldered, rangy man, his body hard, bony and muscular. Herb Shattock was shorter, stouter.

The three men walked away, in their black suits. The boy heard his name called from the house. He did not look back but ran after the horsemen.

★ ★ ★

They stood outside the loose box gazing at the horse. 'He looks so peaceful, don't he?' Herb Shattock said. 'He near enough killed my best young groom two days past. We could a had a pair a funerals this day.'

Leo squeezed between his father and Herb Shattock and looked over the bottom half of the stable door. The horse was a chestnut gelding, tall and hefty, a hunter halfway to being a carthorse, the boy reckoned.

243

'A course I don't have my waistcoat,' Albert said. He meant that he did not have the tiny bottles and tins hidden in its pockets.

'When I was young,' Moses Pincombe said, 'I would a gone in there with a twitch stick and hit im hard between the ears.' He turned to Albert. 'Can you believe that?'

Herb Shattock said, 'Surely you ain't past it, Moses?'

'I'd never do that now,' Moses Pincombe said. 'Even as I could.'

'I'll deal with him,' Albert Sercombe said. 'If you talk to im while I do, Moses.'

'I don't wish neither a you to get clobbered,' Herb said. 'I'd rather shoot im where he stands.'

'No,' said Moses. 'I'll talk to him.'

The boy felt his father's large hand upon his back, patting him, twice. He looked up but his father was studying the horse, then he followed Moses Pincombe inside. He pushed shut the door behind them.

'Come along now, old fellow. Come along, chap.' Moses did not whistle or blow through his teeth, as the boy's father or Herb Shattock did, but spoke to the horse as he would to a man, in the English language. Leo wondered why his father did not. 'There you are, old boy, there you are, no need to fret nor to worry about us, we idn't goin to harm ye.'

The horse fidgeted and trembled and it looked to the boy as if could it run out it would. It seemed about ready to break into a frenzy: it began to whinny and snicker, and shivered as if the men had brought in with them a blast of cold wind. The old man stood close and spoke to the horse and seemed to calm it, a little, or at least restrain it in its state of agitation.

Albert had meanwhile reached the horse's flank, on the left-hand side. He had somehow acquired lengths of rope. He took up the gelding's forefoot and bent its knee until the hoof faced upwards and all but touched its body. He slipped a loop of rope over the knee and up until it was drawn between the hoof and the pastern-joint. He pulled the rope taut and tied it. Moses Pincombe talked to the chestnut gelding the whole while. The horse stood now on three legs, unable to move, nonplussed.

Again the boy felt a pat upon his back, this time from Herb Shattock. He kept his eyes on his father. Albert Sercombe squatted, leaned under the horse and grasped hold of its other front hoof, the right one. He picked it up and lifted it, pulling it towards him as he came back out from under the gelding's belly. The horse toppled slowly and inexorably over away from his father and came to rest lying on its side.

'There, there, young fellow, you's in no danger, you's in good hands.' The old man kept talking to the horse, which lay there, trying but unable to get up. It did not seem to understand why it could not do so. After a while the horse ceased struggling and began to neigh loudly. Leo saw his father remove his large handkerchief from his pocket. He folded it carefully from corner to corner then over itself, making as long a bandage as he could. Then he knelt beside the gelding's head. He closed its mouth, and tied the handkerchief around its jaw, gagging the animal. Moses Pincombe spoke the whole time. 'There be nothin to worry about, old boy, there be no worries at all. Empty thine head, my boy, and calm yourself.'

Albert Sercombe walked to the door, which Herb Shattock opened for him. The two men stood once more side by side, watching the horse now passive on the floor and the old man leaning on his stick, bent over and speaking soothing words.

'I heard a such a method a castin a horse,' said the groom. 'I never seen it till now, Albert. And to a big un. I wouldn't know as you could do it.'

The boy's father shook his head. 'Neither did I,' he said. 'Give Moses another couple or three minutes, I reckon, and he's yours.'

Sure enough, the old man shortly stood up and limped over to the door. He nodded to the groom. 'Try him now,' he said.

Herb Shattock walked slowly into the box. He stood over the horse and studied it. He looked back at the men and the boy leaning against the lower door. 'Talk to him in your own tongue,' Moses Pincombe said. Herb nodded and turned to the horse and made the whistling sounds through his teeth that the boy had heard before. Leo looked at the horse. It was strange but in this hobbled and humiliated state the power of it was even more evident than when it was standing. The force of it seemed somehow ready to explode from its supine form. Herb Shattock kneeled down and with trembling fingers untied the gag of Albert's handkerchief. The gelding made no noise. Herb scrabbled a foot or two on his knees and untied the rope from around the horse's left front hoof and pastern.

'Do you think he's part-way tamed?' Leo heard Moses Pincombe whisper. 'You reckon?'

'I wouldn't like to say,' his father replied.

Herb Shattock kept whistling to the horse as he bound up the handkerchief and the rope in his hands and without looking behind him tossed the bundle towards the door. Albert caught it. Leo felt something press upon him and turned to see that one of the grooms and two of the stable lads had joined them in the doorway. He looked across the yard and saw another walking towards them. He turned back to the box.

The horse lay unmoving. Perhaps it did not realise that it was now unshackled or perhaps it had conceived a liking for this pose. Slowly it unbent its left front leg. It rolled over from its right side to its front, and put both forelegs forward. Its hind legs it brought up under its body when it rolled over. It now pushed itself from its hind quarters, forwards and up. Herb Shattock took a step or two backwards. Perhaps he did so to give the horse the room it needed. He kept whistling and, now that the horse stood upright on its four hooves, stepped towards it. The groom held in his left hand a halter. Leo had not seen him carry it with him nor lift it off a hook on the wall. It was something Herb had conjured. He put the halter on the gelding and the horse let him do so. Then he turned and walked towards the door, leading the horse, who came with him.

Albert opened the door of the box. He and

247

Moses and the boy and the others stepped aside. The lads stood in disbelief. Others had joined them. One shook his head slowly, from side to side. They watched their head groom lead the big savage hunter, now docile as some gentle old cob, out of the yard and down towards the training paddock. Herb said something to one of them, who ran to the tack room. He came out with a saddle and a bridle and trotted after the groom and the chestnut gelding.

One of the lads turned to another. 'If I hadn't seen it with these eyes here,' he said, pointing with the index fingers of both hands at his own eyes, 'I wouldn't a reckoned on that in a hundred years.'

April

At breakfast Albert Sercombe asked the boy if he had time before school to lead the two-year-old filly to the stables. This was the older sister of the colt Leo had brought to halter. The morning was wet with a steady drizzle and the boy walked with hunched shoulders to the field. He stood on tiptoe and was able to reach over the filly's ears. Perhaps the rain rendered her docile but she let him slip the halter over her head and tie it and lead her to the yard.

His father was waiting. He took the rope from the boy and backed the young mare into a stall. He removed the halter and replaced it with a bridle of a kind Leo had not seen before. Its bit was made of wood, but with pieces of iron attached. The carter fed the bit into the filly's mouth. Until this moment all she had taken was food and so she chewed the bit expectantly. Albert reached towards a pillar on one side of the stall and took hold of a length of string hanging there. He pulled the string towards him so that it ran through his fingers and he tied the end of it to the bit ring on that side of the strange bridle. Then he walked around the filly and on her other side did likewise.

The boy's father walked out of the stable without a word. Leo watched him from the doorway, already calling orders to Herbert, embarking upon the day's labour. The boy turned to the filly. She was preoccupied with the strange mouthful she'd been given. He watched her champing at the bit. In time, bubbles of saliva appeared at the sides of her mouth from the lather her chewing provoked. It seemed to Leo that she must have worked out by now that the odd shapes were not edible, but their very presence upon her tongue meant she could not stop steadily chomping at them. He knew he had already watched her too long. He turned, left the stable and trotted out of the yard.

★ ★ ★

On the morning following, the boy fetched the filly and put her to the mouthing bridle himself, and tied the string to the bit rings. On the third morning he did likewise. The fourth day was Saturday and his father put a normal bridle on the filly and harnessed her with the collar. He tied a light rope to the nose band and led her to the paddock. It had not rained for two days, yet there was moisture in the air still and dew upon the grass and the morning was a cool one.

Leo watched his father stand in the grassy dirt and ease the filly in circles around him. Periodically he changed direction. After a while he gestured to his son with a flick of his head to join him. Leo climbed between the fence poles and walked over. His father handed him the rope and walked away, out of the paddock and back to the yard, without once looking behind him.

Leo walked the filly in circles for an hour or more. Whenever he felt giddy he changed direction. Sometimes he walked backwards and the filly altered course and came with him. At other times he walked towards her, or to one side or the other. Each time she responded. He told her what he was doing, and what he wished her to do, but he did not think that accounted for her responsiveness. What issued from his lips was only sound for her, with the vaguest meaning, but he understood that they were both learning, for this, it seemed, was to be the language in which he wished to speak as a horseman. With words, like Moses Pincombe, along with some occasional whistling and clicking of his teeth taken from his father and Herb Shattock.

★ ★ ★

There was another whistle. He turned to see his cousin Herbert opening the gate of the paddock, and waving him over. As Leo led the filly through the gateway Herbert said, 'Don't get carried away, boy. You knows you won't be allowed to work with your old man.'

Leo nodded. Herbert secured the gate and jogged to catch up. 'Why he's learnin you and not me when I'm is lad . . . ' Herbert did not finish the sentence. He did not look at the filly, to see how she was taking to the bit, yet his jaws worked as if he mouthed one of his own. 'You can't tell im nothin, can you?' he said. 'He thinks you's the bee's knees, boy. You know why, don't you?' Herbert asked. He did not wait for Leo to respond but answered the question himself. 'You reminds him of himself, that's why.'

★ ★ ★

His father was waiting for him. Albert took the heavy collar off and had Leo wash the filly down with salt water, to stop her skin breaking from the friction of the harness.

On the afternoon following, a Sunday, they fitted the collar on the filly again and also reins. Leo watched his father walk the young mare around the paddock, working from behind. He called her forward. He pulled both reins to stop her, or on either side to turn her. This time he did not invite Leo to take a turn but had him watch the whole session. Later they took the filly back to the field and let her out with the others. The carter filled his pipe and watched the horses graze the new grass. The boy watched too.

'Every horse has its own character,' his father said. 'No different from men. Some you'll have to break, some like this one here you won't need to. But they all has to have a good mouth. You wants to be able to hold them with light hands. Like this, boy.' Albert put the stem of the pipe between his teeth and stepped behind his son. He pinched the shoulders of Leo's jacket, two fingers on each, and tugged gently on one side, then the other. 'See?' he uttered between his teeth. He let go of the jacket, and took the pipe from his mouth. 'Hold them with yon finger. You don't pull a horse, you guides it.' He put the pipe on the flat top of a fence post, and took hold of

252

his son's hands, turning them one way and another, examining them. 'What a young horse needs, boy,' he said, 'is light hands. A man with light hands and plenty a confidence. And that is about all there is to say on the matter.'

★ ★ ★

On the days of the week following Leo ran out of school and to the yard. He trained the filly with plough-traces then full cart harness, walking her round the paddock. Then they yoked her to a heavy log and had her drag it to get the feel of pulling a weight.

On the following Monday Leo watched his father and Herbert harness the filly alongside Pleasant the old mare, and so begin her working life.

May

The boy walked from the keeper's cottage. He heard a sound and looked up. Three geese flew idly above. They passed over him and on. The sound they made was like that of old friends talking to one another, sightseers commenting on the view below. Perhaps on the weather, too, for it was the warmest day of the year by far. He cradled the skeleton against his chest with his hands as he walked. He believed it was that of a hawk, but it may have been a kestrel, his brother was not sure. A raptor of one kind or another.

He walked slowly through the wood. The sun forced its way here and there through the burgeoning canopy of leaves. He was certain that she would like this one, though he had heard nothing of her response to the others. If there had been one at all. For all he knew she might have thrown each one away at once. Most of this bird's bones were contained in a ball of ribs and wings. Its sternum hung forward and was shaped like the keel of a boat. He wondered if ducks had sternums in like construction, and stopped to have another look at it. The spine extended from the rib-cage to the head, at the front of which the skull was hooked into a bony beak.

At the opposite end of the bird's skeleton, beyond the long, thin legs, with their femurs and

254

tibias and fibulas, along with a third limb it did not share with humans, were four large and terrifying claws. Sharp talons of bone.

The boy heard the sound of drumming. It seemed to come from inside his skull. Then he realised it was outside, and increasing in volume. Approaching him. Not drumbeats but footsteps. A momentary silence.

The runner launched himself. Leo fell, winded, to the ground. He could not move. He lay on his front. He tried to get his breath back but his assailant lay on top of him, a dead weight. He pushed up from his elbows and purchased a little room for his chest, and was able to inhale in short panting gasps, precious pockets of air into his lungs. For a moment it seemed that his attacker was doing exactly the same, mimicking him for amusement, but then he heard laughter and understood that he or she was giggling.

The boy summoned what infuriated power he possessed and, with a grunt like that of a pig, made an enormous effort to push himself and that other upon him off from the ground. He did so, and got to his hands and knees, breathing hard. There Leo took stock and tried to work out what to do next. He propelled himself forward, a four-footed animal, but the other simply rode him. She found this as funny as before, so he stopped, only to feel himself rolling or rather being rolled over. Now he lay above her, his back upon her front, her arms around his neck, her legs wrapped around his torso. He could feel her chest rising and falling beneath him as she laughed. A chuckling spider. He was a fly, immobilised. Breathing hard. His sweat slid into his eyes. In time she was still.

'You are so light, Leo Sercombe,' she said by his ear.

Her arms were tight across his throat. He could not speak, but even if he could there was nothing to say. The master's daughter unwrapped her arms and legs from around his body and released him. He rolled off her and rose and stumbled over to where she'd first jumped him. The skeleton lay amongst twigs and dead leaves and grassy undergrowth, all in pieces, where between them they had crushed it.

The girl came over and stood beside him. 'It was you,' she said. 'I thought it was. Who else? Shattock wouldn't say, but I knew it.'

She turned to him and must have seen his desolation. She knelt down and picked amongst the fragments, studying one broken or dislocated bone after another, as if calculating the order in which she intended to glue them together.

'Hawk,' he whispered.

'I think they're beautiful, Leo Sercombe.'

He looked at her and she said, 'No, it's true, I promise.'

Leo looked back down at the shattered skeleton. It was as if the bird had suffered a second mortality in this desecration of its bones. Or that he grieved for it now as he had not before.

'I promise,' the girl said again. 'Come. I'll show you.'

She took his hand and they walked through the sun-spangled wood. They came out of the trees and crossed a patch of rough lawn towards a brick wall. They were observed from on top of the wall by a peacock, its iridescent feathers draped over the bricks like a long dress. The girl opened a wooden door set into the wall and as they stepped through she let go of his hand.

'Follow close behind me,' she said.

The walled garden was huge. Only a small section was tended. An old man knelt on canvas sacking, carefully sowing some kind of seed in the earth, and he did not seem to be aware of them passing behind him. Much of the garden was wild, weeds and long grasses rampant. Fruit trees stood along one wall, their branches pinned there like Miss Pugsley's insects on display in the schoolroom.

Miss Charlotte led him into a greenhouse. Here the air was twice the temperature it was outside, though some panes of glass were cracked or fallen. The air was pungent too with the smell of soil, and other things — vegetation, turpentine, flowers of which sort he could not identify. Large plants. Leo could taste or feel moisture but that did not seem likely, unless it was his own.

In the middle of the greenhouse were some steps, which they descended. The boy looked up and saw through unclear glass the big house looming above him, and understood as they went through a doorway that they were now beneath it. The cellars smelled dank and musty. They walked along a corridor off which were rooms on either side. Many were empty. Their walls and ceilings had once been whitewashed but it must have been long ago for the paint was flaked and fallen. There were patches of damp from which tiny flowers bloomed. He could not understand how there could be light, murky though it was, but he looked around and saw a long strip of glass panes so covered in moss or algae that all appeared as if inside a pond.

They passed stacks of bottles covered in dust. A room full of furniture: tables, chairs, chests of drawers, beds. It was as if some branch or generation of the master's family had wished to live as certain animals do, underground, only for their successors to abandon the idea. Or perhaps they hadn't. Perhaps they would see some figure that was half human and half badger scurrying away along a darkening passage.

They came to a small door that gave on to an enclosed circular staircase. The girl told him to take off his boots and leave them there. She ascended and he followed. The staircase was narrow; even his bony shoulders brushed its wooden sides periodically. Miss Charlotte climbed fast and he kept up with her, though the stairs went on for an impossible time, as long as any beanstalk. He became dizzy. He could hear her chuckling again above him. Then his head bumped against the backs of her legs. Above them was a roof of dirty glass. She opened a door and poked her head around the frame. One way, then — around the open door — the other. She turned back and reached for his hand and stepped through the door, pulling him up the last stairs behind her. Bending low, he followed her through the doorway.

The room was enormous, larger than the village schoolroom. As large as the nave of the church. Along one side was a fenced-off strip of floor, at the far end of which lay a number of skittles on their sides.

'The nursery,' the master's daughter said. 'Look.'

He followed her to a bookcase. Along its top were the five skeletons he had already passed to her. In front of each was a folded piece of card on which were written, Weasel, Mole, Hare, Shrew, Adder. 'You see?' she said. 'Pride of place, Leo Sercombe. I'm so sorry about the hawk. Stay there. I'm going to have one of the maids fetch us something to eat. Don't look so fearful, boy! I shall bring it up myself.'

The girl left the room through a different door from the one by which they had entered, and which he could no longer see. He looked about him. Across the room stood a house. It was a model of the big house itself, about the size of the upright piano in the Tuckers' parlour. He saw that its façade rested on hinges at one side. Carefully he opened it. Inside were many rooms on five levels, all furnished. At the top in miniature was the room in which he now stood, complete with bowling alley, bookcases, a tiny model of the house.

Leo walked to a window and looked out. He could see past the lawns, over crooked fields, across the estate far into the distance. So gods and masters saw the world. Hawks and other birds likewise. Looking down, he saw two people crossing the shingle between house and lawn, toy-like figures. He turned back to the room. He found a box of lead soldiers. From the Boer War of which his father spoke, or some other? There were dolls in various states of undress. Stuffed animals. A table was laid with a dinner service for eight people, with plates, too many items of cutlery, three glasses of differing shapes. All miniature, and covered in dust.

At the far end of the room was a sofa and chairs, as he had seen once in the vicarage. Huge upholstered shapes, like sacks of grain or squashed-up beds. The vicar had sat in one and half disappeared. It had looked as if it might swallow him up while he sat there, reading his Good Book.

Leo walked past the chairs and sat on the sofa, putting a hand out to each side for balance. He now saw a large, almost human-sized doll seated in the armchair directly ahead of him. It was the doll of an old lady, dressed in white ancient lacy threads. Her powdered skin was too wrinkled to be entirely life-like. Her hands in her lap were little claws. Her tiny feet, far above the ground, were shod in blue slippers. Her cheeks had spots of rouge upon them, which he fancied the girl had daubed there. His sister had but one small doll, passed down from their mother; its body was porcelain, it had a wig made of human hair, and glass eyes. The eyes of this huge doll were dull, perhaps dimmed by its great age. Then they blinked and the boy's heart stopped.

The wizened old lady gazed at him. Leo felt himself pinned to the sofa. He dared not breathe. She blinked again, assessing him, for which she had all the time in the world, before calling for servants to evict him. Leo heard a noise and turned. Miss Charlotte came through the door carrying a tray and he waited. He did not move nor make a sound but he took a breath. She walked over and placed the tray upon the table that stood between the sofa and chairs. 'Milk and biscuits,' she said. 'Oh, I see you've met Great-grandmama.'

The girl sat down next to Leo and offered him the plate. He glanced down and shook his head, returning his gaze to the old woman. She blinked again.

'Great-grandmama lost her mind a long time ago,' the girl told him. 'No one has been able to find it. It's awfully sad. She's outlived all her children. Can you imagine? My grandpa was her youngest son. Great-grandmama had nine children. I sometimes imagine them playing together up here. They're all gone. She should have followed them, but she doesn't know how to die.'

The girl helped herself to a biscuit. She put it between her lips, then opened Leo's left hand, which was clenched into a fist upon the sofa, and placed one on his palm. She took the biscuit from between her lips and bit into it. As she chewed he could hear it crackling between her teeth. He nibbled an edge of his. On his tongue came the taste of lemon.

'We're no longer even sure which century Great-grandmama was born in. Father says that God has forgotten her. He's rather annoyed with Him, actually.'

261

There were two glasses of milk. The girl took one and rose and stepped over to the huge armchair. She knelt upon the threadbare carpet and held the glass to the old lady's lips, while she put her other hand on her little head and tilted it forward, speaking all the while. 'There we are, Great-grandmama, a lovely sip of milk for you, fresh from the dairy herd.' Like Moses Pincombe to the horse. 'Lovely milk to keep your frail bones from breaking. That's it, Great-grandmama, a little more.'

She broke a biscuit too and fed it to the old dowager countess in pieces, as she might to a tamed bird.

The boy watched, nibbling on his own biscuit. His mouth was dry but he did not take the milk until the girl offered it to him. 'It's yours, Leo Sercombe. Great-grandmama and I will share this one, won't we? And then you had better leave. My governess was downstairs. I have to study German soon.'

Leo drained the glass of milk in one long draught. He wiped his lips. The girl stood up and he did likewise. 'Thank you, Miss Charlotte,' he said.

'My name is Lottie,' she said. 'I cannot bear the name Charlotte. I have a new pony, Leo Sercombe. I should like to show her to you. You could accompany me on a picnic. Can you meet me in the wood, where the hawk bones are, in one week's time?'

Leo nodded.

Lottie turned to the door by which she had come with the tray. 'Now you must go. I believe

I can hear her footsteps.'

The boy looked frantically about him.

'Here,' said the girl. She walked over to a panelled wall beneath the eaves. Balling her hand into a fist, she rapped against the panel once. Nothing happened. She did so a second time, a little higher. The panel swung a few inches into the room. The girl opened it fully and the boy stepped through to the narrow staircase. He heard the door click shut behind him as he descended the stairs.

At the bottom he put on his boots. He retraced his steps carefully through the empty cellars, tiptoed into the greenhouse and out to the walled garden. The old gardener was nowhere to be seen. Leo went through the door in the wall, across the rough grass into the wood, and began to breathe easily once again.

June

The days were long. In the hay meadows the grass was rampant. Albert and Fred came home for tea. They ate a stew of bacon bones and cabbage. Kizzie spoke to her father of school and how Miss Pugsley was driven wild by Gideon Sparke. He would not stop showing off and acting stupid.

'He's already known as a twily lad, at his age,' Ruth said. 'He'll have to travel abroad to find work when the time comes.'

'If he's fit to work and wishes to,' said Albert, 'which I doubt he does.'

Kizzie said that when at last Miss Pugsley lost her temper, she screamed at him and her voice was like that of a tomcat in the night, it was frightening. They were all frightened. And then Miss Pugsley wept.

Leo watched a daddy longlegs walk along the window sill on its six spindly legs, daintily choreographing itself.

'I hear your Herbert's in trouble again,' Ruth told her husband. She named a girl in the next village. 'I heard she got herself a bastardy order against him. You never told me.'

'Aye,' Albert said. 'You know I ain't one for gossip. Obliged to pay her a shillin a week. He's been bendin my ear at every opportunity with his

264

moanin. I've ad about as much as I can take.'

'Tell him he should a studied the matter and worked out the consequences before he had his way.'

'Don't think I ain't, mother.'

Dessert was plums preserved in suet. Fred ate a mouthful and told his mother it was his favourite and she hadn't let him down. She told Fred that Herbert's behaviour stood as a fair warning, a fine lesson, and that he could invite a certain young lady she had heard about to tea any Sunday she should like to come. Fred nodded. Then his sister Kizzie yelped, and reached a hand beneath the table to rub her shin.

Albert said that he'd run into the master's groom Herb Shattock today and they had spoken of their boy Leo here. Herb had asked if when the boy was ready he might fancy becoming a strapper at his stables. Leo looked up but it seemed his father might not have known that he was in the room or had ears to hear.

'I told him, if I have anything to do with it, when he leaves school in two years' time he will have a number of offers. But Herb's would be a good one, probably the best.'

★ ★ ★

When the men had finished eating, Albert asked his wife if she might read a little more of the newspaper to him later, then Leo accompanied the men back to the farm. They had left the

265

horses eating their evening bait, which as the grazing was so good was minimal and long since consumed. Herbert brought a message for Fred from his uncle, that Enoch had an errand to run and so Fred should put their horses into the field on his own. Leo volunteered to help his brother, while Albert and Herbert took out the head carter's team.

As the four of them came back into the yard, so they saw in the distance Dunstone approaching, in his customary nervous, bustling haste.

'Here comes our evenin entertainment,' Herbert said.

'T'will have to do for you,' Fred told him. To his father and brother he said, 'Lover boy here's forsworn women. Forever, he says.'

'Aye,' said Albert. 'Or till Saturday night, whichever comes sooner.'

'Women ain't worth the expense, uncle,' Herbert said. His face often bore a scowl, occasionally as now a half-grin, as if there were some game going on only he knew of.

Dunstone walked into the yard. He wore a pair of trousers that were far too large for him, turned up at the ankles almost as far as his knees, and flapping all around his skinny legs like sails.

'What you seen, Dunstone?' Herbert addressed him. 'Tell us all what you seen in your travels.'

'I seen im,' Dunstone said. 'I seen im.' He was in a state of agitation, eyes wide, saliva at his lips, but such was not unusual. 'He's goin round 'n' round. Come see,' he said, tugging at Herbert's shirt. 'I'll show you.'

Herbert took Dunstone's wrist and pulled his hand loose. 'I'm busy, old boy,' the youth told him. 'I'd love to else.'

'Goin round in circles,' Dunstone said, turning to Fred. Albert had already disappeared into the tack room. 'Come and see.'

'Show us, old boy,' Herbert said. 'How's it goin?'

'Round 'n' round,' Dunstone said. He trotted, describing the circumference of a circle in the yard, its diameter twice the length of a man. 'Round 'n' round,' he said.

'Keep goin,' Herbert goaded him, grinning. 'Keep goin, old boy.'

'Round 'n' round,' Dunstone said, breathless.

Herbert tried to encourage Dunstone further, but he could barely do so for laughing as the old lad began to stagger.

'Round 'n' round,' Dunstone gasped. 'I'll show e.'

Fred too could not contain himself as Dunstone grew more giddy and the circle he trotted ever less certain.

Herbert stepped forward and took hold of Dunstone. 'That's enough, old boy,' he said. 'You've convinced us. Walk in a straight line and us'll follow.'

Dunstone looked about him with the eyes of a drunken man, took his bearings and set off out of the yard, only to reel giddily, try to right himself, lurch again and fall over. He sat upon the ground, perplexed at what gravity had done to him. Herbert had to lean against Fred to save himself from falling over too, inebriated with the comedy. The two cousins headed for the tack room, Herbert slapping Fred upon the back, sharing the pleasure of their amusement, which he had both predicted and brought forth.

Leo had stood and witnessed proceedings. He walked over to Dunstone and offered his hand, and though he lacked the size or strength to yank him to his feet he helped the man up. Dunstone stood unsteadily, warily, a hand on the boy's shoulder, not yet quite trustful of his ability to stand upon his own two feet.

'What was it?' the boy asked him.

Dunstone gazed back at him as if Leo had spoken in some foreign tongue.

'What went round in circles?' the boy said.

Dunstone's eyes opened wider. 'Sheeps!' he said. 'Sheeps. I'll show you.'

They walked out of the yard and along the lane past the field with the dairy herd and on towards the pastures below Little Wood. The evening was advanced but much light remained. In the small field was a flock of castrated rams Ernest Cudmore had fattening. One of them was indeed going round in circles, much as Dunstone had demonstrated. The animal did not bleat but bore his plight silently.

'Round 'n' round,' the old lad said. 'Dunstone seen it. Round 'n' round.'

★ ★ ★

They found Ernest at the farm. Mrs Tucker was working with her daughters in the vegetable garden and pointed to the kitchen door. Ernest had finished work for the day and was inside the house, for like Isaac Wooland he was a lodger. He sat at the table with Amos Tucker, drinking cider from a pewter mug. Though there were hours of daylight outside, in the kitchen it was dim.

'And for what grand reason do you disturb us at our rest?' Amos asked the old lad and the boy. The farmer looked indeed to be in need of sleep. He had been performing Isaac's labour since the stockman's death. Dunstone described what he had seen, as before, but now he had Leo Sercombe beside him nodding gravely and so was listened to.

Ernest Cudmore shook his head. 'One a they wethers is got the Gid, gaffer,' he said. 'Sounds like.' He drank what remained of his cider and put down the empty mug upon the table and rose and went out. He fetched certain things from his bothy but the boy did not know what they were for when Ernest Cudmore emerged, whatever he'd chosen was now in the pockets of his jacket. They walked with him to the field, the boy in the middle. He looked to either side and reckoned their trio stood the same height.

When he saw the giddy ram Ernest said that there was no gain in carrying him, the wether should walk by his own means to the place of his doom. Ernest deftly hooked his crook behind one of the animal's front legs and tripped him. Then he pulled a length of cord from a pocket and tied it around the sheep's neck and let it stand. He walked back to the farm and the sheep, on a short lead no more than a yard long, followed him.

Dunstone walked at his usual agitated pace in front. Leo walked beside the shepherd and asked him what was wrong with this ram.

'Some kind a maggot,' Ernest told him, 'or worm, has got in and eaten part a his brains. Won't be no good for nothin now, poor feller. Won't know to graze.'

Back at the farm Ernest put the giddy sheep in a makeshift stall he made from hurdles on a patch of grass. He explained to Leo that he would despatch the wether in the morning. The boy wondered why he did not do so now. Was it a mercy to give the doomed animal one last night upon the earth or a cruelty to prolong its suffering, if such it was?

'Gid don't affect the flesh,' Ernest told him. 'Not so far's I know. I'll have time to dress him tomorrow, give the gaffer's wife fresh mutton.'

When they looked around for Dunstone he was gone. 'Off to secure his sleepin spot,' Ernest said. He thanked the boy for alerting him and bade him goodnight, and Leo walked home in the fading light.

June

On Saturday morning at breakfast Leo's father told him that the gaffer needed certain items for his wife collecting from the railway station in Wiveliscombe. Leo could put the filly in the small cart and take her; she was ready for such light work alone, with the right man driving her.

The boy glanced up. His father did not smile but his mother did, as if her son did not already understand the compliment he was being given.

'I cannot,' he said, and all looked towards him, his parents and his brother Fred and sister Kizzie. Albert Sercombe coloured. 'Said I would help Mister Shattock with a horse.'

Ruth Sercombe put her hand upon her husband's. 'Why, that is good news, is it not, father?'

Albert's teeth had clenched. His mouth remained taut as he spoke. 'Aye, and might the boy not have told me so before?'

'Well,' Ruth said. 'Will you apologise to your father, Leo?'

'Sorry, father,' Leo said in his gravelly voice. 'I should a liked to drive the filly.'

'Aye, well, someone else can do it,' Albert said. 'You can go, Fred, later this mornin.'

★ ★ ★

271

The boy trotted across the estate. The sky was a clean unblemished blue all around the earth and the day was already warm. He entered the wood and made his way to the spot where the remains of the hawk skeleton were scattered in the undergrowth. Some parts, he thought, had disappeared. Perhaps ants had studied them and devised some use for certain bones, as tool or decoration, and had their gangs of workers carry them into their hills. Leo wondered whether he had arrived early enough. It must be shortly before or after seven o' clock. She had not specified a time. The idea that he was late and that Miss Charlotte had come here, waited, given up on him, tormented the boy but he remained. He barely moved, but sat upon the ground. Or she had been forced against her will to do something other. Or she had forgotten their arrangement.

The boy studied insects. He found some dandelions and picked them and sucked the nectar from their stems. He heard occasional voices in the distance, and sounds of waggons and horse gear. Of wood being hammered. He listened to birds in the branches above him and attempted to identify them but could not. Wood pigeons he recognised, but smaller birds he knew only by sight, not sound. A cuckoo called, seeming to mock him.

When she came it was not from the direction of the house, as he'd anticipated, but from the stables. She led the pony through the trees. It was already saddled up and across its rump lay a pannier of two bags.

'There you are, Leo Sercombe,' she said. She turned to the pony as if to present it, or make a formal introduction. 'Her name is Blaze,' the girl said. 'You did not have the chance to ride Embarr, but you shall ride Blaze today.'

'Thank you, Miss Charlotte.'

She told him that unless he addressed her as Lottie she would return the pony to the stable and take the picnic in the saddlebags back to the house and eat it with her great-grandmama. Which she did not wish to do.

They walked out of the wood. Then the girl mounted the pony, and the boy walked beside them. The sun was high in the sky and out of the shade of the trees its heat bore down upon them. The boy wore a cap. The girl wore a felt hat in keeping with her boy's attire. Leo could not help wondering how she came by such clothes.

'My cousins come down at Christmas. The year before last, they were ready to leave, their luggage packed. I found the suitcase that belonged to Eustace and stole his clothes.'

The boy put his fingers on the cheek piece of the pony's bridle so that he would at least appear to any who might observe them to have some use, as they walked along. 'Did no one notice the case was empty?' he asked.

'I filled it with skirts and petticoats,' Lottie said. She laughed as if the event were being re-enacted in front of her. 'Fortunately my cousin Eustace has a keen sense of humour. He also loves to play charades. We repeated this game last Christmas, to keep each other stocked up with the items we prefer, and shall no doubt do so again. No one else knows of this arrangement. Indeed, Leo Sercombe, you are the first person I have told, so you must keep your lips sealed.'

They walked along the track between Home Farm's wheat fields and through pasture around the hillocks known as the Burial Mounds and on to the gallops. This stretch of turf and dirt was clear for Herb Shattock's lads had long since exercised the master's hunters and racing horses. Here they laid the panniers upon the ground and rode the young mare, Lottie first to show Leo how it was done, then graciously inviting him to take her place in the saddle. He did not tell her that he'd ridden this horse already, before she ever had. He did not, however, trust his ability to dissemble if he tried to act surprised or delighted and so he was merely quiet and grave, nodding at the words of advice she gave him. He walked the pony a long while before he trotted her, trying Lottie's patience. He trotted Blaze back and forth, back and forth, until eventually after much exhortation from the girl he let the pony canter.

One day, Leo thought, he would be up here on these gallops, riding the master's horses. He would learn all there was to from Herb Shattock, for he was a man the boy believed he could trust like no other. And one day he would take over from him as head groom on the estate, as Lottie Prideaux would take the estate on from her father.

The girl galloped the pony and rode her hard. She brought her over to where Leo stood, and said, panting for breath, 'That will be enough for now. Put back the saddlebags, please. We shall take our picnic.'

She did not tell him where they were going. They walked from the gallops down into the valley, where willows lined the stream, and up past grazing cows into the bluebell wood, the flowers wilting and faded now. Beyond the wood was bleak terrain, the least cultivated on the estate, scrubby copses, thin soil on rocky ground. Here and there was evidence of human occupation: a stone wall covered with moss; the ruin of a shack; a stairway cut into a slope, its stone steps scalloped by the tread of generations. All the stone for all the buildings hereabouts and further distant was said to have come from these quarries.

The heat was such that Leo had to keep removing his cap to wipe his forehead. They followed a winding metalled lane. The young mare plodded along but then her nostrils quivered and she looked up and snickered with pleasure or anticipation, though she could not yet see what she could smell. Then the vista opened before them and they looked down upon the great pool.

The track led to the water's edge and the mare drank. They watched her stretch her neck forward and suck the water into her mouth and swallow. The girl said that when Embarr was a foal and first weaned from taking milk from his mother's teats he did not know how to drink water. He would plunge his mouth in too deep. 'Or he would try to bite the water, as if it was food,' she said, smiling.

On this side of the pool they stood now in the shade of trees. From hoof and claw prints in the mud they could see that other animals had come to drink here before them. There was duckweed on the surface of the water. It smelled dank. Midges hovered, blue-green dragonflies flew above them. This was where Leo had collected polliwogs, which he took in a bucket to the school and left for Miss Pugsley. She had never known it was from him. The class watched the tadpoles develop. Frogs and newts now inhabited the pond. There were many bulrushes and also yellow flowers — flag iris. Leo told Lottie that he and his sister collected its seeds for their mother, which she roasted and used to make a drink for their father they called coffee, though all knew it was no such thing.

They walked out of the shade and circled the pool. On the far side a huge slab of rock jutted out over the water and here Lottie laid the saddlebags. Leo led the filly back away out of the sun. He removed her bridle and replaced it with a halter Lottie had brought and tied the rope to the trunk of a sapling surrounded by grass, and there left her grazing.

The girl unfolded a rug upon the rock and laid their picnic. 'It's very simple, I'm afraid,' she said. Bread, blue-veined cheese, two cold chicken drumsticks, four hard-boiled eggs, tomatoes. A pork pie Lottie cut in half. A flask of lemonade. They ate greedily, then the girl lay back. The rock was hot from the sun such that they could not rest their hands or elbows upon it

276

without scalding them. They spread their jackets and rested on them and still felt the heat in the rock rise through the material.

'Do you know what my governess said, after she saw you in the stable?' the girl asked.

Leo looked towards her. Her light brown eyes were hard to see in the shade of her hat brim. He shook his head.

'She said, 'The carter's boy has an old man's face.' She does say such stupid things. I have to put up with her, it is one thing Papa insists on. I would so prefer to have a chic Parisian governess, imagine that. Or a Florentine, to teach me the most musical language. But, no. Papa claims that one can think more clearly in German, so I must put up with that Prussian cripple. Do you know what I told her? I said, 'He does have a name, the carter's boy, Ingrid. And so does the carter. The family is called Sercombe.' I did not indulge her with my theory. Do you know what my theory is?'

Leo appeared to ponder the matter a while, before slowly shaking his head once more.

'My theory is that it's because you never laugh.' She peered at him from beneath her hat, as if studying his physiognomy, or colour, diagnosing some half-hidden malady. 'Well? Is there a reason for it?'

He let the question sink in. He clearly had no need to answer before considering it fully. His silence was unnerving. Lottie and her cousins and even her governess were quick-witted. The Sercombe boy contemplated the question, regarding it from all sides, revealing a depth or complexity of which she herself had been unaware.

'A reason for what?' he said.

'Why you do not laugh. Or even smile.'

The boy's blank expression did not alter. She would have thought that it might, if only to prove her wrong. He did not look at her, but gazed at the sun-dazzled water before them.

'I smiles from time to time,' Leo said. 'You just can't see it.'

'And why do I not see it?' she demanded.

Again he was quiet, and peered into the distance. He might have been considering her question, or some other topic entirely unrelated, or perhaps his attention had been distracted by a passing heron.

'Do horses smile?' he asked. 'There's some say they seen their dog grin, but I ain't.'

The girl laughed. 'Leo Sercombe,' she said, 'your voice still sounds like it has sand in it.'

They both gazed at the pool. A cloud passed in front of the sun and the water was black.

'How deep is it?' Lottie asked.

Leo stared at the pool, as if his gaze if of sufficient concentration could see to the bottom. 'Old Isaiah Vagges says his grandfather worked here, as a quarryman, but others say the big pool quarry's not been worked in a thousand years.' He turned to the girl. 'Isaiah says he can recall the quarry as a boy and tis the biggest he ever saw.' Leo lifted his gaze and surveyed the rocky perimeters of the pool. On the far side were sheer cliffs of stone. 'Mind you, I shouldn't reckon he's sin a great many.'

Lottie looked at Leo's face for signs of amusement, but it remained as blank and solemn as before. 'Do you know what I think of when I look at it?' she said. 'I think of Avalon. I imagine the sword rising out of the lake.'

Leo looked at her and waited for her to continue.

'Yes, I know it's stupid,' she said. 'Of course there was no pool here in Arthur's time. It was never a lake. But it's so black it makes you wonder what's in here. When I was small I had a nanny who told me there was a monster down there, a kind of octopus or squid.'

The boy stood up and undid the buttons of his waistcoat, from the top, one by one, and let it slide off. He removed the cap from his head. It floated to the rock he stood on.

'What are you doing?' she demanded.

He yanked his braces off his shoulders. They hung at his sides. He undid the buttons of his shirt, pulled the shirt-tails up out of his trousers, shucked it off and bundled it into a loose cotton ball which, bending, he placed beside the waistcoat. 'One way to find out,' he said. He sat down and untied the laces of his boots, loosened them, and cupping the heels pulled off one and then the other, followed by his socks, all different shades of black or grey wool where they'd been darned and re-darned.

'Are you feeble-minded?' she asked him.

The boy said nothing but unbuttoned his trousers and let them fall around his feet. He grasped his underwear and, bending his knees, slid the grubby garment down his legs then let

279

go and stood up, and stepped out of the wodge of material around his ankles. His shoulders were narrow, his back was long, his buttocks and his legs slender. He looked taller naked than clothed. His neck and hands were brown but the rest of his skin was pale. He took a step towards the water.

'Wait,' she said. The girl took off her hat. Her long brown hair fell loose about her shoulders. Then she stood and as he had done divested herself of her clothes, garment by garment the same, waistcoat, shirt, trousers, until she too stood naked. There was a scribble of hair upon her pudenda. Her nipples were larger than his though she had no breasts. The girl squatted on the slab of grey rock and pissed. The boy looked away. Then he looked back. The water trickled across the rock, staining the granite a darker grey.

Leo turned back and walked over the hot granite and dived forward off the rock. She saw that the soles of his feet were dirty. She saw his boy's penis like that of cherubs or putti she had seen in paintings but not in life. She saw his hands thrown before him as if he'd leaped forward to grab something on the surface of the water. Then he entered the pool and in a moment was gone and the broken surface of the black water recomposed itself as before.

The sun beat down. The birds of the air and the beasts of the earth had found shelter and were silent. She called out his name. It came back to her off the grey cliffs of the quarry. Nothing moved. She looked up, squinting, and scanned the top of the cliffs, and saw a little old man there. Then she blinked and looked again and saw nothing. Another cloud blocked the sun. She turned back to the water. The boy had disappeared and there was no help for it. No explanation. The still black water reflected nothing, it absorbed the light into its darkness and had absorbed him.

Then Leo's head burst up out of the water. As it did so he gasped, as if shocked by what he found in this world above. He shook his head, spraying water from his hair all about him, which speckled the surface of the pool like a tiny cloud of rain. Then he trod water, breathing hard.

The girl stood. Leo watched her. He looked away and then he looked back to see her jumping. She could not dive but wished to make no more of a splash than he, so kept her feet together and arms by her sides. She slid into the water. It was warm, at first, but as she fell the temperature plummeted with every inch. The buoyancy of her body in the water perhaps slowed her descent. For a moment she hovered, and could feel her forehead warm and her toes cold, as if her body had been dipped in the pool as the gauge of some strange thermometer. Then she kicked and rose to the surface.

Lottie could swim but like a dog, working all her limbs below the surface and her head above, facing the way she wished to go. Whichever way she faced, so she went. She paddled into the pool some yards, then turned around in a slow arc to see the boy.

They trod water. The girl was shivering. 'Is it cold enough for you, Leo Sercombe?'

The boy tried to speak but found that his teeth were chattering too much and so he nodded.

They looked at each other and around the rocks of the quarry pool and up at the empty blinding sky and back at each other, like conspirators unsure of their purpose.

Leo gritted his teeth and said, 'I seen a light.'

Lottie turned and paddled back to the rock. She reached up and grasped it and hauled herself out. Leo followed. Drops of water fell from their bodies onto the hot rock and evaporated. They lay naked on their clothes and in the hot sun they soon stopped shivering and their skin dried, they no longer gasped from the cold and the need for air in their lungs. Their hair dried last.

'What kind of light?' Lottie asked.

Leo shook his head. 'I don't know.' He stood. 'I'll have another look.'

'Wait.'

'I'll not be long.' He walked to the edge of the rock and this time jumped in with a splash, bobbed on the surface, took a deep breath then spun his body and dived down. He wriggled like a fish to a good depth then righted himself and turned around. He saw it. White light coming from he knew not where. The boy swam towards it. It was a little further than he thought but soon he reached a wall of rock and the light beckoned him into a breach a little wider than himself. He put his arms in front of him and half swam, half pulled himself into and along the tunnel. In some part of his brain he knew the tunnel was becoming more narrow, yet a stronger part ignored it in the light's allure. Then he was stuck. By his shoulders. He tried to push against the rock in front of him to ease himself backwards but his arms did not work well, and he could get no purchase.

To die was not the end of it, but it had come too soon. His lungs burned. He writhed and pressed and tried to struggle free but he could not. Then he felt something odd. The creature of the deep that Lottie had been warned of had wrapped its tentacles around him. No. Her hands around his ankles. He felt himself being pulled, and coming free, and flowing backwards through and out of the tunnel. She let go of his ankles and he turned and kicked and swam up to the surface. As he rose he had to breathe and only swallowed water. He broke the surface and gulped air. Choking and coughing, he flailed towards the rock and grasped it and floated there, unable to move.

The girl swam around him and clambered out of the pool then turned and took one of his hands and helped him struggle onto the rock. There they lay, once more drying in the sun.

Neither of them said a word for a long time. Perhaps for hours. The heat of the day spent itself and the sun began to wane from its height above them. Eventually the girl rose and began to clothe herself. The boy did likewise. They dressed in silence. Then Lottie gathered the remains of their picnic. She had brought a bar of chocolate but it was melted to a brown liquid. One hard-boiled egg remained, a crust of bread, one tomato. Blue-veined cheese, which like the chocolate had melted. All the food she tossed into undergrowth for insects to feast on.

They did not speak. Leo fetched the pony, and tied the bags to the saddle. They walked slowly, one each side of the horse, back the way they had come. Up the winding metalled track, across the scrub and out of the quarried land, through the fading bluebell wood, into the valley of willow trees along the stream. Leo walked on the left-hand side of the horse, his hand once more upon the cheek piece of the bridle. They walked along the gallops, across pasture round the Burial Mounds, then through the wheat fields. There at last they stopped, for the stables were not far distant.

The girl walked around the front of her pony. Leo let go of the bridle and stepped back. He found it hard to look at her. She evidently felt likewise for she fussed with the bridle, checking the straps as if they might have worked loose.

He spoke to the back of her head. 'You saved my life, Miss Lottie.'

The girl gripped the saddle and put her foot in the stirrup and, flexing her leg twice, sprang up from that foot and mounted the pony. She looked down at Leo from under the brim of her hat and smiled. Then she turned the pony and heeled her and within a few yards they were cantering away towards the stables.

*   *   *

Leo walked home across the estate by the same route along which ten or eleven hours earlier he had run. A light breeze had blown up from the direction of the coast and as he walked below the line of poplars their leaves shimmered and whispered to him. A man he recognised but did not know by name passed him at the corner of Home Farm and walked on.

The boy knew some things and others he did not. He was a carter's son and always would be, even after he became a horseman of whatever mettle himself. This he knew.

Had God shone that light or had the Devil? This he did not know. Had not God known Leo even before He formed him in his mother's womb? Before he was born had He not sanctified him, and all others too? Was He not the Alpha and Omega, the beginning and the end, the first and the last? He wished to show the boy His power and His mercy.

Or had Satan been at work, tempting him with what would most draw the boy, which was not the light but his own desire to see it for himself, no matter what. Or perhaps neither was present at the moment of his deliverance. The light was some phenomenon of nature he might usefully study, a riddle to solve. And it was simply his good fortune that the girl had followed him down into the cold water.

As he approached the cottage Leo saw to his surprise that the big new waggon stood outside, Pleasant and Red in the traces. The waggon was piled high with what? As he came close he could see that it was furniture. And then he recognised his mother's dresser from the parlour, denuded though it was of the blue and white china. His narrow bed and that of Fred stacked one upon the other. The kitchen chairs including his father's wooden armchair. He could not comprehend the spectacle. His sister Kizzie came around the far side of the cottage carrying gardening implements, a fork, a hoe. She stowed these in a space in the bed of the waggon. Turning, she glimpsed her brother. Her hand flew to her mouth and she ran into the cottage.

Leo walked through the open front door. The parlour was empty, and but for a broom leaning against a wall the kitchen likewise. The sight was strange, comical. As if someone was pulling his leg. Yet he knew this was not possible. The cottage was larger, empty, than he would have believed it to be. It was dowdy, in need of fresh paint, and the rooms were misshapen. He looked at them uncluttered and saw that walls curved and bulged, timbers were crooked, floors uneven.

The house smelled of dust and charcoal, as if the furniture itself had been imbued with a homely scent, now gone. Leo climbed the stairs. The three bedrooms were emptied likewise. Only flaky debris on the wooden floorboards. If it had not been for the waggon outside he would have thought he'd been hurled out of time, many years into the future.

He heard heavy footsteps on the wooden stairs. His father rushed into the room Leo had shared with his older brother.

'What have you done?' Albert Sercombe yelled, advancing across the boards. 'What have you done, you little bastard?'

He punched his son on the side of his head

and the boy went down.

'You little fucker. You stupid little bastard.' He kicked the boy. Leo curled up to protect himself and felt his father's boot on his back, his thighs, his buttocks.

'You ruined us all . . . your mother . . . all I've done, in ruins,' his father yelled. He kicked his son as if to emphasise certain words.

Leo scrabbled to all fours and stumbled to the door. His father pursued him. He staggered along the landing but at the top of the stairs Albert caught him at the back of his legs and he tripped. The cottage became a toy flung by a giant. It tumbled about him, banging his bones. At the bottom of the stairs he looked up groggily and saw his father coming down after him, and he crawled into the kitchen. The broom leaned against the wall. Albert grabbed it and struck his son. Leo crumpled and fell once more. He begged for mercy but none came. His father beat him with the broomstick.

There were voices. Whose he did not know, except for his father's saying, 'I'll kill him. I'll kill him.' But he was no longer being hit.

The voices went away. Leo lay upon the floor. His mouth was full of blood. He opened his lips and the blood poured out. He could hear groaning. He realised it came from himself.

Leo heard his mother's voice. He understood that she was weeping and pleading but his father told her to come away, to leave him.

He tried to sit up. He could not see well, for some reason. He saw someone come in and heard himself whimpering. It was not his father.

287

Fred knelt beside him. His father yelled, 'Leave him, I said,' but his brother stayed. He had a jug of water. He took a handkerchief from his pocket and balled it into his fist and dipped his hand in the water. He brought out the handkerchief and wrung it out and applied it gently to his brother's face. With his other arm he held Leo sobbing against him.

'Dunstone come into the yard,' he said quietly. 'All atremble. Herbert asked him what he'd sin. Herbert told Uncle Enoch. Enoch went directly to the manor.'

Fred cleaned his brother's face as he spoke and told him how fast it had all happened.

'The master had no choice, see,' Fred said.

Leo asked his brother to help him to his feet. He stood unsteadily. Some parts of him throbbed, others burned. Were no bones broken? Fred supported him. Leo asked in which direction they were headed. Fred told him that their father knew of a farm on the other side of Taunton where he believed they might find work.

'That's east, ain't it?' Leo said. The words his bruised and swollen mouth could form came out misshapen. 'I'll go west.'

He turned and hobbled out of the open back door of the cottage, and through his mother's vegetable patch, and into the lane. There he clambered painfully over the stile and stumbled across the pasture and on, into the west.

June

The boy limped slowly towards the setting sun.
The sound of hooves coming from behind made
him stop and turn. A horse and rider were
approaching through the evening haze, the two
indistinct, a single entity in silhouette. What he
saw was that figure from mythology, half-man,
half-horse. It cantered towards him in the
twilight. He felt a shiver of fear tremble through
his bowels and understood how terrifying it must
have been for people who'd never seen a horse
before to have marauders bear down upon them
out of the east. The hordes of Genghis Khan.

Had enough not been inflicted upon him?
Who was this advancing, to mete out further
punishment?

The creature was forty yards away when all of
a sudden his anxiety gave way to comprehension.
He recognised the straight-backed gait of the
rider atop the pony.

Perhaps she did not see him standing in the
gloom for she did not rein in her mount until
they were almost upon him. The animal seemed
to rear up in surprise but Leo knew it was her
horsemanship and the animal's trust in her and
as the horse stopped and stood, quivering, she
slid from the saddle and stood facing him. He
looked at her then glanced over her shoulder in

289

the direction from which she had come, as if he should look out for some further figures in pursuit of her, or of him.

Then he turned and looked westward once more. A strip of red lay between the black horizon and the grey sky. The girl walked around in front of him so that she could discern him in the vestigial light. She studied his bruised and broken face.

'What have they done to you?' she said. 'What have they done?'

He reached his right hand towards her, though it hurt to lift his arm, and wiped tears from her eyes.

'The horse,' she said. 'Blaze, she's for you.'

The boy tried to mount the horse but could not, for his body and all his limbs ached, but then with her help he managed. There was no saddle. She pulled herself up behind him and they rode together in the dark.

'Will you come back?' she asked.

'Why?'

'I don't know,' she told him. She seemed to rack her brains for the answer though really she knew it but not how to say it. Then she blurted it out. 'For me.'

He nodded slowly. 'A course I will,' he said.

'One day,' she said.

'One day,' he agreed. His voice was more constricted and gravelly than ever, for it hurt to speak. 'Or another.'

She leaned against him and put her arms around his belly. 'Where are you going?' she asked him.

He told her he was heading west, and when she asked why he explained that his father had gone east.

'Ours is a big country,' she said. 'A big island.' It occurred to her how little he must have seen of it. There were those on the estate who reputedly had never seen the sea, so close that on some days you could smell it. 'There's not much that way,' she said. 'Only the southwest peninsula.'

He asked her if she knew of a place called Penzance. She told him she had heard of it, and he said he would aim in that direction.

They rode towards the sunset in the west. In the dark they came up out of the fields. The western horizon curved across the moor ahead of them like the convex rim of the world itself.

She leaned her head against the nape of his neck. He felt the faint sensation of her breath on his skin and it occurred to him all at once that he, Leo Jonas Sercombe, would one day become a man. That until that moment a boy or youth remained a lifeless form, a sleepwalker, to be animated by the breath of another. Such as this girl, Lottie Prideaux, who would become a woman as sure as he would a man.

He tried to think further on this path but could not do so. The horse walked on. He realised in due course that Lottie had fallen asleep, leaning against him. He prised open her fingers gently clasped and took her hands and laid them by her knees. He raised his right leg, the one least injured, and swung it over the neck of the pony, and slid to the ground with a jolt that hurt his ribs.

She did not wake. He took the reins and put them in her hands. He grasped the bridle at the pony's neck and slowly turned her until she was pointing back the way they had come, and then let go. The horse kept walking, at its own pace, making its way home. The girl did not stir but rode on in her sleep.

Leo watched them disappear into the night, and he stared into the darkness some while more until he could no longer hear the horse's hooves. Then he turned and walked on alone.

Acknowledgements

Behind and interwoven through this book are many others.

Those of Fred Archer describing rural life in the Evesham Vale in the early years of the twentieth century were particularly inspiring, fredarcher.co.uk

Also: Herbert L. Day's memories of farm labouring in Yorkshire, and George Ewart Evans' research among horsemen in Norfolk.

Oral histories of country life under the rubric 'Tales of (the Old Gamekeepers, Old Country-women etc.)' published by David & Charles.

The Great Shoots: Britain's Best — Past and Present by Brian P. Martin.

The Working Countryside 1862 — 1945 by Robin Hill and Paul Stamper, wonderful photographs and descriptions of rural life in Shropshire.

Old Farming Days: Life on the Land in Devon and Cornwall by Robin Stanes.

All Around the Year by Michael Morpurgo.

Especially useful horse books were:
The Manual of Horsemanship by the British Horse Society, the *Pony Club Annual 1950* and *Veterinary Notes for Horse Owners* by Captain M. Horace Hayes FRCVS, 1877 and subsequent revised editions.

Special thanks to horsewomen Clover Stroud and my mother Jill Scurfield; to Victoria Hobbs at AM Heath; and to Alexandra Pringle, Angelique Tran Van Sang, Lynn Curtis, and Myra Jones at Bloomsbury.

We do hope that you have enjoyed reading this large print book.

Did you know that all of our titles are available for purchase?

We publish a wide range of high quality large print books including:
Romances, Mysteries, Classics
General Fiction
Non Fiction and Westerns

Special interest titles available in large print are:
The Little Oxford Dictionary
Music Book
Song Book
Hymn Book
Service Book

Also available from us courtesy of Oxford University Press:
Young Readers' Dictionary
(large print edition)
Young Readers' Thesaurus
(large print edition)

For further information or a free brochure, please contact us at:
Ulverscroft Large Print Books Ltd.,
The Green, Bradgate Road, Anstey,
Leicester, LE7 7FU, England.
Tel: (00 44) 0116 236 4325
Fax: (00 44) 0116 234 0205

Other titles published by Ulverscroft:

PILLOW MAN

Nick Coleman

William has a good, steady job in retail. He works in the bedlinen department of an Oxford Street store. He knows everything there is to know about comfy. Lucy has a portfolio career which, in her view, is no kind of career at all. Her life is in a mess; her love life even more unsatisfactory than that. She wouldn't be comfortable if she sat on a sofa in Heal's. Unable to sleep, she thinks a new pillow might be the answer. William and Lucy are not connected. Yet the pair of them share a terrible memory from the past — the sort of joint recollection that changes with the light, depending on who you were and where you were standing at the time. The question is: what to do with it?